A KILLER in Paradise

Also by Tom Hindle

A Fatal Crossing
The Murder Game
Murder on Lake Garda
Death in the Arctic

TOM HINDLE

A KILLER in Paradise

C

CENTURY

CENTURY

UK | USA | Canada | Ireland | Australia
India | New Zealand | South Africa

Century is part of the Penguin Random House group of companies
whose addresses can be found at global.penguinrandomhouse.com

Penguin Random House UK,
One Embassy Gardens, 8 Viaduct Gardens, London SW11 7BW

penguin.co.uk
global.penguinrandomhouse.com

First published 2026
001

Typeset in 13.5/17pt Fournier MT Std by Six Red Marbles UK, Thetford, Norfolk
Printed and bound in Great Britain by Clays Ltd, Elcograf S.p.A.

The authorised representative in the EEA is Penguin Random House Ireland,
Morrison Chambers, 32 Nassau Street, Dublin D02 YH68

A CIP catalogue record for this book is available from the British Library

ISBN: 978–1–529–92725–2 (hardback)
ISBN: 978–1–529–92726–9 (trade paperback)

For Dad.
And for all of our adventures in
places sunny and green.

List of notable individuals present at the
opening of The Midnight Orchid lodge
(list compiled by Inspector Isabella Rojas):

THE BLYTHE FAMILY

Abigail Blythe

Humphrey Blythe

Stevie Blythe

Miley Blythe

ABIGAIL BLYTHE'S FRIENDS

Zachary Ross

Olive Ross

Michael Bickler

Seth Smith

Jasmine Kelly

If the presence of the first two police officers – the advance party – had threatened to dampen the festivities, then Inspector Isabella Rojas knew that the subsequent arrival of a dozen more would bring them to a deafening halt.

Two cops, she thought, you could just about get away with. Two didn't necessarily mean that anything terrible had happened. But any more than that and folks expected trouble. And there was indeed trouble at the grand opening of The Midnight Orchid.

By all rights, this should have been a joyful occasion. The opening night of a gleaming new ecolodge, deep in the Costa Rican rainforest. And as her officers swept into the lobby, sending nervous-looking guests retreating hastily into the restaurant, Rojas could see what a glittering event it was intended to be. But that was over now. A few half-empty champagne flutes lay discarded on the floor. Intricately carved pieces of pine furniture stood askew. In a large potted plant, a couple of canapés had been hastily abandoned.

It was a far cry from the picture-perfect images being shown on the screen behind the reception desk. Rojas stood for a moment, watching sweeping aerial footage of the lodge, nestled within miles of thick jungle. After a few seconds the image changed to that of a private beach, azure water lapping gently upon a strip of perfect white sand. Next came a teardrop-shaped swimming pool with a swim-up bar, a couple dozen deckchairs organised carefully beside it. At the heart of it all was the building in which the officers now stood, its thatched roof pointing towards the sky like a straw pyramid. From it, like the strands of a spider's web, neat paths snaked into the jungle, dotted along the way with smaller wooden huts. There were fifty, Rojas had been told. All full for opening night.

Looking away from the screen, her gaze settled on a small glass vase that stood upon the reception desk. Inside was a single flower, its petals curling like ribbons of pale-blue velvet.

Rojas looked at it, unable to ignore the uneasy feeling in her gut. The flower seemed to have been chosen as an emblem for the hotel. All of the vehicles in the parking lot had it printed on their doors. Likewise, the staff member behind the reception desk wore it as a logo on her shirt. But most striking of all had been the billboard-style sign outside the front of the building. Breaking through the trees, bursting from the two-mile track that connected the hotel to the nearest meagre road, it had been mounted above a small fountain, spotlights ensuring it was still visible in the darkness. On it, the blue petals unfurled above the words

The Midnight Orchid, elegantly inscribed in flowing calligraphy. Beneath, in a smaller font, was written: *A Conrad Blythe resort.*

Conrad Blythe . . . Despite never having visited the United States, Rojas knew the name. At least one hotel in virtually every major city. Tastefully decorated in shades of grey, she imagined it to be favoured by travelling businesspeople with company credit cards and little need for a hotel with personality. Smart. Inoffensive. It was a brand built on conference days, business suites and reward schemes for frequent guests.

The Midnight Orchid was something else entirely.

With the recent surge in demand for ecotourism, Rojas knew all too well that her home country boasted more of such lodges than she dared to count. Likewise, she knew that many of them were American-owned. But she would want to know why, exactly, a company as prudent and sanitised as Conrad Blythe had set its sights on Costa Rica. And with such a radically different offering to the hotels its customers would be accustomed to in the States. There would be opportunity for that later, though. Right now, there were more important questions at hand.

A young man hurried towards her, dressed in a dark cap and a white shirt bearing the words *Policía Turística*.

She could see the relief on his face at her arrival. When the call came through, he and his partner had been closest. Although that wasn't saying much on the Osa Peninsula. A jagged landmass that jutted out into the Pacific like a hook, it was one of the most remote parts of the country. One of the most sparsely populated too, with fewer of the lush fields and sprawling coffee plantations found in the other regions. Instead, the peninsula was given over to wild rainforest and distant beaches. One good road existed, Highway 245, clinging to the coastline as if the land itself were trying to throw it into the ocean.

As for the hotel, it was on the south-easternmost point, about as far from anything as it was possible to be. Surrounded by dense jungle, Rojas imagined that The Midnight Orchid's website would promise privacy and seclusion. That might well be true. But it also meant that, despite being the closest, it had taken the young cop and his partner an hour to get there after the hotel called for help. They had then needed to wait another two hours for Isabella and her reinforcements to join them, holding the fort entirely on their own in the meantime.

She felt sorry for the guy. The most serious crime the tourist police had to deal with would typically be a stolen item from a hotel room. Maybe, at a stretch, a mugging. He'd almost certainly never seen a dead body before.

'*Señora,*' he said. 'I called control a few minutes ago. Have you been told that—'

'Is the body contained?'

He nodded, his expression anxious. '*Sí.* Locked inside a hut. I have the key, here. But, *señora*—'

'How many of the guests know?'

The officer swallowed, his anxiety becoming more palpable by the second. 'Difficult to say. She was found by a group of friends who had noticed she wasn't at the party.

I'm sure others will have realised by now that she hasn't been seen. And, of course, our vehicle's been in the parking lot for the past two hours. With you here now, I'm sure it won't take long for many of the guests to put two and two together.'

Rojas gave a stiff nod. 'OK. Take me to the hut.'

But the officer still looked troubled. '*Señora* . . . There's something else you need to know first. Things have changed while we've been waiting for you. I've been trying to tell you. There's . . .' He winced. 'There's been another.'

'Another?'

'Another death, *señora*. The body was found just a few minutes before you arrived.'

She stared at him. 'Tell me everything,' she said. 'Everything you know so far. From the beginning.'

Part One: The Reunion

The day before the party

1

Olive's body ached from the journey. First there had been the eleven-hour flight from London to San José. Then, thirty minutes sitting aboard a plane so small its half-dozen passengers had full view of the pilot's sandwich tucked down the side of his seat. Finally, an hour aboard a jeep, trailing through jungle so dense it blotted out the sky.

She was already feeling the jetlag and she was fairly certain she'd suffered whiplash somewhere in the jeep, the road so bumpy in this wild part of the country that at several points she'd felt at risk of being thrown from her seat. And yet, as she sat in her private garden, at the back of the hut she was sharing with her husband, Zach, she knew that she would have gladly done it all again. Twice, if needed. She struggled to imagine a distance she wouldn't travel if it meant being at The Midnight Orchid.

Enclosed on all sides by walls of thick jungle, their garden contained a large parasol, a glass coffee table, a pair of wooden sun-loungers and a hammock. The air was warm and still, filled with the distant call of tropical birds.

Olive stretched out in the hammock, her muscles gradually relaxing, and looked at her phone. Filling the screen was a ten-year-old picture that she had dug up on her Facebook page.

She was aware that she was one of the last of her friends to still be using the social media site. Most had long since migrated to Instagram. But in a funny sort of way, Olive was proud of her Facebook account. It wasn't just a means of keeping in touch with family. Each of the chapters of her life was there, carefully documented for her to look back on. There were pictures of her time as a student at York University. Then her and Zach getting married. Buying their first place. Becoming parents to Ryan . . .

This particular photo was special, though. It showed her and Zach beside a campfire, Olive beaming as she held up her left hand to display an engagement ring. Gathered around them were their friends: Seth, Mike, Jazz – and, of course, Abi.

Even now, Olive could remember the moment perfectly. Having lived and studied together for three years in York, the group had spent the summer after their final exams travelling around Central America. Making their way from Mexico City to Costa Rica's Osa Peninsula, it had been two months spent on buses and trains, bouncing between whatever hostels and campsites their shoestring budget would allow.

Olive must have taken well over a thousand pictures on that trip. All the places they'd stayed, the things they'd seen . . . This picture was her favourite, though. Because this one had been taken on the night before they'd flown home – the night that Zach had proposed.

She had found the engagement ring that afternoon, while looking in Zach's rucksack for mosquito spray, and had been watching giddily for the moment he took it out. When it finally happened, her anticipation had built to such a height that he didn't even have a chance to ask the question. At the sight of the box, she'd leapt to her feet and shouted, 'Yes!'

She remembered the surprise on his face, the speech she imagined he'd been about to deliver suddenly moot. She recalled laughing as she asked if he was going to put the ring on her finger. Calling her mum straight away to deliver the news . . .

Ten years. Sometimes it felt like a lifetime ago. But now they were back – reuniting in the exact same place. Only this time it wasn't a no-frills campsite. It was the site of The Midnight Orchid. Abi's gleaming new lodge.

Closing Facebook, Olive opened Instagram, going straight to The Midnight Orchid's profile and scrolling with practised confidence to a particular post.

The caption read:

Meet our team!

The Midnight Orchid is jointly founded by brother and sister Humphrey and Abigail Blythe. Together, they set

out to create a luxury rainforest retreat where guests
can be at one with nature.

In the accompanying photo, Humphrey and Abi stood
side by side, his arm around her shoulders. They were
posing on what looked to be a restaurant terrace somewhere in the hotel, with dining tables on either side of
them, jungle in the background, and then beyond it a strip
of blue ocean stretching off into the distance.

Olive had only met Abi's brother, Humphrey, on one
occasion. During their second year at York, he'd been
over in the UK for a music festival, and had caught the
train up from London to visit his sister before flying home
to the States. In the photo he appeared more or less as
Olive remembered him. Tall and lean, with blonde hair
and a grin that most other men would have killed for, he
looked as if he'd been pulled away from a beach party in
order to have the photo taken, dressed in a flowery shirt
and flip-flops. Perhaps he had been. During that weekend
in York, the impression he'd given was of an overactive
teenager refusing to grow up. Olive had thought he was
fun, knocking back shots and cracking jokes. Seth had
agreed. Not everyone had warmed to him, though. Mike
had said he was immature. Jazz had called him a creep.

But it wasn't for Humphrey that Olive kept returning
to this post.

An international student who had come from America
to study history of art, Olive had befriended Abi at the

beginning of their first year, and she had quickly become part of their group.

Abi had never been one for social media, much to Olive's dismay when she'd returned to the States at the end of their summer in Central America. No Instagram. No Twitter. Not even Facebook. As such, the photo that been included in this post was the first new picture of her friend that Olive had seen in ten years.

Simply dressed in a sleeveless top and flowing skirt, Abi was every bit as beautiful as Olive remembered. Her blonde hair was tied back, green eyes on full display while a pair of silver necklaces rested on her slender collar bone. And that smile . . . Olive knew it so well she could have painted it. It was small compared to Humphrey's wide grin. Subtle. But her eyes seemed to bore into the camera, fixing you in place. They were eyes that missed nothing. From which you could *hide* nothing. To be in a room with Abi was to know that everything you did – no matter how inconsequential – would be noticed.

Olive stared at the photo.

Ten years since they'd last seen her. Ten years since they'd parted ways at San José airport.

Holding the phone in her hand, Olive had to fight the urge to reach out and touch the screen. 'Where did you go?' she murmured to herself. 'Why did you go quiet?' Then, so softly it was barely a whisper, '*What did I do wrong?*'

At that moment, the picture disappeared, her phone

beginning to buzz. A video call was coming through, a photo of her mum now filling the screen.

Immediately Olive sat up in the hammock, a smile coming to her lips as she swung her feet onto the ground. She had already tried twice to call home, her heart sinking both times as the call had rung out. Surely he would still be up, she had told herself. Surely she hadn't missed him?

As she accepted the call, the head and shoulders of a woman in her fifties came into view.

'Hey, Mum!' Olive said eagerly. 'You OK?'

'Hello, love. Sorry we missed you earlier. Ryan was just having a bath.' She turned and called over her shoulder. 'Ryan! Your mum's on the phone!'

In the background Olive could see the kitchen in which she had grown up. A pair of glass doors looking out onto a neat garden. A large table with crocheted place settings. An oak shelving unit that housed a polka-dot teapot and a collection of well-thumbed recipe books. It made her endlessly happy to think of her own son now spending time in the same place.

Her mum looked back into the camera. 'Have you arrived, then?'

'Yep. This is our place.' Olive spun the phone round, showing off the garden. 'Isn't it beautiful?'

Before her mother could reply, another voice came bounding out of the phone.

'Mummy!'

A second later a boy of five came running into shot. He beamed into the camera, gaps showing between little teeth. He was still damp from his bath, blond hair sticking to his scalp and a towel around his shoulders.

Olive felt herself light up at the sight of him. She was excited for the reunion with her friends. Likewise, she was excited about the prospect of a holiday with Zach – their first without Ryan in the five years since he'd been born. But she'd never been this far from her son before. The prospect of him going to bed without her having spoken to him all day had been heartbreaking.

'Hey, darling!' she said. 'How are you doing? Are you having fun with Grandma and Grandad?'

'Yeah. We went to see the fish today.'

'The fish?' Olive gave a pantomime gasp, well aware of how keenly her animal-loving son had wanted his grandparents to take him to the aquarium. 'Which was your favourite?'

'I liked the sharks. We went through this big tunnel, and they all swam over our heads.'

'Gosh, that must have been scary.'

'No!' Ryan giggled, eyes crinkling. Olive must have heard it a thousand times, but it was still the most beautiful sound in the world.

'Is Daddy there?'

Olive looked inside the hut. Zach was in the en-suite bathroom, door closed. A few minutes ago she had heard him unpacking their toiletries. Now she thought she might just hear the sound of the shower running.

'I think he might be having a wash, sweetheart. But I'm sure he won't be long.'

17

'OK.'

Her heart sank at the disappointment in her son's voice.

'Hey,' she said quickly. 'Guess how many monkeys I've seen since we got here.'

'Monkeys?'

'Yep. Guess how many.'

Ryan thought for a second, a look of intense concentration on his face. 'Fifty?'

'Fifty!' Olive laughed. 'Maybe not as many as fifty. But we've definitely seen—'

'Ryan!' Somewhere in the background, Olive heard her father's voice. 'Come here, little man. Let's get you in your PJs.'

'But Mummy's telling me about the monkeys!'

'It's OK, sweetie,' said Olive. 'You go and get ready for bed. I'll call you tomorrow. And I'll see if I can take a picture of the monkeys to send you.'

Ryan beamed at this idea, and once Olive had told him she loved him he went scampering away.

'Has he been OK?' Olive asked.

'Good as gold,' her mother replied. 'We might have to do the aquarium again before you come home. He was so desperate to stay past closing time that I thought they'd have to kick us out.' She raised a mug of tea, taking a sip. 'So how was the journey?'

'Long. I managed to get a little sleep, though. And the internal flight was amazing. We flew half an hour from San José to the peninsula on this tiny little plane. I didn't think to count at the time, but it can't have had more than ten seats. At one point Seth got out his speaker and started playing the *Indiana Jones* music! I'll send you some pictures, the views were stunning.'

'That sounds exciting. And is it nice to see your friends again?'

'Oh, it's the best. Zach's seen Seth and Mike a few times over the years, although never at the same time. And of course I see a lot of Jazz. But having us all back together . . . You'd think it had been ten minutes. Not ten years.'

'What about Abi?'

Immediately Olive noticed the shift in her mother's tone. It was subtle, but it was undeniably there. The disapproval. The suspicion.

She chewed her lip, thinking for a second about lying.

'We, uh . . .' She cleared her throat. 'We actually haven't seen Abi yet.'

Her mother frowned. 'I thought you said you'd arrived?'

'We have. But Abi hasn't been free to come and meet us. She's got so much going on, coordinating the preparations for tomorrow's party. She left a really sweet note in our room, though, saying we'll all have dinner tonight. And she's booked Jazz and me in for a spa treatment this afternoon.'

Her mother didn't reply. Olive could see her lips pursing.

'It's fine, Mum.'

'Is it?'

'Yes.'

Her mum pulled a face. 'I don't know, love,' she said. 'You can't blame me for being wary.'

'There's nothing to be wary of. Abi was my best friend during uni and now she's invited us all for a reunion. Why would we need to be wary?'

Her mum sighed. 'Olive, I know you can make your own decisions. But think of how it looks from where I'm standing. This girl spends every minute of every day with you while you're at York. She goes backpacking with you all around Central America. Then the minute she goes home to New Hampshire she decides she wants nothing to do with you. No messages. No phone calls. Doesn't even respond to an invitation to your *wedding*, for goodness' sake. And now, ten years later, she asks you all to fly half-way round the world to come and stay free of charge at her swanky rainforest hotel, but she apparently can't find five minutes to say hello when you arrive.' She held up her hands, palms to the camera. 'I know you don't like to hear me saying it, Olive. But your cousin's right.'

'Jazz doesn't—'

'She's *right*. This Abi woman is bad news. And you'd have been better off turning this trip down.'

Olive bit her lip again, the words stinging.

'We had to pay for our own flights,' she said, weakly.

'I'm well aware. I've had to hear all about *that* from your husband.'

Olive winced. 'I'm sure there's an explanation, Mum. There'll be a reason why she went quiet after we went our separate ways. Maybe it was just too painful to keep in

20

touch after she went home to the States and we all came back to the UK.'

'Well, if there *is* an explanation I hope it's better than that. All I'm saying is that I remember how upset you were when Abi disappeared on you. I remember how devastated you were when you asked her to be a bridesmaid at your wedding and she didn't so much as send a reply. And I don't like that you're letting her swan so easily back into your life.'

Olive said nothing, and for a moment they fell into an uncomfortable silence. Then, at last, her mum sighed.

'How *is* Zach? Has he cheered up at all about the flights now that you've arrived?'

Olive looked up. Zach was just coming out of the bathroom, a light cloud of steam following him. He was dressed in shorts and a loose-fitting shirt, his hair still wet, with a towel in one hand and his phone in the other. She wondered if he might come out and join her in the garden. Instead, he stayed inside the hut, settling into one of the wicker chairs beside the coffee table.

'Yeah,' she said. 'Yeah, he's really happy to see everyone.'

She hoped she sounded more convincing than she felt. But she thought it best not to mention the bad mood Zach had been in since they'd left home the previous morning. The way he'd spend the majority of the flight from Heathrow to San José either scowling out of the window or glued silently to his phone, a pair of earbuds wedged firmly into place for most of the eleven-hour journey.

'I'm sorry, sweetheart,' said her mum. 'I don't mean to be a spoilsport. I just worry about you.'

'I know. It's all right, Mum.' Olive cleared her throat, unsure how much longer she could keep this up. 'Listen,' she said, 'I think I'm going to ring off. Can I call you tomorrow?'

'OK, love. Have a good time. Speak tomorrow.'

Ending the call, Olive tipped back her head and closed her eyes.

Feeling the sun on her skin, listening to the sounds of the surrounding jungle, she tried to focus on how good it had been to speak with Ryan. Her one reservation about coming on the trip had been leaving him behind. She and Zach had never been away from him for more than a couple of nights. And they had certainly never been so far. Desperate as she'd been to come to The Midnight Orchid – to reunite with Abi – she'd worried that their absence would upset him. That when she video-called home, he would tearfully ask when they were coming back. It had been a relief to see that he was OK.

But try as she might to think only of her son, it was the latter part of the call that rang in her ears.

She didn't need her mum to remind her of how painful it had been when Abi went quiet on them. She could so clearly remember the weeks after they'd gone home. The echoing silence that she'd received in response to every attempt she'd made to reach out. And she could still remember, word for word, the message she had finally received after she'd eventually contacted Humphrey, asking why Abi wasn't replying.

Sorry, Olive. I won't make the wedding. Hope you guys have an amazing day. Take care.

Take care.

Never had two words felt more final. Three years of friendship. Three years in which they had spent virtually every day together. Olive had been hurt, of course. She'd been devastated. But she was sure there would be an explanation. And she hoped that in the coming days she would hear it.

Her thoughts were interrupted by the sound of a door opening, a short distance to her left. Opening her eyes, she turned her head. It was the people in the neighbouring hut. She couldn't see them – the foliage was too thick – but she heard them stepping out of their hut, gasping and whooping in delight at the sight of their garden.

She listened to them for a short while, the separating wall of jungle plants doing nothing to disguise the sound. Then she looked back towards her own hut. She could see Zach through the glass doors, eyes glued to his phone.

For a few moments she just watched him. He couldn't be angry with her for the entire trip, could he?

Withholding a sigh, she rose to her feet, crossed the little garden and stood in the doorway of the hut. It was cool inside, a ceiling-mounted fan moving sandalwood-scented air around an open-plan bedroom and living area. An ornate coffee table stood on polished floorboards, upon which sat a bottle of champagne. White rose petals had been scattered over a sumptuous king-sized bed.

Olive paused, her brow creasing into a frown.

When they'd first set eyes upon the room she had been too giddy to notice. But now, with an hour having passed, it occurred to her that in several pictures she had seen on The Midnight Orchid's Instagram profile the petals upon the beds had been blue. The same shade of blue as the flower that had been chosen as the hotel's emblem. It was bound to have been a deliberate choice. So why, she wondered, might it have changed for the grand opening?

She gave a little shake of her head, putting the thought from her mind. Whatever the colour of the petals on her bed, the hut was a far cry from the three-star all-inclusive they'd stay in during their last trip abroad. Olive had wanted to go to Italy, but had seen a deal online for Turkey that they couldn't pass up. Not that she was complaining. She'd loved that week, photos of Ryan splashing in the sea and grinning at the buffet now plastered all around their house. But The Midnight Orchid was a different animal. It was a world, if Olive was honest, that she simply wasn't used to. And while she was ecstatic to be there, she kept catching herself moving cautiously around the hut, handling everything delicately as if she were worried she might break something.

'I just spoke to Ryan,' she said. 'Mum and Dad took him to the aquarium today.'

'Bet he loved that.'

'I think he did, yeah.'

Zach didn't reply, eyes still glued to his phone.

'Why don't you come outside?' she said. 'It's beautiful out here.'

'That's OK. I'm happy here.'

'Do you want to have a nap? I know you didn't sleep much on the flight.'

'No, I'm good.'

She watched him a moment longer. As she did so, she thought about apologising once more for getting carried away. For telling Abi that they would come without so much as asking him first. For insisting that they should go when she had been well aware they couldn't really afford the flights.

But she knew it would be no use. Not when she had apologised for these things a hundred times already.

Instead, she reached for her phone, fetching up the engagement picture she'd found on Facebook. Then she stepped inside and sat down in the wicker chair beside his.

'Hey,' she said. 'Look at this.' She held up the phone, showing him the photo. 'Did you ever think we'd make it back?'

She searched his face, wondering which way this was going to go. Eventually, his expression softened.

'God,' he said. 'You wouldn't know it was the same place, would you?'

'Not a chance. You don't think Abi fancied keeping the crumbling barn or some of the rusting vehicles?'

'Don't forget the dirty outbuildings.'

'Of course. Who could forget the dirty outbuildings?' Olive smiled. 'I can't believe how much things have changed since then. We all have busy jobs. We're living in different places. We have Ryan . . .' She paused, her smile becoming suddenly cheeky. 'Do you think Mike still has comic books under his bed?'

'I reckon Seth definitely still hides a bag of weed under his.'

She laughed.

If she tried, she could still picture their respective rooms, back in their halls of residence. Mike's with four different gaming consoles, his alphabetised Blu-ray collection and a stack of fantasy novels on the bedside table. Seth's with an array of potted plants on the windowsill and a battered acoustic guitar propped up in the corner.

As for Zach's room . . . Well, she could remember that one clearest of all. Next door to her own, she had spent plenty of nights in it during their first year. It had felt so grown up. Eighteen years old, away from home, in a flat of their own . . .

She had been pleased, on the journey, by how quickly her friends seemed to have picked up from where they'd left off. Seth had once said that she and Zach were the parents of the group, the only people to have set out on a serious relationship during their very first week of uni. If that had been true, Olive had often thought it made the others their squabbling kids, with Seth being the joker and Mike the punchline. Even Jazz fitted a certain mould – that of the grumpy older sister who rolled her eyes at everything the boys did.

Olive smiled to herself, thinking for a second about Abi. What role had she played in their little family? The beautiful American heiress who'd come into their midst.

In a funny sort of way it had often felt as if they had adopted her. Taken her in when she'd had nowhere to go. Even now, Olive could remember meeting her at a students' union event. She had been alone, an international student who hadn't yet made any worthwhile friends. That same evening, Olive had brought her back to the flat and introduced her to the others. After that, she had simply stayed. A part of the group.

'Do you think he's OK?' she asked. 'Ryan, I mean.'

'Of course he is.'

'How do you know?'

'Because your mum's probably spoiling him rotten. He looked happy enough on your video call, didn't he?'

'Yeah.'

'There you are, then. If anything I reckon he'll be sad when we get home.'

She thumped him on the arm.

'Babe,' she said. 'I really am sorry. I know I got carried away. But you will try to enjoy this trip, won't you? Now that we're here . . . you're going to get into the spirit of things?'

Suddenly his expression clouded over once more.

'Babe?'

He didn't answer. Instead, he got to his feet and went into the bathroom, closing the door behind him.

2

Sheltering from the sun beneath the woven roof of the poolside bar, Jazz sat with a pair of AirPods lodged in her ears, eyes closed behind her designer sunglasses.

To any observers it might have appeared that she was trying to block out Mike and Seth, who were busy bickering on the bar stools beside her. In reality, she was listening intently to a podcast she'd found on the flight – an American show called *Hello Hospitality*.

It was far from the sort of thing she'd usually tune in to on holiday. In an ideal world she would be listening to one of the various health and fitness shows to which she subscribed, or maybe Radio 1 if there was anything decent in the charts. But this wasn't a normal holiday. Jazz had no interest in enjoying the luxury of The Midnight Orchid. Nor did she have any desire to catch up with the boys. She had come to make sure nothing happened to her cousin. Specifically, she had come to protect her from Abi.

It had been a while since Jazz had felt the need to watch Olive's back. But as kids, growing up in the same corner of Cheshire, it had been a regular state of affairs. Born six months apart, Jazz might have been younger but she had always been savvier. Olive had always been too pure a soul. Sheltered from the moment she had been born, she was too trusting. Too impressionable. The fact that she had often been lonely as a child – not quite bullied but certainly never popular – hadn't helped. Instead, as a teen-ager she'd developed a desire to impress beautiful people, as well as a tendency to idolise those who didn't deserve it.

The result was that Olive's parents – Jazz's aunt and uncle – had spent much of their daughter's life doing any-thing they could to shelter her from the world. Jazz still remembered the look of relief on their faces when she announced that she hoped to join Olive in studying at the University of York. It was only two hours from where they lived in Cheshire. Still, they had been so worried about Olive moving away from home that they had apparently entertained the idea of moving to the area for the duration of her studies. They had dropped that idea, though, when they learned that Jazz, too, had applied to go to York. With Jazz there to keep an eye on her, they could rest easy.

With hindsight, Jazz often felt that she had let them down.

First there had been Zach. A little self-absorbed but not necessarily a bad guy, he and Olive had been placed in a flat together with Seth and Mike. On the days when she was feeling charitable Jazz could convince herself that he and Olive were right for one another. But she couldn't help feeling deep down that no one ought to be setting

30

out on a serious relationship during their first week at university. Let alone with the guy in the room next door. Zach hadn't been trouble per se, but he hadn't immediately seemed like someone worth committing your life to. And the speed with which he and Olive had coupled up had perhaps been the first sign of how severely Jazz would have her work cut out for her during their time at York.

Where Jazz felt she had really let Olive's parents down, though, was Abi – the American student who had taken an instant interest in Olive. Beautiful, smart, wealthy . . . She was exactly the sort of friend Olive had spent her teenage years yearning for.

Even now, Jazz could still remember the night Olive had brought her new friend to the flat. The way she'd so proudly introduced her, beaming from ear to ear as if Abi were a work of art that she had painstakingly crafted.

The others had been welcoming. Zach had been friendly enough, offering her a beer. Seth had asked Abi if she'd wanted to smoke some weed, nodding his approval when she'd given a nonchalant *Sure*. Mike, the poor boy, had fallen immediately in love. But Jazz had known. From the beginning, she had seen it: this girl was trouble.

How right she had been.

More than once, Jazz had blamed herself for what had happened the last time they were in Costa Rica. For not seeing the events Abi had set in motion until it was far too late.

And now here they were. Back together. At the scene of the crime.

What did Abi want, though? Ten years without a word,

and then suddenly she invites them all out for a reunion? And in the very place where she had sabotaged Olive's life in about as cruel a way as Jazz could imagine?

Olive might have been blind to the fact that Abi wasn't to be trusted – even now, she still had no idea of what Abi had done on that last day of their summer in Central America – but Jazz was not.

It was these suspicions that had compelled her to listen to *Hello Hospitality*. She wasn't sure what she expected to find. Nothing, most likely. It wasn't even recent, the episode she was listening to being a little over three months old. But she wanted to know everything she could about this place – about what Abi had been doing during the years since they'd last seen her – before she had decided to grace them with her presence once again.

'OK,' said one of the presenters. 'With the news section wrapped up it's time for this week's industry interview. Taylor, do you want to introduce our guests?'

'Sure thing. So today we're lucky to be joined by Humphrey and Abigail Blythe, brother and sister, and joint heirs to the world-renowned Conrad Blythe hotel group. Abi. Humphrey. Thanks so much for joining us.'

'Thanks for having us.'

It was Abi who'd replied, her voice like silk. Without intending to, Jazz scowled.

'So we all know Conrad Blythe,' Taylor said cheerfully. 'Founded by your father, Frank Blythe, it's one of the biggest hotel chains here in the US, with dozens of locations in every state. I'm sure everyone listening has visited at least one for a conference or a spa day—'

'Shacked up for a dirty weekend.'

It was Humphrey who'd spoken this time. Again, Jazz scowled, recalling the visit he had paid Abi at York. A man-child through and through, he hadn't made a gleaming first impression, spending much of the weekend hitting on Jazz and knocking back shots with Seth. Aware that she would likely be seeing him again at The Midnight Orchid, Jazz had vaguely wondered on the flight to San José if he might have grown up over the past ten years. She quickly abandoned this idea, imagining his stupid grin as he'd made this comment on the podcast.

'Well,' said the host, humouring Humphrey with a polite laugh, 'I'm sure there will be some listeners who could perhaps relate to that. But to get to my question . . . We know that your father passed away quite suddenly last fall. We were incredibly sorry to hear about that. He was a real titan of the industry, and we'll talk about him a little more in a few minutes. But tell us first about how you came to join him at Conrad Blythe. Was that always the plan?'

'Well, first,' said Abi, 'let me just thank you for those kind words about our dad. It really means a lot. As for joining him at Conrad Blythe – more or less. It had been made clear to us as teenagers that there was a career path there if we wanted it.'

'With a view to one day taking Frank's place as joint heads of the company?'

'Again, if that was what we wanted. And, crucially, if

we were willing to earn it. Dad always said that he'd give us the ladder but if we wanted to get to the top we'd have to climb it ourselves. But he encouraged us to explore other interests as well. Humphrey did a lot of travelling and I went to study in York, England. It was only after finishing my studies and coming home that I think we decided joining the company was something we definitely wanted to do.'

'He sounds like a very special man.'

'He was. Yeah.'

'OK,' said the other host, Beth. 'So we know how you joined the company. And we know what Conrad Blythe has always been about. But it sounds like change is coming. You two have been working together on your first project, and you're looking to do something really different. So tell us. What does the future look like?'

'That's right,' said Abi. 'Before our dad passed away we'd been working on the next chapter in the company's story, and we'd decided to create something pretty different. As you say, we've grown to become one of the best-known hotel franchises in the United States, and that's exactly what Dad set out to do when he founded the company thirty-five years ago. But there's only so long you can keep doing the same thing. You have to keep moving. Keep evolving. And that's what we want to do with this site in Costa Rica. Our first hotel outside of the US.'

'It sounds incredible,' said Beth. 'And it looks it, too. I've got some images here. Tee, take a look.'

'Oh my God,' Taylor drawled. 'This is gorgeous.'

'Isn't it? For the folks at home, this place is *stunning*. I'm seeing huts in the rainforest, I'm seeing a private beach, I'm seeing a terrace overlooking the most beautiful garden.'

'And I love the logo. The blue flower. So classy.'

Abi laughed politely. 'I'm so glad you think so. It grows in the grounds. The only place in the world, as far as we're aware. It's actually where the name of the hotel comes from. The name we gave the flower while we were building the hotel was the midnight orchid.'

'I love that!' said Beth. 'Not at all dramatic, though. *The midnight orchid*.'

Again, Abi laughed. 'What's wrong with a little drama now and again?'

'Nothing, Abi,' said Taylor. 'Nothing. At. All. Now, obviously the lodge itself is brand new. But is it true that you'd been to this plot of land before? Have I got that right?'

'You've done your research! Yes, that's right. After finishing my studies in the UK, I spent the summer backpacking with some British friends around Central America. On the last night of the trip, the hostel we were due to stay in ended up being full, so we found ourselves on this campsite. Real humble sort of place, but it was so beautiful. I never forgot it. When Dad agreed it was time for Conrad Blythe to go down the ecotourism route, I knew straight away that it would be the perfect place for our first lodge. As it happened, the family who owned the estate had been trying to sell for nearly a year, so we snapped it right up—'

Unable to stomach any more, Jazz took out her AirPods.

Sipping on a Cuba libre, she swept a quick glance around the pool. Then, she faced forward again, looking out at the view.

Situated somewhere at the back of the lodge, they had needed to go into the garden and then through a short tunnel of palms and ferns in order to access the pool, giving it a secluded feeling that Jazz was loath to admit she found incredibly effective. On three sides it was enclosed by thick foliage. On the fourth, the jungle had been cleared to allow a view of the ocean. Spread out before her, the rainforest sloped downward for a mile or so, the green turning to blue as it met the water.

Looking down on the view, Jazz had been aware of the jeep climbing for much of the journey from the airstrip, but she hadn't realised just how far above sea-level the lodge was situated. She could see for miles, the jungle canopy comprised of a thousand different shades of green. Beyond it, the water shimmered, twinkling in the sunlight. For a brief moment she imagined a paraglider leaping from the poolside bar, riding the warm air all the way down to the shoreline.

She checked her smartwatch. Half-past two. Thirty minutes until she and Olive were due to receive the spa treatment Abi had booked for them.

Beside her, Seth had taken off his shirt, revealing a slender, tattooed frame that spoke of little in the way of nutrition or exercise. Mike, meanwhile, had exchanged the *Star Wars* T-shirt he'd worn on the flight for a Black

Sabbath one. He looked curious, the only man at the pool with a shirt still on in the pressing heat. But Jazz wasn't surprised. With his ghostly-pale complexion, she remembered how easily he'd burn on a summer's day in York. He was unlikely to be spending much of their week in Costa Rica sunbathing. As for Jazz herself, she had changed from the leggings and Nike-branded hoody that she'd worn on the journey into a sleeveless top and sarong, her blonde hair held back in a clip.

Taking a bite of a quesadilla that had been brought down for him from the lodge, Seth was flicking through a book entitled *Flowers and Fauna of Central America*. He also had a Bluetooth speaker, playing a Bob Marley song which was drawing to a close. As it did so, a heavier drum-and-bass track began to play, drawing a disapproving look from one of the pool's other patrons.

'Mate,' said Mike sternly. 'You've *got* to turn that down. What's Abi going to say if she hears we've been upsetting other guests?' He looked at Jazz, fixing her with a pleading expression. 'Will you tell him? He never listens to me.'

'I say turn it up,' said Jazz. 'We travel halfway around the world to see Abi's fancy new lodge and she's so busy prepping this party that she can't so much as greet us when we arrive? If upsetting a few other guests gets her attention, then I say good.'

Mike scowled. 'Why did you even come? You never liked Abi. You clearly aren't happy to be here.'

Jazz shrugged. 'It's a reunion, isn't it? Doesn't exactly work if you don't turn up.'

'Well, I hope you put on a happier face when she's able to join us. She's invited us to this amazing place, put us all up for free . . . The least you can do is look like you want to be here.'

'Give it a rest, Mikey.' Finishing his quesadilla, Seth put the plate to one side, brushing crumbs off his swimming trunks. 'Abi didn't need you to fight her battles back at York and she surely doesn't now.'

Mike pursed his lips. No one else called him Mikey. Only Seth. Jazz could remember all too clearly how much it had irritated him as a student. And she was certain, from the small smile on Seth's face, that he remembered too.

'All I'm saying,' said Mike, 'is that we could do with seeming a little more grateful to be here.'

Seth didn't reply, a smirk crossing his lips.

'What?' said Mike.

Seth shook his head, still saying nothing.

'*What?*' Mike asked again.

Seth sighed, although the smile remained in place. 'Mikey. Tell me you haven't come all the way out here because you're hoping you and Abi might hook up again.'

Mike tried to laugh, but it came out wrong. 'I haven't . . . I mean, I'm not . . .' He clenched his jaw, looking down at his Coke Zero. 'Where do you reckon Zach and Olive got to?'

Seth shrugged. 'Shagging, probably.'

'Seth!'

'What do you want me to say? They're on their first

ever holiday without Ryan. In the place they got engaged. What else do you think they're likely to be doing?'

Mike didn't reply. He did, however, notice two other patrons of the pool begin to leave, casting a disapproving look in the direction of Seth's speaker.

'Seth, will you *please* turn that music down? People are *leaving*—'

'Let them. I'm not doing anything wrong.'

Jazz watched as the two men stared at each other, not sufficiently interested to intervene but curious enough that she wanted to see what happened next. In the end it was Mike who backed down, muttering something under his breath as he began to climb to his feet. Before he could make his dramatic exit, though, there came the sudden pattering of feet. Then, a girl, no older than ten, charged from somewhere behind the bar, colliding with Mike as he rose from his bar stool.

It seemed to happen in slow motion. Jazz watched as Mike swayed for a moment on the spot, arms flailing, before toppling backwards into the pool.

She raised a hand to her mouth as he came spluttering from the water, trying not to let him see her laugh. Seth made no such effort, laughing loudly before raising his phone to photograph Mike as he waded towards the edge of the pool.

A second later, a woman rounded the corner. Dressed in a Midnight Orchid uniform, she was clearly a member of staff, aged somewhere in her twenties and with a name tag on her shirt reading *Alana*. Slightly out of breath, she took

in the scene, her hassled expression immediately morph-
ing into one of horror.

'*Mierda!*' she cried out. '*Señor.* Please, *señor.* I'm so
sorry . . .'

She hurried to the side of the pool, dropping to her knees
to help Mike climb out. Putting out her hand, he reached
up to take it, only to slip and fall backwards a second time
into the water.

Finding it impossible now to hide her amusement, Jazz
turned away, eyes settling on the girl. Brushing a strand of
dark hair out of her face, she watched nonchalantly from
behind a pair of pink-rimmed sunglasses, as if it had somehow been Mike's fault for being in her way.

For the most part, Jazz didn't get on with kids. She
didn't have the patience for them, nor the inclination to
develop it. But she found herself warming to this girl
immediately.

Alana, who had by now succeeded in helping Mike from
the pool, threw a look over her shoulder.

'Miley!' she hissed.

'Sorry,' the girl replied. 'I didn't know he would be there.'

American, Jazz thought, clocking her accent. Probably
here with a parent who'd been invited to the party. Once
again, Jazz had to try not to laugh, this time at Miley's
complete lack of remorse.

Grimacing, Alana turned back to Mike, offering apolo-
gies and platitudes at a hundred miles an hour.

'It's fine,' he said, in a tone that suggested it was anything
but. '*It's fine.*' Managing, at last, to climb from the pool, he

glared at Seth, whose phone was still raised. 'Could you put that away?'

Seth didn't reply, beaming from ear to ear.

'Seth! Could you . . .'

Apparently realising that it was no use, he stopped mid-sentence and stormed away in the direction of the garden. Alana, meanwhile, who now appeared close to dying of embarrassment, turned for some reason to Jazz.

'I'm so sorry,' she said. 'I've asked her not to run. But I couldn't—'

'Why?' Miley demanded. 'I told him I'm sorry. He shouldn't have been standing there.'

Alana raised a hand to her face. 'Come on,' she said. 'Let's get that milkshake before you upset anyone else. And *please* don't—'

Before she could finish, Miley had already begun to run towards the lodge, leaving Alana to hurry along in her wake.

Jazz watched her go, thinking of Ryan. She loved him, of course. He was Olive's son, after all. Jazz loved her cousin, and so by extension she loved Ryan. And he could be fun from time to time. But not like Miley had been just then. Even within the space of a few short minutes, Jazz could see that this kid was a rock star.

She turned back to Seth. He was typing into his phone, a satisfied smile plastered across his face.

'Where are you sending that?' she asked.

'The WhatsApp group. I'm sure Zach and Olive would like to see it. Maybe I'll pop it on Instagram, too.'

Jazz watched him for a moment as he continued to tap at his screen.

'You aren't going to spend this whole trip winding him up,' she said. 'Are you?'

'Maybe.'

'For God's sake, Seth. We're in our thirties now. Do you really have to behave like such a child?'

'Hey – I wouldn't have spent half as much time winding Mikey up back at York if he didn't let himself *get* so wound up. So really it's his own fault.'

Jazz sighed. 'Do you honestly think Mike's come all this way because he's hoping something will happen with Abi?'

'Who knows? I wouldn't put it past him.' Seemingly finished, Seth laid his phone down on the bar before looking Jazz in the eye. 'What about you? Why have you come? 'Cause Mike's not wrong. You've never liked Abi. But Olive says you insisted on coming on this trip.'

'I told you—'

'I know. But I don't buy you being interested in reuniting with any of us. I haven't heard from you in years, and the whole journey you barely said a word to anyone but Olive. So why have you really come?'

Jazz thought for a moment. Eventually she said, 'You know why.'

'Do I?'

'What happened on the coach.'

Seth's expression suddenly became serious.

'Come on, Seth,' she said. 'We both know what we saw.'

'We didn't see anything.'

'We saw her—'

'No,' he cut across her. 'We didn't. You know it. I know it. And you'd be a lot happier if you just accepted it.'

'I can't believe you're being so naive.'

'And I can't believe you're still thinking about this.' He shook his head. 'Is that *really* why you're here? Are you looking for proof or something?'

'No,' said Jazz. 'It's too late for that. If I dragged it back up now it would destroy Olive. I came because Abi can't be trusted. I came to keep an eye on her, because the last time we saw her, Olive ended up—'

'All right,' said Seth, raising his voice slightly before she could finish. 'All right, let's leave it there, shall we?'

They sat for a few seconds in silence, Seth looking painfully uncomfortable.

'You don't think that you're being a little crazy?' he said. 'Coming all this way just to keep an eye on her. I mean . . . shouldn't that be Zach's job? He's her husband, after all.'

Jazz glared at him. 'I'm not leaving Olive's wellbeing to Zach. If he had even *half* a spine we wouldn't be here in the first place.'

She glanced down at her smartwatch again. Fifteen minutes until her spa treatment with Olive.

'Gotta go,' she said, draining what remained of her Cuba libre and leaving before Seth had any time to respond.

3

The route from the pool back to the huts required The Midnight Orchid's guests to walk first through the garden at the back of the main lodge, and then through the lobby itself, before joining one of the paths that weaved through the jungle, huts placed evenly on either side.

This was unfortunate for Mike, as it meant there was no way of going for a shower and a change of clothes without drawing dozens of curious looks from other guests.

The whole way, he forced himself to look straight ahead, gritting his teeth. With his clothes sopping and his cheeks flushed red with embarrassment, he heard people chuckle as he walked past. Felt their smiles as they watched him go.

With each step, he found his mind beginning to swim with questions he hadn't asked in years. Why were Zach and Olive so fond of Seth? Why did they insist on keeping him around?

At university, Seth had made winding Mike up a near full-time occupation. Pranks, taunts, jokes at his expense . . . It had seemed there was nothing that Seth enjoyed more. There were moments when Mike had been so frustrated that he'd even wondered if it was worth remaining part of the group. He'd always kept those thoughts at bay, though. In part this was because he would never forgive himself for letting Seth beat him. But he was also desperate not to lose Zach and Olive. They were his best friends. Why should he have to give them up because of Seth?

More than once, during their time at York, Olive had told him not to rise to Seth's jabs. That he only did it because Mike always reacted so strongly.

If you just stop giving him the satisfaction he'll get bored.

That had only wound Mike up more. How could he not rise to it when it was so utterly relentless?

In the ten years since they had graduated, he'd seen Seth just three times. The first had been at Zach's stag do, the second at the wedding. The third had been during an ill-fated reunion at a cottage Olive had booked in the Cotswolds. On that particular weekend, Seth had succeeded in winding Mike up to such an extent that by the end of the trip Mike had deleted his number and blocked him on every possible social media platform, vowing never to see him again.

So his heart had sunk when he'd learned that Seth had also been invited to The Midnight Orchid.

He'd tried to convince himself that things might be different. That in the years since they'd last seen each other, Seth might have grown up a little. How wrong he'd been.

They hadn't even been able to make it through security at Heathrow without Seth sneaking something into his hand luggage.

Mike remembered his confusion as the security personnel took him to one side and asked him to open his bag. The way everyone queueing behind him had grinned – some breaking into laughter – as he reached inside and produced an enormous bottle of lube. Even the security official, who had clearly realised what was happening, struggled to keep a straight face as he asked Mike to explain what it had been doing in his hand luggage.

Jaw clenched, Mike remembered catching Seth's eye, his grin the biggest of all.

Just you wait, that smirk had seemed to say. *We've got seven years of this to catch up on, Mikey*.

Finally arriving back at his hut, Mike peeled off his sodden clothes. Taking them into the bathroom, he paused at the mirror, despairing at the sight of a faint T-shirt tan.

How had that happened? They'd barely been there three hours, and he'd been slathered in factor 50 since the moment they'd touched down. And was that a mosquito bite, too? He looked a little closer. No. Not one mosquito bite. There were two. Wait – three.

He growled somewhere in the back of this throat. This place hadn't agreed with him last time, either. The sunburn, the insects . . . It was as if the jungle itself didn't want him there. Although it was perhaps the heat that he hated most. The others all seemed to luxuriate in it, but he hated the way he couldn't so much as step outside without breaking into a sweat. For a second Mike wished that he hadn't come. He quickly quelled that idea, though, forcing himself to think of the reason he'd accepted the invitation.

The reunion. The chance to reconnect with Abi.

Before he could stop them, Seth's words from the poolside bar echoed, unbidden, in Mike's mind.

Tell me you haven't come all the way out here because you're hoping you and Abi might hook up again.

God, how did Seth always find just the right thing to say? The one thing that would boil Mike's blood like nothing else?

Balling up his T-shirt and hurling it into the corner of the bathroom, Mike told himself that, of course, Seth was wrong. What had happened between him and Abi, on the last night of that trip, had been a one-off. He hadn't travelled halfway round the world in the hope that, ten years later, she might want to get together a second time. That would be madness.

Mike told himself these things. But he struggled to believe them.

He still remembered the first time Olive had brought Abi back to their flat. The first time he'd set eyes on her . . . At just eighteen years old, he'd never been in love before. Not properly. But he'd known, straight away, what he'd felt. Looking at Abi, it was as if she'd been put in the world just for him.

Not that those feelings had ever been returned. During their three years at the University of York, she hadn't shown him a scrap of interest. Until, of course, that final night in Costa Rica. That was when it had happened.

He knew how overly dramatic it sounded to say that Abi had thrown herself at him, but it was the truth.

For ten years he'd thought about that moment. Had analysed it and picked it apart in his head. There had been a couple of girlfriends since, but neither relationship had lasted more than a year. And when each had come to an end Mike had found himself drifting back to that moment in the jungle. The moment with Abi.

He'd tried to tell himself that he was over it. That it was a wild moment which he'd romanticised and idealised with the magic of hindsight. But when that invite had come – when Abi's name had appeared on his phone for the first time in a decade – he'd known without a second's hesitation that he would be going. That the hold Abi had had on him at York was very much still in play.

He recalled the rush that he'd felt. The way he'd immediately messaged Zach and Olive, demanding to know if they were planning to go.

And before he could stop himself, he thought again of Seth. He thought of that smirk, imagining how hilarious he would find it to know that Mike was still besotted.

Fucking Seth.

Forcing the image of that smirk from his mind, he finished undressing and stepped into the shower. The water pounding against his head, he tried once more to tell himself that Seth was wrong. That he hadn't come all this way in the hope that something might happen between himself and Abi.

He told himself he was succeeding. That he believed it. But as with every other time he'd tried to tell himself this line, he knew just how futile it was.

4

The moment Olive closed the door to leave for her spa treatment, and Zach had the hut to himself, he breathed such a sigh of relief that he felt himself tremble. In an instant, it was as if all of the anger, the stress and the fear that he had been fighting to conceal since leaving the tarmac at Heathrow were now finally free to come to the surface.

He leapt to his feet, gritting his teeth as he began to pace around the little space.

Why had Abi brought them back there? For ten years she'd been quiet, meeting each and every one of Olive's numerous attempts to get in touch with total silence. What had changed that meant she suddenly needed to see them? Had she not already done enough harm?

He screwed his eyes shut, recalling the day, three months ago, when Abi had sent them all their invites. It had been lunchtime. Zach had spent the break in his classroom, holding back a group of Year 10s who had spent the previous lesson arsing around. When, finally, he'd had a chance to check his phone over a quick sandwich, he'd been surprised to find that Mike had added him to a Whats-App group called Reunion!

It had been perhaps eighteen months since Zach last saw Mike. The two of them had met up in Birmingham for a curry and to attend a gig, something they'd done frequently after graduating, but had started doing less and less as the years ticked by. Upon seeing the WhatsApp group, Zach had assumed that something similar was about to be proposed. Instead, the horror that he'd felt as he'd caught up on the messages and realised what was actually happening had been so sudden and so intense that he'd briefly thought he might be sick.

Abi had resurfaced. After ten years of silence – no messages, no phone calls, no posts on social media – she had been in touch, inviting them all to the opening of her brand-new lodge in Costa Rica.

At this point, Zach had frantically looked for his own invitation, desperate for more information. It quickly emerged that he hadn't received one. Instead, Abi had sent one to Olive, addressed to the pair of them. And Olive, so frantic with excitement, had accepted without so much as asking him what he thought.

He had tried, of course, to talk her out of it. It was all very well Abi offering to let them stay for free at the hotel, but they couldn't possibly afford the flights. They couldn't travel so far from Ryan. They had too many responsibilities to go swanning off to Costa Rica at just a few months' notice.

He'd made any excuse that he could think of. Offered any reason that he thought might sway her. In the end, though, it hadn't mattered. For Olive, the lure of seeing Abi again was too much. The chance to rekindle that friendship. The chance to find out why, exactly, she had been quiet for all that time.

Well, Zach couldn't allow it. They might well have arrived, but he could still try to keep Olive and Abi from speaking alone. He had to. If Olive were to learn the truth of what Abi had done the last time they'd been together, the life that Zach had steadfastly built for them would surely fall apart. His home, his son . . . He would lose it all.

So far, that particular goal had proven achievable. With Abi personally overseeing the preparations for the following evening's party, she was apparently so busy that she couldn't even come to greet them as they'd checked in. But once the festivities were out of the way, he would need to be on guard. They would have five nights left before flying home, during which he needed to watch them both like a hawk. And if the opportunity presented itself – if it seemed that *he* might somehow be able to get Abi alone – he would need to confront her. To make her tell him why she had brought them all together.

Forcing himself to stop pacing, he took several deep breaths and reached for his phone, seeing that there was some new activity on the WhatsApp group. Seth had posted a video of some kind, with a caption about Mike testing out the pool. Olive had just replied: Oh no! Poor Mike!

Zach didn't bother hitting play on the video. He could see clearly enough what had happened from the single frame that was available in the chat — a static image of a fully dressed Mike standing in the pool, face twisted into a scowl. Instead, he locked the phone again, pausing for a moment at the sight of his screensaver. It was a photo of Ryan, smiling into the camera with those wide hazel-coloured eyes.

At once, the fear returned. More than that, it seemed to swell, as Zach thought once more of all he stood to lose if Olive were to find out what Abi had done.

It was going to be all right, he told himself. It was going to be OK. Whatever Abi was up to — whatever reason she had for bringing them together — she wasn't going to tell Olive the truth.

He wasn't going to let her.

5

The rest of the afternoon passed by in a blur.

Meeting Jazz at a little wooden building deep in the jungle, the spa treatment had felt to Olive like something out of a magazine. Breathing in the scent of lavender and aloe vera, Jazz had wanted to try a mud treatment, but in the end they'd gone for a neck-and-shoulder massage. They were there for a week, Olive told herself. There would be plenty of time to be adventurous.

Later, on the walk back to the huts, it had rained. Olive had known to expect that. She remembered from their summer spent travelling that Costa Rica had only two seasons: dry and rainy. August, as it happened, was right in the middle of the rainy season.

It hadn't been like the kind of rain they knew at home, though; cold and persistent, with miserable little showers that would chill you to the bone and could last all day without ever letting up. The rain that afternoon had barely lasted five minutes. It had been urgent and powerful, as if the sky had been holding its breath and couldn't hang on a moment longer.

The funny thing, though, was that no one minded. The rain in this place felt almost like a celebration. A momentary downpour after which everything seemed to feel suddenly more alive. The jungle looked lusher and more verdant, leaves heavy with plump beads of water. The wildlife called out in a newly revived chorus. Even the air felt lighter, the humidity easing as if reset for the day.

When seven o'clock came rolling around, darkness having fallen and the evening beginning to draw in, Olive sat with Zach in the lobby, waiting for the others to join them for dinner.

The hotel didn't seem quieter for the arrival of nightfall. If anything, it was even busier than it had been when they had checked in that morning. The guests she had seen bustling around the garden and relaxing beside the pool now made their way to the restaurant, polo shirts and swimming costumes exchanged for blazers and glittering dresses. Staff, likewise, hurried around, ferrying objects in preparation for the launch event the next evening, as well as for the dinner service.

'This is the main lodge.'

Turning her head, Olive saw that a short distance away, at the reception desk, a member of staff was checking in a couple of new arrivals. Leaning forward slightly, she drew a circle on a printed map of the hotel.

'You'll find the huts on the path that goes left out of the

building. I've marked yours on the map. And here . . .' She drew three more small circles. 'You have the garden, the pool and the spa.'

The receptionist was clearly a *tica* – the local word, apparently, for a native Costa Rican – but her English was flawless. It occurred to Olive that the same could be said of every staff member she had met so far. The driver who had ferried them from the airstrip to the lodge, a *tico* called Hector, had frequently apologised for the quality of his English, despite, as far as Olive could tell, it being near perfect. She wondered if it was a requirement Abi imposed on any applicants for jobs at The Midnight Orchid.

'How do we get to the beach?' asked the man. They were American, well-dressed, each with greying hair. Even their luggage, it seemed to Olive, looked expensive.

The receptionist held her pen over an area of the map. 'The beach is in this direction. There is a beautiful trail through the jungle, if you would like to walk. Otherwise one of our staff can drive you.' She lowered her voice a fraction, her smile stretching wider. 'It's downhill all the way, so the most popular option is to walk down there and then call for a ride back up. If you do enjoy walking, though, you'll find a nature trail through the jungle at the back of the lodge. You'll see lots of different birds, maybe even sloths or iguanas. The waterfall is that way, too. Just go through the garden and follow the gravel path into the forest. The trail is marked, with a good path all the way round. Or if you would like a guided walk our staff lead daily wildlife tours every afternoon and evening.'

'That all sounds great,' said the man.

The receptionist smiled. '*Pura vida.*'

Pura vida.

So far, Olive had heard this expression used to mean 'hello', 'goodbye', 'thank you' and 'you're welcome'. At one point on the journey they had passed a roadside stall selling towels and sunhats on which it had been printed in bright letters. Calling over his shoulder from the driver's seat, Hector had explained that it was something of a national saying. It stood for wellbeing and gratitude, representing what he described as Costa Rica's positive outlook on life.

In that moment, Olive felt as if she could do with some *pura vida*. While she was of course looking forward to the evening ahead, the truth was that she was intensely nervous.

In a few minutes they would see Abi. *Abi.* For the first time in ten years. Olive's head spun with all the questions she would ask. But a dozen frightening possibilities also rattled around inside her mind. What if they had changed in a way that left Abi unimpressed? What if, by the end of the evening, she regretted inviting them? And perhaps most terrifying of all – what if the reason for her disappearance didn't put Olive at ease, as she hoped it would?

As the American couple headed off in search of their hut, Olive locked eyes with a woman across the lobby. She, too, seemed to be waiting for companions, sitting alone with her foot tapping almost nervously against the floor.

Exchanging smiles, Olive studied her for a moment.

She was a couple of years younger than Olive was herself. Late twenties, perhaps. She was also slight – Olive doubted that when she stood up she would be much more than five feet tall – and incredibly pale, surveying the lobby from behind a large pair of round glasses. Dark hair hung at her shoulders, and she was dressed simply, kitted out in sneakers and sage-green dungarees.

Hearing Zach laugh beside her, Olive turned to face him. For the past few minutes he'd been scrolling on Instagram. But now he was watching the video that Seth had put on their reunion WhatsApp group. Glancing at the screen Olive winced as she saw the furious Mike wading towards the side of the pool.

'I wish Seth hadn't filmed that,' she said. 'You know how embarrassed Mike gets.'

Zach waved her concern away. 'It's just what they're like. Mike will get over it.'

Olive thought about protesting – asking Zach if he would say something to Seth about teasing Mike. She was desperate for this reunion to be a success. That was hardly likely to happen if Seth and Mike came to blows on the first day.

But she decided to say nothing, all too aware that she would be met with grumbling and complaining. Instead, she turned her attention once more to the woman across the lobby. As she did so, she made a sudden realisation. This woman had been on the internal flight with them from San José.

She had sat quietly at the back of the plane, a chunky

pair of headphones over her ears as she'd looked out of the window. And then she had ridden with them to the lodge in the jeeps. Two vehicles had been sent to collect them. Olive had ridden in one with Zach and Jazz. The woman across the lobby had joined Mike and Seth in the other.

Now thoroughly intrigued, Olive watched the woman for a few seconds longer. She was clearly looking for someone, her eyes twitching every few seconds in the direction of the path that led towards the huts. More than that, she seemed nervous. She was chewing the corner of her lower lip, tapping the floor repeatedly with one foot.

Olive thought for a moment. Then, she rose to her feet.

Zach's eyes flicked suddenly up from his phone. 'Where are you going?'

'That woman was on our flight. I'm going to see if she'd like some company.'

'Why?'

Olive didn't answer, knowing he would only tell her that she was being silly. Instead, she made her way across the lobby, ignoring him as he hissed at her to come back.

Meeting the woman's eye, she offered a smile.

'Hi,' she said. 'Sorry, I don't mean to bother you. I couldn't help noticing you were on your own and I wondered if you might like some company. We were all on the same internal flight.'

At first the woman appeared confused. She looked past Olive, peering at Zach. Then she glanced down at herself. Apparently noticing the tapping foot – realising what had brought Olive her way – she gave a nervous laugh.

'Thanks,' she said. 'That's kind of you.'

Olive sat down beside her, settling into a second wicker chair.

'I'm Olive,' she said. 'That's my husband, Zach.'

'Stevie,' the woman replied.

Immediately Olive picked up on her accent. American, she thought.

The woman – Stevie – cleared her throat. 'It, uh . . . It sounded in the jeep like you guys might have been here before. I think I heard your friends talking about a reunion of some kind?'

Olive nodded, looking around the lobby in disbelief. 'That's right. Although you'd never know it was the same place. When we last came it was just a rundown campsite. Looking at it now . . .' She smiled. 'Not that it mattered. Campsite or not, this place means a lot to us – we actually got engaged here.'

'No way?'

'Mm-hm. Zach and I.' She nodded towards Zach, who was watching them warily from across the lobby. 'That was ten years ago now. We'd spent two months travelling down here from Mexico City, when we—'

'Stevie!'

A male voice came echoing across the lobby. Turning to face it, Olive saw Humphrey striding towards them. Dressed in designer shorts and a linen shirt, he ran a hand through his hair, the other tucked into his pocket.

'Sorry I'm late,' he said. 'Totally lost track of time and I— Oh, hey! Olive! How're you doing?' His face lit up, pulling Olive abruptly into a hug. 'Look at the two of you. I didn't know you'd already met.'

'Only just,' said Olive. 'We were on the plane together this morning.'

'Cool,' said Humphrey. 'Well, in that case, let me make a proper introduction. Stevie, Olive is Abi's best friend from England. We met a few years back, when I went to visit for a weekend.'

Olive found that she was beaming at the suggestion that she was Abi's best friend. 'And you two?' she said. 'You're together?'

Stevie and Humphrey shot each other a quick look.

'No,' he laughed. 'No, this is Stevie. Our sister.'

Olive blinked at him.

What had he just said? Sister? That couldn't be right. She must have misheard.

Humphrey frowned at her. 'Olive? Everything OK?'

'Yes,' she said quickly. 'Yes, of course. It's just . . .' She chewed her lip, narrowing her eyes as if concentrating intently. 'Sorry. But did you say *sister*?'

She said the word like she'd never heard it before, staring at Stevie as if she were some mythical creature that had just appeared from the jungle.

'Yeah . . .' Humphrey, too, now looked confused. 'Our parents adopted Stevie when she was four.'

Again, Olive stared, finding herself feeling only more confused. Could that really be right? How could she not have known that Abi and Humphrey had an adopted sister?

And then it seemed to dawn on all three of them at once.

Abi had never told her. In three years as a student at York — three years in which Olive had apparently been Abi's closest friend — she hadn't once mentioned that she had an adopted sister.

For a brief moment, Olive wasn't sure what to do with this revelation. She felt her jaw clench, her knees suddenly going a little weak at the thought of not having known something so significant about her best friend. But she didn't have long to think about it. At that moment another voice rang out across the lobby.

'Humphrey!'

Turning, Olive saw Seth and Mike making their way over. Dressed in shorts and flip-flops, Seth had a white shirt open down to his abdomen. Olive's heart sank as she saw that he was carrying a pair of swimming goggles. Trailing behind him was Mike. Clean-shaven and already a little sunburnt, with a checked shirt open over an Iron Maiden T-shirt, he looked hot, uncomfortable and considerably less pleased than Seth to see Humphrey.

'Seth!' Humphrey called back. 'How you doing, man?'

Olive watched as the two men embraced, clapping each other heartily on the back.

'Are you eating?' asked Seth. 'We should put a few tables together.'

'You know it. What are the goggles in aid of?'

'Oh, they're for Mikey. I thought he might need them at dinner.'

He tried to hand Mike the goggles, who was now scowling.

'I've told you,' said Mike. 'I'm not taking those. You might as well throw them in the bin.'

As Seth grinned, promising to show Humphrey the video, Olive's head spun. She was aware of the effort that she was making not to meet Stevie's eye – to look just about anywhere else as she tried to collect herself.

How could Abi not have mentioned a sister? Why had she not said anything? What else had she not told them?

'Aunt Stevie!'

As if in answer to her question, there came the pattering of feet, and Olive turned to see a young girl sprinting towards them.

'Hey, Aunt Stevie!' she cried out again, before launching herself at Stevie and throwing her arms around her middle.

Immediately, Olive recognised the girl, her heart leaping into her throat.

'I don't believe it,' said Seth. 'Mikey, look. It's your pal!'

Olive watched as his face lit up with delight. She couldn't help but notice that Mike, meanwhile, seemed so unhappy at the girl's arrival that he took a sudden step back, his own expression one of horror.

The girl looked up at Stevie, the biggest grin across her face.

'They said you were coming,' she said. 'They said you were!'

Aware of the ashen expression that she must be wearing,

Olive looked to Humphrey, forcing her features into what she hoped was a smile.

'Aunt Stevie,' she said. 'So you must be her dad.'

Humphrey shook his head, that grin still in place. 'Not me.'

'Then who . . . ?'

'Miley.'

One last voice came ringing out across the lobby. Clear and clean, it was the voice that Olive had been waiting all day to hear.

Slowly, she turned, and for the first time in a decade she looked upon her best friend.

Abi looked just as effortlessly perfect as Olive had known she would. Hair tied back, her green eyes were heavily shadowed, porcelain skin somehow untouched by the beating sun. She moved towards them like a breath of cool air, a loose skirt waving around her as she crossed the lobby. In each ear, a collection of silver piercings twinkled like stars.

Olive stared at her. In the months since receiving their invitation she had pictured this moment so many times. Imagined how perfect it would feel to be finally reunited. Instead, she found herself overwhelmed. She looked from Abi to Stevie, and then to the girl. Her mind raced at a hundred miles an hour as she pieced together everything she had missed since they'd parted ways. Everything she hadn't *known* during their time together at York.

'Come away, kiddo,' said Abi. 'Let's give Stevie some space.'

'But I want to—'

'Now, please, Miley.'

Miley resisted for a moment longer, her bottom lip sticking out in a defiant pout. But she did, eventually, do as she was told. Relinquishing her grip on Stevie's waist, she went to Abi, who placed her hands on the girl's shoulders.

Olive felt sick. She wanted this to stop. Wanted it all to be perfect, just as she'd imagined.

'Abi . . .' said Seth. 'Is she . . . ?'

Abi smiled. 'Hey, everyone. Sorry to keep you waiting. And yes.' She looked down at the girl, a proud smile touching her lips. 'This is Miley. My daughter.'

Part Two: The Sister

6

Two months earlier, Stevie Blythe sat on her bed, in the Camden apartment that she shared with her house-mate, Max.

The room itself was full to bursting, every available surface occupied. To anyone who didn't know Stevie, there would appear to be no discernible theme, each of the objects carefully organised but with little at first glance to connect them. Those who did, however, would understand the truth – that virtually everything in sight had at one point been rescued or rehomed.

On the windowsill there were several potted plants in various raggedy states. On top of an antique desk that had seen better days stood a gramophone that didn't work. Even Patch, the scruffy old cat who was snoozing on the bed, had been saved from a one-way ticket to Battersea. A colleague was being forced by their landlord to get rid of him, and in the absence of any other willing homes Stevie had taken him in. Her own landlord wasn't aware of Patch's existence. Nor did he allow his tenants to keep pets. But that was a problem Stevie would address if the time ever came.

As Max had once put it, it seemed there wasn't a lost or abandoned thing that Stevie could knowingly walk past.

At that moment, Stevie held her phone out in front of her. She was waiting on a call from Abi, having received a message that afternoon saying that they needed to talk. As she waited, she was watching a video that Humphrey had posted on Instagram two weeks earlier. In the footage, he was walking with purpose, blonde hair bouncing as he went. Dressed in a hoody and a pair of Ray-Ban sunglasses, she could see the straps of a rucksack on his shoulders, an airport terminal visible behind him.

'Well, boys and girls,' he said to the camera, 'here I am, at the airport in Manchester, New Hampshire, where I'm catching a flight to Thailand. Not something I was planning on doing when I woke up this morning, but guess what? As of about three hours ago, I don't have a job any more. Because the assholes on the board of directors at Conrad Blythe have seen fit to kick me out of my own goddamn company.'

Over the past fortnight, Stevie had watched this video more times than she could count. Still, she winced at the malice in his voice. She had, on occasion, seen her brother frustrated before, but never like this. The Humphrey she knew was full of life and laughter. For all intents and purposes, the furious young man in this video could have been a stranger.

'The company my dad built,' Humphrey continued. 'The company that was supposed to be his legacy to me and my sister. The company with my *goddamn name* over the door. But it seems being a Blythe isn't enough any more. Apparently I'm not good enough to be there. Apparently I've *never* been good enough. And now that Dad's six feet under, these sons of bitches feel it's finally safe to tell me they don't want me around.'

At this point he turned his head a fraction, looking directly into the camera.

'Here's the real kicker, though. Are you ready for this? It seems my sister isn't getting the same treatment. Oh no. For some reason, Abi's allowed to stay. Well, you know what? Fuck that. Fuck those old men on the board. Fuck this whole screwed-up situation. Now I'm about to get on a plane. If anyone needs me, I'll be in Bangkok blowing off some steam. Peace out, motherfuckers.'

As the video came to an end Stevie grimaced, swiping across to a second that Humphrey had posted just a few days later. It showed him in a nightclub, fluorescent paint in his hair and half a dozen different-coloured glowsticks around each of his wrists. Dressed in a designer shirt, the sleeves rolled back to show tanned forearms, he stood at a bar, a line of shots standing ready before him.

'Are we good?' he asked whoever was holding the camera. 'Are we filming?'

He had to shout over the thumping music that was playing in the club. Again, Stevie winced, this time at how drunk he appeared.

'OK,' he continued, swaying slightly as he reached for the first shot. 'Here's to all of you fuckers on the board.'

He tipped it back, reaching for the second.

'Here's to Abi, and all the hard work she's done that I apparently haven't.'

He tipped back the second shot.

'Here's to my dad, who, I'm sure, if he was still here to see it would be incredibly fucking unhappy with how his company's being run.'

He tipped back the third.

'And you know what? Here's to me not giving a fuck about any of it.'

There came a rapturous cheer as Humphrey grinned into the camera, perfect teeth on display. He tipped back the final shot. Then, the video came abruptly to a halt.

Stevie sighed. There were others that she could watch. Abi had saved them all. But she didn't want to see them. Not again. Instead, she put the phone to one side, eyes glazing over as she scratched Patch behind the ears.

She was certain that Abi wanted to talk about Humphrey. She could think of no other reason for her sister to call. Earlier that afternoon, it had occurred to her that she could think of no other *occasion* on which her sister had ever called her. Because Stevie, after all, was not a true Blythe. Not, at least, as far as Abi was concerned. Stevie was the family cuckoo, brought home, in Abi's own words, like a gerbil from a pet store. And Abi had resented her from the moment she'd arrived.

Born to a teenaged single mother who'd been unable

to cope with the demands of parenthood, Stevie had been just three when she was put up for adoption. Four when Frank and Jane Blythe had brought her home. And while Humphrey, as the eldest, had gladly welcomed the arrival of a new sibling, Abi, aged seven at the time, had made it clear from day one that she didn't want Stevie in their lives.

For years Abi had begged their parents to send Stevie back, going so far as to hide things in Stevie's room, in the hope of portraying her as a thief. As teenagers, their relationship had only become more strained. With Jane Blythe passing away shortly after Stevie turned fourteen – succumbing to the same disease that had taken her own mother before her – the seventeen-year-old Abi's resentment had reached a peak, accusations coming thick and fast that Stevie had stolen precious years that should rightfully have belonged to her and Humphrey. A few peaceful years had then followed when Abi went to university in the UK. A peace that was resumed when, a couple of years after Abi's studies had ended and she'd returned to the Blythe family's hometown of Concord, New Hampshire, Stevie herself had gone to work for a genealogy firm in London, turning down Frank's offer to join Abi and Humphrey at Conrad Blythe to instead help strangers trace their family histories.

This, it seemed to Stevie, was the ideal arrangement. Frank and Humphrey would visit her in London whenever they could. Likewise, she would go home for Christmas, Thanksgiving and the occasional birthday, visits that she would look forward to immensely and which it seemed Abi would just about tolerate.

For three years, that was the way it had been. Stevie in London. Her adoptive family an ocean away in New Hampshire. But things had changed when Frank, seemingly without warning, had suffered a fatal heart attack the previous fall. Flying home to Concord for the funeral, Stevie had stood in the graveyard, watching the coffin being lowered into a plot beside their mother's, and wondered if Abi might finally get her wish. If, with both Frank and Jane now gone, she and Stevie really might sever ties for ever.

For the best part of a year, that certainly seemed to have been the case. After the funeral, Stevie had returned to London, where she proceeded to hear not a word from Abi for nine months. Then had come Humphrey's removal from Conrad Blythe. Immediately after had come the videos on his Instagram. And then, that afternoon, there had come a message from Abi, saying they needed to talk.

Stevie sat there in silence, waiting for the phone to ring. In the kitchen, on the other side of her wall, it sounded as if Max might be emptying the dishwasher. An aspiring actor from County Cork, she sang to herself as she worked, a show tune just audible over the sound of clattering crockery and banging cupboard doors.

Stevie hummed along, trying to distract herself. Even so, it took a few moments to realise what it was that she was feeling as she waited for Abi's call. She was nervous.

74

Even with an ocean between them, the prospect of just speaking to her sister was enough to put her on edge.

When the phone did eventually ring, and Stevie brought it to her ear, her heart began to thump against her ribs.

'Humphrey's just been here,' said Abi. No greeting. No small talk. Not a shred of warmth in her tone.

Stevie blinked. 'He's home?'

'That's right.'

'What happened?'

'He's apologised. He's taken down those videos and he's told me he overreacted. He says he's sorry.'

'Well, that's . . . That's good. Isn't it?'

Abi didn't reply, and for a moment Stevie wondered if the call had been disconnected. Then, at last, her sister said four words that she had never imagined she might ever hear.

'I need your help.'

Stevie was so taken aback that she didn't know what to say. Over the years, Abi had requested that Stevie leave their family, that she stop using the Blythe name, and even that she not speak to her. But not once had Abi ever asked for her help.

'He wants to come to the launch,' Abi continued. 'Of the hotel. He claims to understand the board's decision. He's out. Non-negotiable. And he says he knows that. But he's insisting he still wants to come to the launch party.'

'What for?' Stevie asked.

'He says he wants to support me. That he wants to make up for flying off the handle.'

75

'And you don't believe him?'

'Not for a second. I'm terrified he's going to try something, but I'm just as frightened of what he'll do if I tell him he can't come. Now, for some reason, much as it pains me, he listens to you. If the truth is that he's planning to try something reckless, I think you might be the only one who could talk some sense into him. So I need . . .' There was a pause. Stevie could almost feel Abi's repulsion as she said the next words. 'So I need you to come. To Costa Rica. I need you to keep an eye on him, and if it looks like he's going to try anything, I need you to stop him.'

Stevie didn't know what to say. Even when Humphrey had been involved in the hotel, she hadn't bothered asking if she might be invited to the launch party. She had known all too well that Abi would want her nowhere near it. So to be asked to come – regardless of the circumstances – felt little short of unbelievable.

'Why's this happening?' she eventually asked. 'Why has the board kicked Humphrey out?'

'Why do you think?' Abi spat down the line. 'Because he's a nightmare to work with. He's lazy and he doesn't take anything seriously. Just look at the lodge. Dad gave it to us as a test and Humphrey's just sat around taking credit for everyone else's work. *My* work, specifically. Now that Dad's no longer here to protect him the board has decided they don't want to deal with him any more.'

Stevie's eyes were wide with disbelief.

'So what do you say?' asked Abi.

'About what?'

'About the lodge. Are you coming or not?'

Stevie had said she would. Abi had booked her a flight. And now there she was. In Costa Rica. Tasked with preventing Humphrey from doing something she had no way of knowing if he was even considering.

Sitting alone at a table in the corner of the restaurant terrace, an hour had now passed since dinner had ended, with Abi's friends having dispersed and gone back to their huts for the night. Her phone was pressed to her ear, Max demanding to know all that had happened during her first day at The Midnight Orchid.

'So let me get this straight,' said Max. 'You're saying that in the three years Abi spent at York, she didn't tell her friends that you so much as existed.'

'Seems that way,' Stevie replied. 'I guess it's stupid of me to be so surprised. Growing up, she used to hate when her friends asked questions about me. She probably relished being somewhere people didn't know.'

'Mate,' said Max. 'This sister of yours is a piece of work.'

Stevie gave a hollow laugh. 'How's Patch?'

'He's fine. Although the way he was trying to mug me for my lunch this afternoon he'll be lucky if he's still here when you get back. Don't change the subject, though, Stevie. Tell me more about this dinner you had with them all. Was it weird?'

Stevie thought for a moment. 'A little,' she said. 'I mean . . . Listening to them all catch up, Abi clearly hasn't seen any of these guys in the ten years they've been apart. Hasn't even *spoken* to them, I don't think. So why has she invited them all out here for a reunion?'

'Isn't that sort of the point of a reunion? To catch up with people you haven't seen in a long time?'

'Sure. But inviting them halfway round the world? And they've *come*? Can you think of any friends you haven't spoken to in ten years who you'd do that for?'

'They probably just wanted a holiday. Hold on. Just a sec, Stevie.'

For a few moments Stevie heard muffled movement on the other end of the line. Then the sound of a door, a scrap of muffled conversation and the rustling of a plastic bag.

'Sorry about that,' said Max.

'Deliveroo again?'

'Maybe.'

'I thought you were broke?'

'I am. But I'm hardly going to learn to cook just because you're not here.'

Stevie gave a small laugh.

'How's Humphrey been?' said Max. 'You had any trouble watching over him today?'

'I've barely needed to. I got here at midday, and he's been out ziplining all afternoon. I didn't catch up with him until we all met up for dinner.'

'And do you think Abi's right? Do you really think he's there to try something?'

'I don't know. I don't think so. He's not the vindictive type. But I suppose . . .' She tailed off, thinking of

Humphrey's fury in the videos. Then, she sighed. 'What am I doing here, Max? Why didn't I just tell Abi I had a conference or something?'

'Because you're a good person. And you don't want to see your brother doing something he'll regret.'

Stevie didn't reply.

'It's his own fault this is happening,' Max pressed. 'I know you love him, but Humphrey can't just coast his way through life. If your crazy-rich dad wanted to offer him a ready-made career path to one day becoming the joint CEO of one of the largest hotel empires in America, and he then decides to spaff that all away, that's on him. And if he can't see that then maybe he deserves to get into a bit of trouble.'

Again, Stevie didn't reply.

'Hey,' Max continued. 'I have a question for you. Something I've been thinking about since you set off. You say your old man brought Humphrey and Abi into the family business, with a view to them potentially taking his place at the top someday.'

'Sure.'

'So why didn't *you* join too? Was the option never there for you or . . . ?'

Stevie hesitated.

'It was,' she said at last. 'Dad asked me to join. More than once. But I guess it was just never something I wanted to do.'

'Why not?'

'I don't know.'

'*Stevie.*'

Stevie closed her eyes. 'If you must know, I guess I felt I didn't have the right.'

'The right?'

'Yeah. Like . . . It was something for Abi and for Humphrey. But not for me.'

'And I take it you know who's responsible for you feeling that way?'

'I have a pretty good idea.'

She heard Max make an unhappy noise. 'This sister of yours, Stevie.'

'In fairness——'

'No, Stevie. No *in fairness*——'

'Just hear me out!' Stevie laughed. 'In fairness, I don't know how much I would have really wanted to work for the company. I think I'd known for a long time that I wanted to do something that would help people like me. People who didn't know where they came from.'

'So you ended up in genealogy.'

'Exactly.'

'And why take a job in London? I'm sure there must be people in New Hampshire who want help tracing their family history.'

This time, Stevie struggled for an answer.

'Oh, God,' said Max. 'Don't tell me Abi drove you away.'

'She didn't say anything,' Stevie said quickly. 'She didn't *tell* me to go or anything like that——'

'But she made you feel like you should.' Something

changed in Max's voice, a hint of desperation starting to creep in. 'Seriously, Stevie. Why are you thinking about going back to these people?'

Stevie didn't reply. She didn't know if she could. Wasn't sure she had the words to articulate the various conflicting feelings that gripped her whenever she considered going home.

For a moment she pictured herself back in New Hampshire. She thought of horse farms and hockey matches. Lake swimming in the summer and ski trips in the winter. Laughing at the leaf-peepers who flocked from out of state to see the autumn colours.

And then she imagined where she might live. A nice little condo, maybe. Somewhere in Concord. She imagined inviting Humphrey over for dinner during the week. Babysitting Miley at weekends.

Most clearly of all, though, she imagined Abi embracing her. Telling her, at last, that she truly was a Blythe.

'Stevie?' said Max. 'Are you there?'

'Yeah,' she said. 'Yeah, sorry. I'm here.' Suddenly frustrated, she wiped a tear roughly from the corner of her eye.

'Listen, Stevie. Try to—'

Before she could go any further, Max's voice abruptly cut out.

'Max?' said Stevie. 'Max?'

No answer came.

Sighing, Stevie set her phone down on the table. She knew exactly what had ended the call. Never in her life had she met anyone so averse to charging their own phone as Max.

Clasping her hands, she leaned back in her seat until her head touched the window. From the restaurant's elevated position, the garden at the back of the lodge was spread out before her. Gravel paths weaved neatly between perfectly tended bushes and trees, upon which a small number of guests were seemingly out on after-dinner walks. In the centre, Stevie could see a small plaza with benches and a large fountain. Off to the right, where the garden ended, she could just about see lights glowing from the swimming pool area. And at the far end, a temporary stage had been constructed, upon which there would presumably be some entertainment during the launch party. Behind the stage, where in the daylight there had been a mass of jungle, trees and ferns of a hundred different species and hues woven together to form an impenetrable wall, there was now just darkness. She could scarcely make out the canopy, stretching towards the ocean. She could, however, see the light of a full moon reflected on the distant surface of the Pacific.

Reaching again for her phone, she tapped open her work emails, scrolling through a selection of replies and updates on various projects. There was the woman in Cardiff hoping to confirm the identity of her great-grandfather, a European labourer who had visited England only briefly before returning to his home country without ever knowing that the young sweetheart he'd met was carrying his child. Then there was the man in Scarborough, a devoted student of the First World War, who was trying to paint a clearer picture of the lives of several distant relations who had laid down their lives in the Somme. There was even a slightly more scandalous affair, with a woman in London having recently learned that her grandmother had given up an illegitimate child, before meeting the man who would later become her husband. Stevie's role in that particular project was to locate the child – now, presumably, aged somewhere in their sixties – and find out what had become of them.

She skimmed through each email, sending replies where needed, before stopping on one message in particular. Sent by her boss, Alex, she could see that it had arrived the previous afternoon, shortly after she'd boarded the Heathrow flight to San José. Tapping it open, she read:

Fwd: Subject: Thank you!

Dear Stevie,

It was great chatting with you yesterday. As discussed, I'm sending this email to put in writing the offer of a promotion to Project Lead, effective immediately upon your acceptance.

I do hope you'll consider it. You've been an exemplary member of the team these past three years, and the Directors are all agreed that you're more than ready to take this leap. That said, I know what a commitment this would be, given that you have recently been considering returning home to the US, and I don't want you to rush into making a decision. So give it some thought while you're away this week and perhaps chat it over with your family. We can wait for an answer until your return.

For the time being, please do try not to look at your inbox. You deserve this break. As this is the last note I hope to send you until you're back at your desk, let me take the opportunity to just highlight the email below, which arrived from Neil this morning. You're going to be modest and say that it was a team effort, but we all know you did the lion's share on this one, so I think it's lovely that he's thanked you personally. You should be proud.

Have a lovely break, and see you next week.
Alex

Director
Living History Ltd
St Martin's House
Chancery Lane
London

Uncover your story

Begin forwarded message:

Subject: Thank you!

Dear Alex,

Hope you're keeping well. I just wanted to share the attached photo from my meeting with Simon this morning.

It was an amazing couple of hours. He looks even more like me in person than in the picture you found. We even have a couple of the same mannerisms. Honestly, I'm still buzzing from it. Incredible to think that just a few weeks ago I had no idea he existed.

Thanks again, to you and your team, for making this happen. And a special thank you to Stevie for all of her hard work. It's changed my life.

Best wishes,
Neil

Opening the attachment that Alex had forwarded, Stevie saw a photo of two men in their fifties. Sitting in a coffee shop, they beamed into the camera, each with an arm around the other's shoulders. Neil was right. The resemblance was uncanny. She could see it in the bridge of their noses and the shape of their chins. But it was their eyes that clinched it. Not only were they the same colour, but as the long-lost brothers smiled for the camera their eyes crinkled in just the same way at the corners.

Smiling, Stevie typed out a quick reply, thanking Alex for the message and promising that she would try to keep out of her emails. Then, she put down the phone once more.

If she was honest with herself, in the two days since Alex had taken her into a meeting room to offer the promotion, Stevie had been trying hard not to think about it. But with the question of her future now brought firmly to the front of her mind, she thought of the conversation she'd had with Max after the offer had been made.

Seriously, Stevie, why are you wavering on this? Why would you even consider going back to the States?

Because it's my home.

Is it? You've got a sister who hates you just for existing, a brother who's doing his utmost to screw his life up . . . Why can't London be your home?

Was Max right? Sitting there now, in The Midnight Orchid, Stevie couldn't help but wonder why she wasn't accepting this promotion on the spot. What would be so bad about committing to staying in London? Why did she cling to the idea of one day going home? Why was she even there, in Costa Rica?

She told herself that she had come to The Midnight Orchid for Humphrey. Because for all of his flaws – his laziness, his recklessness, his occasional bouts of jealousy and impetuousness – he was a good person. He made people laugh, and whereas Abi had rejected Stevie as a sibling from the very beginning, Humphrey, meanwhile, had welcomed her. She loved her brother and she didn't want to see him get himself into trouble.

This was what she kept telling herself. Because the alternative was that she had come for Abi's benefit. That, no matter how futile it might seem, she still hadn't given up on winning the approval of her adoptive sister. And she wasn't ready to admit that just yet.

Perhaps Max was right. Perhaps she really should give up on the idea of returning to the States. On Abi accepting her as a Blythe. Perhaps London was her home now. Would that really be so terrible?

She reflected on how she'd come to join the Blythe family in the first place. Desperate for a large family, but unable to have any more children of their own after Humphrey and Abi, Frank and Jane had been ecstatic to bring home four-year-old Stevie. Ten years later, Jane had died, taken by the same disease that had killed Humphrey and Abi's grandmother. Now twenty-eight, Stevie was acutely aware that more time had since passed than they had actually spent together as a family unit. And now Frank was gone too, taken suddenly one afternoon by a heart attack.

It had been Frank and Jane who had made her a Blythe. With them gone, maybe it really was time for her to make a home elsewhere.

Sighing, she began to think about returning to her hut. It was late and she was worn out from the journey, a quick shower and a good night's sleep calling out to her.

She closed her eyes, mustering the willpower to move her weary legs. Any second, she thought to herself. Any second now, I'll make myself go to bed.

But it was at that moment that her thoughts were interrupted by the sound of footsteps. Her eyes snapping open, she was just in time to see Olive sweep onto the terrace.

7

From the outside, the group's first dinner together in The Midnight Orchid's restaurant must have looked exactly as Olive had hoped.

Once the initial shock of Miley's identity had abated, and the group had spent a few minutes introducing themselves to her, Abi asked her daughter to bid her friends goodnight before a member of the lodge's staff – the same staff member, Olive noticed, from Seth's poolside video – took her off to bed.

After Miley had departed, they'd gone through to the restaurant, pushing a couple of tables together on the outdoor terrace. Wooden boards underfoot, they were seated at the far end of the terrace, with a glass barrier offering a clear view down on the large garden at the rear of the lodge.

A waiter came within moments of them sitting down, and Abi ordered three bottles of wine and a selection of sharing platters for the table without so much as glancing at a menu. As they waited for the food to arrive, she regaled them with the story of how she had acquired the land, of the two years that had been spent building the hotel, and of the various preparations she was personally overseeing for the launch. She told them about how the hotel ran almost entirely on solar power and how they drew their own fresh water from a local spring. She knew each staff member by name and could recall where each ingredient for every dish had been sourced. In essence, it became evident that The Midnight Orchid wasn't just a project for her. It was her kingdom.

The food soon arrived, the waiters setting down plates of fish wrapped in banana leaves, tacos drizzled in a vivid lime-green salsa, and traditional combinations of rice, plantain and black beans. Dessert, when it came, consisted of ice cream and fruit served on crushed ice.

As they ate, the conversation was lively. Mike fawned over Abi, laughing too loudly at every joke and seizing any opportunity to compliment her on the hotel. Seth told her about some of the raves and music festivals he'd attended over the past decade. Even Humphrey got stuck in, knocking back tequila shots with Seth and attempting unsuccessfully to flirt with Jazz.

Yes, to any observers the dinner would have appeared the perfect start to a long-awaited reunion. But underneath it all, Olive was feeling utterly blindsided by the appearances of Stevie and Miley. Looking around the table, she could see in each of their faces how badly they all wanted to ask Abi about her daughter and her sister. But no one seemed brave enough. Not when it appeared to be the one subject on which Abi refused to volunteer any information. And certainly not with Stevie herself sitting there at the table.

In the end it was Mike who took the plunge. At one point between the main course and the desserts, while Abi left the table to answer a call, he turned to Humphrey and said, 'I don't understand. Why didn't she ever tell us she had a child? How can she have gone all this time without ever *saying*?'

Humphrey shrugged, taking a sip of wine. 'She's always been protective over Miley. Never allowed anyone to put pictures of her on social media. Won't even let me take her out on a daytrip to Echo Lake. It's just the way she is. I guess that with you guys back in the UK she just decided it would be easiest not to say anything.'

Mike nodded. Then he asked the question that no one had been brave enough to ask.

'So who's her dad?'

Humphrey adopted a grim expression. 'I don't think that's my story to tell.'

'Did someone hurt her?' It was Olive herself who'd spoken this time, making no effort to hide the concern in her voice.

'No,' Humphrey said quickly. 'No, it's nothing like that. It's just . . .' He sighed. 'We don't know.'

'You don't know?' Jazz cocked an eyebrow.

'Abi doesn't like to talk about it,' said Humphrey. 'I think she's embarrassed by it all. But the long and short of it is that after your trip – after you guys went back to the

UK and she'd come home to New Hampshire – she was in a bad way. Really down. And about a week or two after she got back, she hooked up with a guy from a bar. Wasn't interested in his name. Apparently he was just passing through, back on the road in the morning. A month later, she gathers me and Dad at the house and tells us she's pregnant.'

'Did she not try to find him?' asked Jazz.

'Sure. But as I say, she didn't know anything about him. She didn't know where he'd come from, wasn't sure where he was headed in the morning. She didn't even get the guy's last name. She went back to the bar but no one could help.'

Abi returned before they could press Humphrey further, abruptly removing the opportunity to ask any more questions about Miley. Instead they talked a little more about the hotel. They discussed the decor, the building, the plans for the party . . .

And it was here that Olive said it.

'Well, listen,' she said. 'I think you two have done the most amazing job here. I didn't know him, of course, but I'm sure your dad would be very proud of you – I'm sure *both* of your parents would. And I think we should raise a toast to you, and to the lodge, and to everything you're going to do together going forward.'

Abi gave a pained smile. 'Olive . . . There's something—'

'Thanks, Olive.' Humphrey cut over her. 'That's very kind. But I think I need to come clean before I take any

91

credit that isn't deserved.' He then grinned, before saying, 'It's just Abi who needs congratulating. I'm no longer part of the company.'

Olive frowned. 'But I thought you'd both worked on this place? Didn't your dad bring the two of you in together?'

'He did,' Humphrey agreed. 'But the board had other ideas. They kicked me out a couple months ago. I'm only here this week to support Abi.'

Olive hadn't had the first idea of what to say to this, scolding herself for not somehow knowing. When, a few minutes later, Abi rose a second time from her seat, announcing that she needed to call a few more suppliers ahead of the party and was unlikely to be back, she felt both relieved and devastated that the evening had ended on such an uncomfortable note.

The others began to peel off soon after Abi left, Mike departing first, followed by Jazz. But Olive, whose head was still spinning, touched Zach gently on the arm.

'I don't think I'm quite ready,' she said. 'For bed. I want to stay up for a bit. Maybe go for a walk. Will you come with me?'

Zach grimaced. 'I don't know, Liv. I'm shattered. You go for your walk. I'll join you for one tomorrow.'

She forced a smile, removing her hand, and after he'd gone she did as she'd said she would. She walked around the garden and then beside the pool, the parasols having been taken down and the water lit up in an impossible shade of blue. Each time she completed her loop, she started it again, the action of walking helping to calm her racing mind.

The truth was that she felt confused. Betrayed, even, by the discovery of Abi's seemingly secret family members.

In many ways Miley's existence explained a lot. For a start, it explained what Abi had been doing these past ten years. Why, in the months after their trip, she hadn't so much as responded to the invitations to her and Zach's wedding. But at the same time the story of Miley's conception didn't sound like the Abi that Olive knew. Back at York, Olive remembered Abi regularly turning up at the students' union in old joggers, hair scraped back and without a smudge of make-up, and still she'd turn just about every male head in the room. But she had never been interested in any of them. Had never had a boyfriend or even taken a guy home for the night while they were students. For her to have been so low after the end of their trip that she'd found herself falling pregnant by a man she didn't even know . . . Olive felt an intense rush of guilt, thinking of how *she* had been spending that same period of time, eagerly planning her wedding to Zach. But why had Abi never said anything? Never confided in her? Never asked for help?

And then there was Stevie.

How, in all the time they had spent together at York, could Abi not have told them about Stevie? Had Olive done something wrong, for Abi to feel she couldn't share Stevie's existence? Had she really known her friend at all?

Having lost count of the number of circuits she had completed of the garden, but still not yet ready to return to her hut, Olive went back into the main lodge, passing straight through the restaurant and out onto the terrace. Finding that she had the place to herself, she walked across the wooden boards to the glass barrier, looking down on the garden below.

Even in darkness, it was beautiful. And as she stood there taking it in Olive wanted to enjoy it. To breathe it all in and be carefree once more, as they had been ten years ago. As she'd hoped they would be when they arrived here again. But try as she might, she was struggling.

In the weeks leading up to the trip, she had refused to listen to Jazz's suspicions. To the idea that Abi must surely have some ulterior motive for wanting to bring the group together after all this time. But now, upon learning of the existence of Miley and Stevie, there was a gnawing feeling in her stomach that this impromptu reunion might not be as innocent as it had first seemed. Why, exactly, had Abi gathered them?

She turned away from the view, intending to make her way back to the hut and to Zach. Instead, she leapt half out of her skin at the sight of Stevie, watching her intently from the corner of the terrace.

8

For several moments, Stevie had been sitting completely still, trying to determine what to do about the fact that Olive clearly didn't realise she was with her on the terrace.

At first she had thought about somehow drawing Olive's attention. Calling out her name, perhaps, or clearing her throat. But already, in the seconds she had spent contemplating what she might do, it felt as if too much time had passed. So now she was considering whether there might be a chance that she could sneak away without being noticed.

Yes. That was the thing to do. Olive stood at the barrier, looking down on the garden. If Stevie could stand up without being heard, and then cling to the restaurant wall, she could make it to the door and disappear back inside without—

But before she could give any further thought to her escape plan, Olive turned, promptly jumping out of her skin.

'Oh, God!'

'Sorry!' Stevie leapt to her feet. 'I'm so sorry. I didn't want to disturb you. I was trying to see if I could—'

'No,' said Olive. 'No, it's fine. You didn't . . . I should have . . .'

An uncomfortable silence settled, Stevie now acutely aware of how Olive was staring at her.

'I'll, um . . .' Stevie motioned towards the restaurant. 'I'll leave you to it.'

'No!' Olive said quickly. 'No, you stay. You were here first. I was just . . . I wasn't ready to go to bed yet.'

'You sure?'

'Yes,' Olive insisted. 'Please. Stay.'

Stevie nodded. 'OK. Thank you.'

She sat back down, Olive turning to leave. Just as she was about to step inside, though, she looked back.

'I'm sorry about earlier. About not knowing who you were.'

Stevie smiled. 'No need to apologise. How could you have known if you hadn't been told?'

'I know. But I just . . .' Olive looked troubled. 'Can I be honest? It's bothering me that I didn't know. Abi was my best friend. I saw her every day for three years. I told her everything there was to know about myself. I just don't know what it means for her to have never told me about having another sibling. And now to have found out that she has a *child* too . . . That instead of telling us about Miley – instead of asking us for help – she decided to go quiet . . .'

Stevie was silent, trying to think of something she could say that would offer some comfort.

'I can't speak for Miley,' she said at last. 'But as for Abi not telling you about me . . . I think it's more to do with me than you.' She sighed. 'It was difficult for Abi. Having me around.'

'How so?'

Stevie shook her head. 'I don't think she would like me talking to you about this.'

'Seriously? It's so bad that she wouldn't even want us talking?'

Yes, Stevie thought. It is absolutely as bad as that.

She didn't say it out loud, though. Instead, she looked Olive in the eye, deliberating over how dangerous it would be for her to speak out of turn to Abi's supposed best friend.

'Did you say that you guys got engaged here?'

Olive didn't reply immediately. Stevie was trying to change the subject and they both knew it.

'Yeah,' she said eventually. 'We did.' Apparently playing along, she turned back to the glass barrier, gazing out over the garden. 'You know, I've been thinking about the layout of this place. I'm actually pretty sure it happened somewhere in that garden. It wasn't a garden then, of course. And there was an old farmhouse. Just there, I think.' She pointed towards the pool. 'The place really was a dive. It's no wonder Abi and Humphrey managed to buy the land so cheaply. But it was where it happened.' Olive smiled to herself, bowing her head slightly as if embarrassed. 'I'd found the ring. A couple of hours beforehand. I'd gone into Zach's rucksack looking for some mosquito spray and I found it squirrelled away in one of the pockets.'

'That must have been quite a surprise,' said Stevie.

'It was. I mean, we'd been together three years, but we were still only twenty-one. I had no idea he was even *thinking* about proposing.'

'You met at university?'

'That's right. We lived together in halls. One of those flats where six of you share a kitchen. Our rooms were next door to each other. I remember bumping into him in the corridor the day I arrived, while my parents were helping me carry my stuff up from the car. And that was it.'

'Love at first sight,' said Stevie.

'Exactly. Seth was in that flat, too. The three of us became friends. And then Zach met Mike through his course.'

'When did Abi come into it?'

'I met her at a students' union thing in freshers' week. She hadn't made many friends yet, and we all got along really quickly, so she became part of our little group too. I think . . .' She took a deep breath. 'I didn't have many friends as a kid. I was never popular. That's probably why this group meant so much to me. And why, in hindsight, I went all in on my relationship with Zach. I'd always had Jazz, of course. We're cousins. We grew up together. But I'd never had a group of friends like that. Never had a boyfriend. And then, when I met Abi, and she seemed to want to be part of our group too . . . Well, I just couldn't believe it.'

Stevie nodded, understanding. She knew a thing or two about loneliness.

'You know,' Olive continued, 'it still seems like the most surreal moment. A few hours passed between me finding the ring and him fetching it out. I'd become pretty giddy in that time. When we were all around the campfire, and he did, finally, go into his rucksack, I was so excited that I didn't even wait to hear him ask the question. I saw the box in his hand, and the second he opened it I just shouted, "Yes!" You should have seen the look on his face. He must have thought that he was going to take me by surprise. At the very least, I'm sure he had a little speech prepared, but I couldn't help myself. It just came out. It took him a minute to recover. In the end I had to say, "Go on then. Put the ring on me."'

Stevie smiled. 'Sounds like quite the moment.'

'It was,' Olive agreed. 'We called my mum straight away.'

'You called her there and then?'

'We had to. I'd already messaged her that afternoon to say I'd found the ring. We were close like that. And . . . she was sick at the time. Really sick. She's better now, thank God. But she was in the hospital when we called her. She put us on speakerphone and we heard the nurses give a little cheer. The next day, when we flew home, some of my family were waiting for us in the airport. They took us home and threw us a little surprise engagement party.'

'Sounds like a dream,' said Stevie.

'Yeah,' Olive replied. 'Yeah, it was.'

They stood together, leaning against the barrier. Olive had enjoyed telling the story. Stevie could see that. But she still looked troubled.

'Did Abi ever mention Joel?'

Olive frowned. 'Joel? Who's Joel?'

Stevie chewed her lip, deliberating over how much was wise to share.

'Who's Joel?' Olive asked again, a hint of panic now sounding in her voice. 'You don't have *another* sibling she never told me about, do you?'

Stevie took a deep breath.

Then, she paused, noticing movement in the garden.

'Hey,' she said. 'Is your friend OK?'

She pointed into the garden. Towards Mike. He was clearly drunk, tottering towards the jungle at the far edge of the garden.

Olive frowned. 'Where's he going?'

Stevie didn't reply. She had no idea.

Together, the two women watched as Mike took out his phone, turned on the torch and disappeared into the jungle.

9

Having agreed with Olive that they should follow the clearly inebriated Mike and make sure he was OK, Stevie led the way towards the far edge of the garden.

As they continued into jungle, they found that the path was well defined, Stevie remembering how there had been talk of a nature trail for guests to explore. It was a relief, but a gravel path underfoot didn't make the crushing darkness of the surrounding rainforest feel any less intimidating. With the moonlight barely able to penetrate the canopy that sat thick above their heads, Stevie wished more than once for a better torch than the narrow strip of light being cast by her phone. The sounds of the night filled her ears, unseen creatures rustling leaves and branches, and she forced herself to keep her eyes firmly on the path, trying hard not to think of whatever might be watching them pass. Snakes. Tarantulas. Possibly even jaguars. What was the comment Humphrey had made over dinner? *The most interesting critters come out after dark.*

Olive called out Mike's name a few times as they

walked. The lack of a response did nothing to put Stevie at ease. But after a minute or two, a sound emerged through the trees. It was a faint hissing, reminding Stevie of radio static.

Olive's eyes widened. 'The waterfall,' she said. 'Of course. I know where this leads, now. There wasn't much of a path to it when we were last here, so it all feels a little different. But if the garden is where we had our camp-fire, then I'm pretty certain this takes us to the waterfall.'

Stevie didn't reply, although she agreed that it made sense. If that was where Mike had gone, and if he was close enough now to this waterfall, then there was a strong chance he wouldn't have heard them calling out to him.

The path began to slope downward, at one point on a surprisingly steep incline. But after another few minutes, the canopy cleared, moonlight finally providing a little extra visibility. Ahead was a clearing, containing a pool large enough in which to swim. Water tumbled into it from a cliff edge perhaps thirty feet above them.

And there was Mike. He was walking from tree to tree, seemingly inspecting them each in turn. Looking at him now, it was immediately clear that their suspicions on the terrace had been correct – he'd undoubtedly had a lot to drink. As he moved between the trees he muttered to himself, looking more than once as if he might trip or lose his balance.

Olive squinted, keeping her voice to a whisper. 'What's he doing?'

Stevie shook her head. 'I've no idea.'

At that point, Mike turned, and upon seeing the light from Olive's phone gave a violent start.

'Who's there?' he cried out. 'Who is it?'

'It's OK!' Olive sprang forward, turning her light around so that he could see her face. 'It's OK, Mike. It's just us.'

'Olive?' Mike's face creased into a frown. 'What're you doing?'

'I'm sorry. We saw you disappearing into the trees and thought we'd best make sure you're OK. You looked . . . Well, you looked like you might be a little drunk.'

Mike gave a short laugh, swaying slightly. 'Just a bit. Been thinking.' Words slurring, he turned away and stumbled off in the direction of a particular tree. 'This is it,' he murmured. 'Yeah, this is the one.' He ran his hands over the bark, before calling over his shoulder, 'Do you think she looks like me? Miley, I mean?'

'Miley?' said Olive. 'Why would Miley look like you?'

'Didn't Seth ever tell you what happened here?' Mike asked. 'What he walked in on? He said he wouldn't, but I always wondered . . .'

Olive looked perplexed. 'Seth?' she repeated. 'No, Seth hasn't told us anything.'

Mike didn't answer. He pressed his hand to the tree, eyes distant. In the gloom, it looked to Stevie as if he was trying not to cry.

'Mike . . .' said Olive. 'Why would Miley look like you? What hasn't Seth told us?' She took a step closer.

'Did something happen with you and Abi? Did the two of you . . . ?'

Still Mike didn't reply. He hardly needed to. Olive was still talking, piecing it together as she went.

'Oh, God,' she said. 'I think I remember . . .'

She pulled a face, working hard to cast her mind back. Then, as if suddenly remembering that Stevie was there too, she looked back, lowering her voice so that Mike wouldn't hear.

'After Zach proposed, and I called my mum to tell her the news, Abi went for a walk in the forest. I wanted to take a photo with everyone, so Mike went to find her. When *he* didn't come back either, Seth went to look too.'

She stared at Mike. 'Did something happen with you and Abi? Is that what Seth hasn't told us? Did he find you here?'

Mike nodded. 'She was upset,' he said. 'When I found her. Something had upset her. I asked what it was, but she wouldn't tell me. So I said, "Let's get back to the others." She didn't want to go. When I asked her again to come back with me, she . . .' He frowned, as if he himself couldn't believe what he was about to say. 'She threw herself at me.'

He closed his eyes. Stevie, meanwhile, winced, trying hard not to picture her sister and Mike against the tree that he was still touching.

'I didn't know what to do,' Mike continued. 'I suppose I should've stopped it. But I'd been in love with her since the night you first brought her back to the flat in halls. I'd *dreamed* of this happening someday. So I went with it. Only . . .'

He tailed off.

'What?' Olive pressed. 'What happened, Mike?'

He swallowed. 'That's when Seth found us. It must have only been a minute or two. I didn't think I'd . . . I didn't think I'd *finished*. I was sure of it. But now that we're here again . . . Now that we know about Miley, I can't help thinking that the dates add up. They *do* add up.'

He seemed to reach the end of his story, once again having to fight back tears. Stevie, meanwhile, found that her mind was racing. She was looking at Mike intently, eyes bulging as she tried to determine if he bore any resemblance to her niece.

'Mike,' Olive said gently, 'if you were Miley's dad, why would Abi keep that from you? Why wouldn't she say anything?'

'I don't know,' he said. 'I didn't . . .' He looked Olive in the eye. 'I'm in love with her. Even now. I've always been in love with her.'

'Mike . . .' Olive said again. 'You haven't seen her in ten years.'

'But that's how you know, isn't it? If it lasts. If the feeling's still there.' He took a breath. 'I always wondered. When we went back to the UK. Was it a one-off thing? Was she just sad and in need of something to distract her? Or was there a chance that, on some level, she felt it too? Felt the same as I did about her? That's why I was so desperate to come out here. When she invited us to the hotel, it's why I was so eager . . . I needed to know if she might feel the same. To know if there was any chance she might want to pick up where we left off.'

At this point, he did, finally, start to cry, and Olive had to step forward and pull him into a hug. Stevie watched as he buried his face in Olive's shoulder. Then he looked up and met her eye.

'Sorry,' he mumbled.

'What for?'

'Dunno. She's your sister. It's probably weird hearing about her hooking up with someone.'

Stevie didn't reply. While Olive did her best to comfort Mike, she walked around the edge of the water, using her torch to light the way. After a few moments, the ground changed. All of a sudden there was a flash of pale blue. It was then that Stevie saw them. Beside the waterfall, an entire carpet of pale-blue petals.

'Come on,' she heard Olive saying to Mike. 'Let's get you back up to the lodge. I heard at the reception desk that they offer nighttime nature walks. If a group comes through here I don't suppose a pissed-up Englishman is quite the wildlife sighting they'll have had in mind.'

Mike mumbled something unintelligible in reply.

'Stevie!' Olive called. 'I'm taking Mike back to the lodge. Are you coming?'

It took Stevie a second to reply. She was enraptured by the flowers that had materialised before her. They were beautiful. She could easily see why Abi had chosen them as the hotel's emblem.

'Stevie?' Olive pressed. 'I wouldn't mind a hand here?'

'Sure,' Stevie called. 'Be right there.'

But she didn't turn back. Something else had caught her attention. It was ahead of her, just out of her torch's reach but close enough still that she could be certain it was there.

There was something in the grove. A motionless shape among the flowers.

Stevie took a tentative step forward. Then another. Wary of stepping on the flowers themselves, she walked around the outside of the grove, skirting the blue carpet. She was aware of Olive calling out to her again, but this time she didn't respond. Her heart thumped in her ears, the light from her phone creeping slowly closer until the lump in the flowers finally took shape.

She felt her stomach drop.

Completely still, its eyes glassy, lying among the flowers was the corpse of a deer.

Part Three: The Flower

The day of the party

10

Early the following morning, Stevie sat on The Midnight Orchid's private beach, her feet in the sand as she watched the sun rise over the gently lapping water.

She'd slept lightly, waking to the distant bellowing of howler monkeys as dawn broke. Lying in bed, the white sheets soft against her skin, she'd listened to it for a while, muted only slightly by the windows, before eventually deciding to get up. It was far earlier than she would have liked, especially with the jetlag starting to really kick in, but she'd known she wouldn't drift back off. Not while her mind still swam with the previous day's events. And so she'd thrown on some loose-fitting clothes, laced up a pair of hiking boots and trekked down through the jungle to the beach.

When Max occasionally asked her what she missed about home, the landscape was often one of the first answers she gave. As a teenager, she had made countless trips with Humphrey to New Hampshire's legendary national parks. Setting off early, before the sun had even risen, they would make it to the White Mountains or to Echo Lake while the early-morning mist still clung to the surface of the water.

She remembered feeling a unique sense of calm on those hikes, and had hoped that being beside the water at The Midnight Orchid would set her mind similarly at ease. But as beautiful as the ocean was, the effect wasn't the same. Walking through the forest back home, she could have named every tree. Told every pine from each maple and birch. But the hike to the beach had taken her past count-less ferns and palms that she couldn't hope to identify. When she'd reached the water, she'd found sand under her feet, T-shirt clinging to her back from the humidity. Ahead of her, the Pacific stretched towards the horizon. A pelican flew overhead, two surfers catching the early-morning waves.

It was beautiful, of course – paradise, even. She couldn't deny that. But in that moment, paradise wasn't what she wanted. She longed for fresh earth and a calm lake. Mist on the water and cold air in her lungs. She wanted to be home.

Looking out at the water, she reflected on the night's revelations. After convincing Mike to return to the lodge, and reporting the remains of the deer to the reception desk, she and Olive had gone their separate ways, Olive taking Mike back to his hut while Stevie had returned to her own, where she'd spent a considerable amount of time mulling over the possibility of Mike being Miley's father.

Could it be true? Was there really a chance?

The timeline made sense. She had to give him that. For

nearly ten years Abi had claimed to have fallen pregnant with Miley as the result of a one-night stand, less than a fortnight after the end of their summer spent backpacking around Central America. If she and Mike really had got together by the waterfall, on the last night of that trip, then it seemed entirely possible that this could be a viable alternative. More possible, perhaps, than a nameless man who'd just been passing through?

Yes, Stevie thought. It was possible. It wouldn't even be the most outlandish story she had heard in her working life. Earlier that year, the agency she worked for had been commissioned by a forty-year-old mailman to find the teenage mother who had given him up at birth. Not only had they found her, but they had discovered that she lived on his daily route. For years they had said good morning to each other without ever knowing that they were mother and son.

So Stevie knew better than most just how plausible the two stories were — both Mike's account by the waterfall and, likewise, that of Abi's stranger from the bar. But if Mike was Miley's father, why Abi would keep it from him?

It certainly sounded as if his affections for Abi had been staunchly one-sided during their time at York. Mike himself had likely been more surprised than anyone when she had thrown herself upon him by the waterfall. So was that the answer? Had Abi simply not wanted Mike to be involved? Had she wanted Miley all to herself? Or perhaps had she wanted to avoid the challenges of parenting a child with someone on the other side of the Atlantic?

Lying in bed the previous night, it had crossed Stevie's mind that this might be the reason for Abi calling the reunion: to finally tell Mike the truth about Miley. Why not just tell him, though? Why go through the charade of staging a group reunion? Stevie understood it being a conversation to be had in person. But why not simply invite Mike to come alone? Had she been worried that he would say no? Given how enamoured Mike seemed, Stevie thought it unlikely.

And in any case, in her heart of hearts, did Stevie really believe that Mike could be Miley's father?

No. It was possible, sure. But Stevie spent a great deal of time looking at pictures of long-lost parents and siblings. She was good at identifying family resemblances. And while she understood that resemblance wasn't everything, no matter how she tried she could see nothing of Mike in Miley.

She had even turned to Facebook, hoping to find a younger photo of Mike on the off chance there might once have been a closer resemblance that he had since grown out of. She had found Mike's own Facebook page to be private, accessible only to his approved friends. But when Stevie had tried Olive's profile, she had found not only that her privacy settings were set to public, but that her photos were so plentiful and so neatly organised it had barely taken a minute to track down several images of a much-younger Mike.

Starting with an album full of photos from their summer

in Central America, she had scrolled quickly through, pausing for a few seconds on each image that featured Mike. She couldn't see any resemblance to Miley. She did, however, find one interesting photo towards the end of the album. In it, Zach and Olive stood around a campfire with the rest of the group. Olive beamed into the camera, holding up her left hand to display an engagement ring. Beneath the picture, a caption read:

We're engaged!!!

Nearly three years exactly since the day we met. The perfect end to an amazing summer. Last night, Zach surprised me with this ring in Costa Rica, our final stop before we head home. It was the most beautiful moment, made all the better by having our friends there to share it with us.

I love you Zach. And I can't wait to be your wife.

Beneath the post, Stevie saw all manner of comments from ecstatic friends and family.

OMG!!! Congratulations hunni. So so happy for you xxxx

CONGRATULATIONS! You deserve this so much. You're going to be the most beautiful bride.

They were all suitably excited. But one comment in particular caught Stevie's eye, posted by a Charlotte Morgan.

Congratulations darling daughter. You're a perfect couple.
I'm so proud of the woman you have become and will be
proud to call Zach my son-in-law. He could of given us
some warning tho lol

It was a sweet comment, Stevie thought. It must have
been a beautiful moment, when Zach and Olive had
phoned her in the hospital to deliver the good news, the
nurses cheering in the background.

At this point, Stevie had decided to try one more Facebook album. Her mind was already half made up about
Mike and Miley, but her agency research had taught her
the importance of due diligence and the foolishness of
overlooking such a gift as Olive's carefully curated, pub-
licly available Facebook profile. As such, she turned to an
album full of photos from the group's time at York.

Just as with the Central America album, she could find
no pictures of Mike that suggested a familial resemblance
to Miley. But she did find several of Abi that intrigued her.
She lingered for a while on one in particular. With a caption that read My two favourite people, the picture showed
Olive, one arm around Zach's shoulders and the other
around Abi's. All three were in fancy dress, and from the
background, it appeared that they were in a pub.

It had been curious seeing this chapter of her sister's life.
Stevie remembered spending those years simply enjoying
that Abi was gone. But as she looked at this picture, of Abi,
Zach and Olive, a feeling stirred in her gut that she hadn't
expected.

She was jealous.

What was it about Olive? Sure, she was nice. But why had Abi clung to her so closely during their student years? What had made her so deserving of Abi's love, when Stevie hadn't been?

It was here that Stevie had eventually abandoned Facebook, uncomfortable with the thoughts it was causing her to entertain. She had for the most part, though, answered her own question. She did not believe that Mike was Miley's father. Or at the very least, she would not believe it without some persuasive DNA results.

Staring now at the water, Stevie closed her eyes, her thoughts turning to the day ahead.

With the launch party now less than twelve hours away, this was the day when it would be most crucial for her to keep an eye on Humphrey. The day when, if Abi's suspicions were correct, and he really was planning some act of sabotage, he would surely strike.

In fairness to Humphrey, watching him had so far been an easy job. Before they'd parted ways the previous evening he had suggested a morning hike, with one of the lodge's wildlife experts taking them into the jungle surrounding the lodge. Stevie had leapt at the idea, seeing an opportunity to keep him away from Abi for a few hours as no bad thing.

Still, she sighed at the thought of heading back up to the lodge, the sinking feeling in her stomach causing her to revisit the question Max had asked her the previous evening.

Why did she want to go back to New Hampshire? Why was she wavering over staying in London? She enjoyed her life there. She enjoyed her job. And she enjoyed living with Max.

She figured that, to answer that question, she needed to ask why she had left in the first place. And the simple truth, which she tried hard to think of as infrequently as possible, was that she had run away. Her parents, who had been the ones to suggest adopting her in the first place, were gone. Her sister didn't want her around. She had a niece who she loved but who Abi was loath to let her see. And she had a brother who loved her but who was such a free spirit that she barely saw him, given how frequently he was jet-setting around the world.

In short, she had felt like an intruder. Like she didn't deserve to be among them. She had thought that her genealogy job would be the answer. That helping people uncover the secrets of their families would give her the fulfilment she had longed for. But while she was proud of her work, she did not feel fulfilled. The truth was that she wanted to belong. The Blythes had taken her in. Given her a name. She wanted to be one of them. Wanted it all to work. She just didn't know how to make that happen.

At that moment, she heard her phone ping. Taking it out of her pocket, she found a message from Abi:

How does Humphrey seem? Anything to worry about?

Stevie typed out a quick reply:

He seems fine. No sign so far that he's planning anything. We're going on a hike soon, so he'll be away from the lodge for a while.

Abi's reply came within seconds:

OK. Keep watching him.

Again, Stevie sighed.

She should head back, she thought. She wanted some breakfast before meeting Humphrey. Possibly even a shower, too. And it would take a good half-hour to get back to the lodge, the walk uphill all the way.

Climbing to her feet, she brushed sand from her shorts. As she took one last look at the ocean she heard movement behind her, turning just in time to see Seth emerging from the jungle.

She jumped at his sudden appearance. He, likewise, took a hurried step back.

'Whoa!' he said. 'Fuck. Sorry, Stevie.'

Dressed in shorts and a T-shirt, with a rucksack over his shoulder and a guidebook of some kind in his hand, he recovered quickly, grinning at her from behind a pair of bright yellow Ray-Bans.

Stevie fought the urge to glare at him, heart pounding. She hadn't warmed to him over dinner. Hadn't failed to notice, as he'd knocked back shot after shot with Humphrey, the way his eyes had so often lingered on her and Jazz. Now she found herself irritated by the startled noise she had made at his sudden arrival, and the way he seemed to be grinning at it.

'You're up early,' he said. 'Couldn't sleep?'

'That's right.'

'The howlers?'

'Something like that. You?'

'Yeah, something like that. They're noisy little guys.'

Shrugging the rucksack off his shoulder, he unzipped it and slipped the book inside. It was a guide to the flora and fauna of Costa Rica. Well-thumbed by the look of it, with the corners of several pages already folded down. With the book tucked away he fetched a bottle of water from the bag.

'I spoke to Olive. Sounds like Mikey gave you two the runaround last night.'

'Is he OK?'

'He'll be fine. I'll bet he's got a stonking headache, but nothing he won't recover from. I wouldn't be surprised if you find him avoiding you the rest of the week, though. Telling you about his rendezvous with Abi by the waterfall . . . Knowing Mikey, he'll be mortified.'

Stevie tried to smile, noting the amusement in Seth's voice.

'Has he said anything about Miley?' she asked.

'Abi's kid?' Seth shook his head. 'No, I don't think so. Should he have?'

'Not necessarily. I only wondered . . . He was saying last night that . . .' She tailed off. 'Forget about it. I don't think it's my place to repeat it.'

120

She could tell already that it was too late, though. As Seth took a swig from the water bottle, she saw the gears turning in his mind, and then the moment of realisation as his eyes flew wide.

'No!' he cried out.

Stevie flinched, looking up and down the beach as if the surfers might somehow be able to hear their conversation.

'Please don't say anything,' she said. 'Not if he hasn't—'

'No fucking way!' Seth continued. 'Mikey really thinks—'

'He's not sure,' Stevie said sharply. 'He thinks it could be possible. But he isn't sure.'

Seth shook his head, laughing to himself. 'Fuck,' he said. 'No, he hasn't mentioned that. I mean, I wouldn't have said there was a resemblance. But I guess the timeline would make sense. You have to wonder why Abi wouldn't tell him though. And why make up that story about the guy in the bar?' He met Stevie's eye. 'Is he planning to say something to her?'

Stevie chewed her lip, unhappy with just how much Seth seemed to be enjoying this.

'I don't know. He was very drunk. And as I say, he can't be sure. He said that he thought you interrupted them before he could . . .' She winced. 'You know.'

An agonising few seconds went by as she waited for Seth to realise what she was saying. But after a moment his expression suggested that he understood.

'Well,' he said. 'I guess he'll also be thinking about when they hooked up again later that night. In her tent.'

'They got together twice?'

'Oh yeah. My tent was next to Abi's. After we'd finished celebrating Zach and Olive getting engaged, and we'd all gone to bed, I heard the two of them whispering for a few minutes. Next thing I knew, they were going into Abi's tent.'

'What were they saying?'

'Not sure. From what I remember, though, they actually sounded quite pissed off with each other. I wondered if Abi was somehow blaming Mike for my catching them by the waterfall. Whatever they were talking about, after a few minutes they stopped talking and they started . . . Well. Not to put too fine a point on it, but it certainly sounded to me like they were finishing what I'd interrupted earlier.' He pulled a face. 'Sorry. You probably don't want to hear this.'

'It's fine,' said Stevie, more confused than grossed out. 'Are you sure that's what you heard? Mike didn't mention that at all last night. He only spoke about the time by the waterfall.'

'About as sure as you can be when you're trying to sleep and feeling the effects of half a bottle of rum. I slept in a room next to Zach's for three years. I'm familiar with the sound of two people trying to hook up without anyone hearing. But I guess . . .'

A brief, slightly awkward silence fell, during which

Stevie's phone pinged. Glancing at the screen, she saw it was Humphrey:

Still up for the hike? Meet at 11:00 in the garden?

'Listen,' said Seth, leaping on the distraction, 'I'm going to keep moving, if that's OK. The others want to meet for breakfast, but I'm keen to get a walk in first.'

'Yeah,' said Stevie. 'Sure. No problem.'

With a smile and a nod, he swung his rucksack back onto his shoulder, before stepping past her and making his way down the beach. For a few moments, Stevie watched him, reflecting on all he'd said. Then, she turned and began the mile-long walk back up the hill, feeling more confused than ever.

11

'Honestly, Jazz,' said Olive, 'I really think I should meet you later, in the spa. When Abi messaged she asked me to come and see her alone . . .'

Walking side by side in the direction of Abi's hut, Jazz waved Olive's concern away.

'It's all right,' she said. 'She won't mind.'

Olive scowled. 'Fine. But just back off a little when we're in there, will you? Don't grill her or anything.'

Jazz didn't reply, noting the hostility in her cousin's voice. It sounded alien. Unnatural. As if Olive, who was usually so full of light and laughter, shouldn't know how to speak in such a way.

They walked for a few seconds in silence, the path winding through the jungle. Every few yards or so they passed a wooden hut, each separated from the next by a thick wall of lush green foliage. A happy-looking couple emerged from the nearest one, towels over their shoulders and beach bags in their hands. Hearing movement overhead,

Jazz looked up to see a pair of capuchin monkeys chasing one another through the jungle canopy.

'Is everything OK?' she asked at last. 'You don't seem yourself this morning.'

Olive was silent for a moment, her scowl still fixed in place. Then she sighed.

'Sorry. I don't mean to be snippy. It's just . . . I was so looking forward to this trip. To all of us being together again. To seeing Abi. I wanted it to be special, but it's only been a day and already Mike and Seth are at each other's throats. We've learned Abi has an entire sibling she never told us about at York, and I can't understand why. She's had a *child*, for God's sake, but she chose to go quiet on us all rather than tell us she was pregnant. And then there's Zach.'

'What about him?'

'We had a row. This morning. I was having a coffee in our garden when he came barging out of the hut and told me he wants to go home. Honestly, Jazz, he was in such a state. He started going on about how he's been looking at flights and that there's one this afternoon he wants us to get on.'

'Did he say why?'

'Apparently it's stressing him out being so far away from Ryan. He thinks we made a mistake coming. But Ryan's *fine*. He loves spending time with my parents. They're spoiling him rotten.'

'Has something happened? Has Zach *heard* something or—'

125

'No! He'd only been awake about an hour when he said it, and something can't have happened last night because he went back to the hut after dinner and straight to bed rather than coming out with me on a walk.'

They walked in silence for a moment.

'How is Ryan?' Jazz asked. 'Have you spoken to him much?'

'Yeah, I called him again this morning. Mum and Dad are taking him to see a Chelsea match. He's super excited. It's very cute.'

'I didn't know he was into football?'

'Oh yeah. He's always asking us to take him to see the games, but he only gets to go when my parents take him. Zach says the tickets are too expensive.'

Jazz, who remembered Zach's lack of interest in any kind of sport from their time at York, didn't reply, deciding it best not to comment on his smartwatch, his gleaming iPhone and what looked to be a brand-new pair of Adidas trainers that she had seen him wearing around the lodge. She was intrigued, though, by Zach's sudden desire to leave.

'So what did you say?' she asked. 'To going home?'

'I told him no. Said that he was being silly and that I wasn't going anywhere. He pushed back pretty hard. He said that I was being heartless and disregarding his feelings. And when I wouldn't budge he stormed off up to the lodge for breakfast.'

Jazz narrowed her eyes, watching her cousin carefully.

'It just feels like so far nothing is as it should be,' Olive continued. 'As I *hoped* it would be. And I just . . .' She winced. 'Abi was my best friend. And I thought I was hers. But I can't understand why she kept Stevie secret from us at York. Three years we spent together. We saw each other every day. And I told her everything about myself in that time. *Everything*. So how could she not even have mentioned an entire sibling she had back home? Talking to Stevie last night, it seems she might not even be the only one.'

Jazz frowned. 'What do you mean?'

'Just before we saw Mike going into the jungle, she asked if Abi had ever mentioned someone called Joel. She didn't have a chance to tell me who he was, but we'd been talking about why Abi hadn't told us about her. So does that mean this Joel is *another* secret sibling?' Olive shook her head. 'I just can't understand why she never said anything about Stevie. Or this Joel. And I can't understand why, instead of telling us about Miley – instead of asking us for help, if that's what she needed – she decided to go quiet when she went back to the States. To cut us off completely.'

For a little while, Jazz was silent. When at last she replied, she said quietly, 'Is it possible that Abi might not have been the person you thought she was?'

Olive looked pained. 'Please, Jazz . . . Don't go there.'

'Why not? Seriously, what are we doing right now, Olive? Why has Abi brought us out here? We don't hear a peep from her in ten years, then all of a sudden it's *Let's have a reunion! On the other side of the world!* Who does that?'

'There must be a reason,' Olive said. 'Something she needs us for.'

'Do you really think that?'

'Yes.' Olive fixed her with a pleading expression. 'She's a good person, Jazz. I wish you wouldn't doubt her.'

'And I wish you wouldn't defend her.'

They fell into silence, and for a moment, as they continued to walk together through the jungle, Jazz thought about telling Olive everything she'd suspected about the final day of that summer trip. But she meant what she'd said to Seth. She hadn't come to drag up the past. There was nothing to be gained from that. She was there only as Olive's protector.

Again Jazz thought of the conversation she and Seth had shared by the pool bar the day before.

We didn't see anything. You know it. I know it. And you'd be a lot happier if you just accepted it.

I can't believe you're being so naive.

And I can't believe you're still thinking about this.

She fought to contain a scowl. He knows what we saw, she thought to herself. He absolutely fucking knows.

They remained in silence until they arrived at the hut that was apparently Abi's. Stepping up to knock on the door, Olive lit up when it swung open.

'Hey!' she called out. 'How are you this morning? Excited for your big night?' She stepped forward and pulled Abi into a hug.

'Hey,' Abi replied, not a trace of enthusiasm in her

voice. She looked suspiciously at Jazz. 'I only asked for Olive to come.'

'I know,' Jazz replied.

'This needs to be a private conversation.'

Jazz said nothing, holding Abi's gaze.

'It's only Jazz,' said Olive. 'You can trust her with anything you'd tell me.'

Abi thought for a few seconds. She was clearly unhappy, the resentment on her face causing Jazz a flicker of pleasure.

'Fine,' she said eventually. 'Come in.'

Olive followed her into the hut, shooting Jazz a look as she stepped over the threshold.

Jazz stifled a sigh. Fine, she thought to herself. For you, cousin. There will be no grilling this morning.

Her immediate thought, as she stepped inside, was that the hut certainly looked like the residence of someone who had a lot on their plate. The place was bigger than her own hut, with two bedrooms as opposed to one open-plan space. Despite being larger, though, the amount of clutter somehow made it feel more cramped. Clothes were strewn all over the place, a pile of children's books sitting beside a laptop and a stack of paperwork that was piled up on the coffee table.

'Where's Miley?' asked Olive.

'She's spending the day with Alana again. I don't think either of them are thrilled to have been buddied up for the next couple days, but they'll just have to deal with it. I think they're out looking for sloths at the moment.' As she spoke, Abi whipped around the hut, moving things from surfaces and closing the doors to hide the unmade beds. She motioned towards a drinks station beside the minibar. 'Either of you want a coffee or something? Machine's over there if you do.'

As Olive set about making herself a herbal tea, Abi encouraged them to sit in the wicker chairs. She looked stressed, Jazz thought. The preparations for the party were clearly taking their toll.

'Shall we go outside?' asked Olive. 'It's a beautiful—'

'No,' Abi replied quickly. 'No. As I say, this needs to be a private conversation.' She looked once more at Jazz. 'Do you really have to be here?'

Jazz nodded. She knew this would irritate Abi, but she didn't care. Under no circumstances was she leaving this woman alone with Olive.

Abi was clearly unhappy, but again she didn't resist. Tossing a pile of Miley's clothes into a bedroom, she seemed almost to be done tidying the place up. The last thing she removed was a strip of tablets, which she snatched up from the coffee table, before carrying them into the en-suite bathroom and depositing them into a paper bag with a green cross.

'What are they?' asked Olive. She knew she might be overstepping in asking, but couldn't help herself.

'What are what?'

'Those pills?'

Abi waved the question away. 'Nothing,' she said. 'Don't worry about it.' Closing the bathroom door behind her, she came to sit in one of the wicker chairs. 'OK. Here's the thing. I asked you to come here this morning because I have questions about what you found by the waterfall last night.'

'You mean the deer?' said Olive.

Abi nodded. 'You said that it was lying among the blue flowers. Are you absolutely certain of that?'

Jazz watched, intrigued, as her cousin frowned. 'Yeah,' said Olive. 'I mean . . . I'm pretty sure. But I suppose it was Stevie who actually found it. I was busy trying to convince Mike to come back up to the lodge.'

Abi grimaced. 'And could you see anything to suggest that the deer had been eating the flowers?'

'Eating them?' Olive repeated.

'That's right. Try to remember, Olive. It's really important.'

Olive looked perplexed. 'I don't . . . I mean, I'm not sure.'

Abi swore.

'I don't understand,' said Olive. 'What's wrong with the flowers?'

'Nothing's wrong with them. I just need to know if the deer had been eating them.'

'Are they dangerous?'

It was Jazz who'd spoken this time, asking the question partly out of genuine curiosity, partly to see how Abi would respond. It got a reaction, with Jazz quickly finding herself on the receiving end of a vicious look.

'They're *not* dangerous,' she insisted.

'Then why are you so keen to know if the deer ate them?'

Abi was silent, glaring at Jazz across the coffee table.

'Tell us, Abi,' Olive pressed. 'Please. You're making me nervous.'

Abi looked at her, deliberating. Finally, after a long pause, she said, 'This stays between us.'

'Of course,' said Olive.

'I mean it,' Abi snapped. 'No one else knows about this. Not the staff, not the board members. So if any rumours start spreading at tonight's party, I'll know exactly who started them.'

She fixed Jazz with another glare.

'This is the only place,' she said, 'that the flower grows. The only place we're aware of, that is. It's why we chose it as the emblem for the hotel. A beautiful, previously unknown species that can only be found in our grounds. It seemed too good an opportunity to miss. But when we unveiled it, a short while ago, a local wildlife expert got in touch to warn us that it's poisonous.'

'Poisonous?' Olive's eyes flew wide.

'That's right.'

'How poisonous?'

Abi grimaced. 'The locals seem to think that if consumed it could be life-threatening. From what they've described it seems to have a similar effect to cyanide. Respiratory shutdown. Foaming at the mouth. That sort of thing.'

'Oh, God . . .' Olive raised a hand to her mouth. 'And do they have evidence? Has someone died recently, or . . . ?'

'None,' said Abi. 'Nothing, apparently, beyond local knowledge. And conveniently enough there's nothing on the internet or in any book. As I say, it's an undiscovered species.'

'But if there's no evidence,' said Jazz, 'then it could all just be superstition. What are the chances of a genuinely poisonous plant going truly undiscovered?'

'My thoughts exactly,' said Abi. 'But when I raised this with the locals they just said there's no evidence because everyone who knows it exists understands they need to steer clear. The farm we camped on ten years ago had been in the same family for generations before we bought the land, and apparently the folks who worked there just kept away from it. It hasn't killed anyone in well over a hundred years, just by virtue of people giving it a wide berth.'

'When did this happen?' asked Olive. 'When did you find out, I mean?'

'Recently,' Abi replied. 'About a month before the board made their decision about Humphrey. As if I didn't already have enough on my plate.' She shook her head. 'Obviously this has the potential to be a huge problem. Not only do we have a whole grove of these plants growing beside the waterfall, on a nature trail that we actively encourage our guests to use, but we've designed the branding of the entire lodge around it. Every uniform, every towel, every brochure is branded with that blue flower. Every image that we've sent to every travel operator we're planning to work with contains it in some form or another. If it does turn out to be poisonous, it would be a total fucking nightmare.'

'So what are you doing about it?' asked Jazz.

'I sent it off to be tested. See if we could confirm whether the rumours are true.'

'And?'

'And it came back from the lab exactly as we'd been warned. Highly toxic. Not to be consumed.'

Olive's eyes widened. 'That's why you changed the petals in our rooms,' she said. 'On Instagram there are photos of the huts made up with blue petals on the beds. But I noticed when we checked in yesterday that the petals on ours were white.'

Abi nodded, sighing as she did so.

'So what now?' asked Jazz.

'Still deciding. I'm waiting on the results of a couple more tests—'

'More tests?'

Abi grimaced. 'I can't make a change as monumental as this off the back of one set of results. I need to get more data before we do anything, so yes. I've sent off for some more tests. But if that deer had been eating the flowers . . .'

She left the rest unsaid. If the deer really had been eating the flowers, it seemed the results of the tests would be indisputable.

'And no one knows about this?' said Olive.

Abi shook her head. 'Until now it's just been Humphrey and me. As I say, this all happened just before the board decided to remove him from the company, so we'd been looking into it together. I don't even want any of the staff to know until we can be sure of what we're dealing with. But now . . .' She paused for a beat. 'The two of you know as well.'

The hut fell silent, with not even Jazz venturing a comment.

'So not a word,' said Abi, rising to her feet. 'To anyone. Now if you don't mind, I have a lot to be getting on with for tonight.'

12

Sitting out on the restaurant terrace, at the same table where they'd eaten dinner the night before, Mike's head throbbed.

The place was buzzing with activity. Virtually every table was occupied, diners talking excitedly over plates of eggs, bacon and fresh fruit. A few were even sampling the traditional *gallo pinto*, plates piled high with rice and black beans. In the reception area, a group of new arrivals had just been fetched from the airstrip and were now checking in at the desk. Down in the garden, a group was taking part in a yoga session, a dozen guests stretching out on identical exercise mats. Beyond them, the temporary stage that had been set up for the launch party that evening was in the process of being kitted out with DJ decks, along with strobe lights and an enormous PA system.

Mike, meanwhile, was quietly nursing an orange juice and a large bottle of water, hoping the paracetamol he'd knocked back would kick in soon. Zach sat across from him, eyes slightly glazed as he looked down at a lizard that had taken up residence beside their table. It stared up at them, a little over a foot in length, apparently hoping for breakfast scraps like a seagull might back home.

'I just don't know what came over me,' said Mike. 'I never usually drink like that. To be honest, I barely drink anything at home these days. I think I was just so shocked by Miley . . .' He shook his head. 'And who knows what I was thinking, going off by myself to the waterfall. Thank God Olive and Stevie followed me. Stumbling around in the dark . . . It's a small miracle I didn't trip on a root and break my neck.'

At that point a waiter came over and cleared their plates, the lizard watching intently as the remains of their breakfast were carried away. Neither of them had eaten much. Mike knew his hangover was preventing him from stomaching a great deal. He couldn't say what was troubling Zach.

'Does Abi know?' he asked. 'What I was talking about, that is? Has Olive told her?'

He waited a moment for Zach to reply.

'Zach?' he said. Then, when still no reply came, '*Zach*.'

'What?' Zach flicked him a look, a hint of irritation in his tone.

Mike frowned. 'What's up with you today?'

'Nothing.'

'Are you sure?'

'Yes, I'm sure. What were you saying?'

Mike studied his friend, unconvinced.

137

'I was asking if Olive has told Abi what I said at the waterfall last night.'

'No idea. We haven't spoken about it.'

Mike thought about pressing him further. If he was honest, he was disappointed in Zach's apparent lack of interest in his dilemma. He'd been hoping for words of support, maybe even advice. But since joining him in the restaurant Zach seemed barely to have listened to a word he'd said.

Mike tried to keep a level head. He had already clocked both Zach's bad mood and Olive's absence from break-fast. It seemed he wasn't the only one with problems to contend with that morning.

Hearing a now-familiar shriek, he looked down into the garden to see Miley running in the direction of the pool, startling a couple of the yogis as she passed. Alana, the staff member who had been assigned to watch her, hurried after, doing her best to keep up. Mike watched them go. Only once they were out of sight, disappearing into the tunnel of foliage that led towards the pool, did he turn to Zach again.

'What am I going to do?' he asked.

'About what?'

'About *what*? What do you—' Mike paused, wincing as the throbbing in his head flared up again. Waiting for it to subside, he took a deep breath, trying hard to gather his thoughts. 'What do you think?' he said. 'About the Miley situation. Should I speak to Abi or should I see if she says something to me? What would *you* do?'

Zach pulled a face. 'I think you might be overthinking this, mate.'

'How can I not when there's a chance she could be my child?' He pressed his hands to his face. 'By the waterfall. All those years ago. When I went to find Abi and we ended up together. I'd been so sure that we'd stopped . . . That there was no chance of . . .' He winced. 'But now? I mean, you can remember things wrong, can't you? Especially when the thing you're trying to remember happened ten years ago. We'd all been drinking – it happened in such a rush . . .'

He sipped his water as he collected his thoughts. 'When I went into the jungle it really was just to *find* her. To bring her back to the campsite so that Olive could take her group photo. It's not like I thought anything would happen.'

He shook his head, looking down at the bar. 'Part of me wishes now that I'd never gone looking for her. That I'd let Seth go instead. I just wish I could *know*.'

Again, he waited for Zach to offer some guidance. And again he received nothing.

'All right,' he said sharply. 'What's going on here, Zach? Have you and Olive had some kind of a fight? Because it's becoming a little difficult not to feel offended by your lack of interest.'

'What do you want me to say?' Zach snapped. 'Humphrey told us last night who the dad is.'

'Right. The nameless guy from the bar. Doesn't that sound just a little convenient? The guy who was only there one night, and whose name Abi never caught?

139

Just a couple of weeks after she and I got together at the waterfall?'

'You don't think it's true?'

'No! I don't!' Mike took a breath. 'Look. I've been thinking. What if this is the reason Abi went quiet after that summer?'

'Of course it's the reason she went quiet. She'd just found out she was pregnant. She had things on her mind.'

'I don't mean Miley. I mean *me*.' Mike's gaze fell to the table. 'We all know she was never interested in me back at York. When we got together by the waterfall she was clearly just looking for a distraction. Maybe she was feeling sad about going home and she knew I'd never turn her down. What I'm saying, Zach, is what if she decided she was going to keep the baby, but she didn't want me to know about it? Because she didn't want me involved. Perhaps she didn't want to have to manage having a kid with a mother in the States and father in the UK. Or perhaps she was just embarrassed that it was me she'd got together with?'

They fell once again into silence, each lost in their own thoughts. Zach's phone buzzed on the table. He looked at the screen, swearing under his breath.

'Who is it?' asked Mike.

'It's Olive. She wants to know if we're coming on this fucking hike.'

Mike frowned. 'Will you just tell me what's happened? What have you two fallen out over?'

Zach didn't reply, eyes glued to his phone.

Mike sighed. 'Just go,' he said. 'If she wants you there you'll only make things worse by skipping it.'

Zach grimaced. 'What about you?'

'When have you ever known me to go on a hike?'

'True. It might do you some good, though. Help take your mind off Miley.'

Mike thought for a moment. 'Is Seth going?'

'What?'

'Seth. Is he going with you?'

'I think so. Olive only found out that it was happening because Humphrey invited Seth, and then Seth mentioned it to us.'

'I'll give it a miss, then.'

If he'd hoped that Zach would protest at this – tell him that they would all want him to join them – then, once more, he was disappointed. Instead, his friend nodded, stood and left the restaurant.

For a few moments Mike sat alone, surrounded by cheerful couples as he contemplated how he was going to entertain himself. The party wasn't kicking off until seven o'clock that evening. He had an entire day to fill.

Perhaps going on the hike would help to take his mind off Miley. Was he really as desperate as that, though? To go trekking through the jungle with Seth?

Another shriek sounded from the garden below, and once more he turned to see the girl who might be his daughter running away from her minder, this time in the direction of the fountain in the centre of the garden. He watched as she barged past a pair of middle-aged couples, his mind immediately flooded with all the questions that had tormented him during dinner. The questions he couldn't answer without confronting Abi.

Swearing under his breath, he finished his water and got to his feet.

He supposed he was going on a hike.

13

It was only when Stevie met Humphrey in the garden at the back of the lodge, arriving at bang on eleven o' clock, that she realised it wouldn't be just the two of them heading out on their hike.

For a start there was their guide, a *tico* called Luis, who would be showing them the way and helping them to spot some of the local wildlife. A smiling man of around forty, he wore a pair of sturdy-looking hiking boots, a wide-brimmed hat and a long-sleeved shirt, the cuffs rolled back over a pair of lean forearms. Like every other member of staff, Stevie couldn't help but notice that The Midnight Orchid's distinctive blue flower was printed on his breast pocket.

But as she made her way to the stone fountain in the centre of the garden, it quickly emerged that Humphrey must have invited Seth along too, and that he had in turn invited the rest of Abi's friends. It was only Seth, though, Stevie thought, who looked happy to be there. She noticed the space that Zach and Olive seemed to be leaving between themselves, her arms tightly crossed while his hands were thrust into his pockets. Mike, meanwhile, looked to be severely hungover, wincing as Seth laughed loudly at something on Humphrey's phone. He was doing everything he could to avoid catching Stevie's eye, and she found herself recalling her conversation with Seth on the beach about how embarrassed he would be by his confession beside the waterfall.

'Shall we begin?' Luis asked brightly, once Stevie had fallen in beside her brother.

'Hold up,' Humphrey replied. 'I think we're waiting on just one more.'

'Aunt Stevie!'

Stevie, who had assumed he must be referring to Jazz, turned at once at the sound of Miley's voice. Her niece hurried towards them, grinning broadly from behind her star-shaped sunglasses. As she came skidding to a halt beside the fountain, she hopped excitedly from one foot to the other.

'Uncle Hump says we're going looking for tarantulas!'

'We sure are!' Humphrey scooped her up into his arms, turning to the guide. 'Think you can find a tarantula for us, Luis?'

The guide laughed. 'I'll do my best.'

Stevie leaned in close, dropping her voice to a murmur. 'Is Abi good with this? I thought she wouldn't even let you take Miley to Echo Lake?'

'Sure,' Humphrey replied. 'She knows there's a group of us to keep an eye on her. And Alana's coming too.'

Stevie glanced at the young woman from the lodge who had seemingly been assigned to watch over Miley. She didn't look thrilled with her role, slightly out of breath from having presumably spent the morning chasing Miley around the garden.

With the group assembled, Luis led them into the jungle, setting out on the same path that Stevie and Olive had used to follow Mike the previous evening. The place looked different in the daylight. Where before there had been nothing but the inky outline of the surrounding foliage, now there were a hundred different shades of green on display. Luis explained that the vibrancy was down to the time of year. The 'green season', it was apparently called, when the daily rainfall meant that the jungle managed to appear even more lush and alive.

At the waterfall, they left the neatly defined gravel path, taking a dirt trail deeper into the jungle. Stevie tried, for Mike's sake, to avoiding looking in his direction, mindful of embarrassing him further. But she couldn't help glancing towards the blue flowers, as if checking that the receptionist had indeed arranged for the deer to be taken away. Of course, it was gone. She thought, though, that she could perhaps see the imprint of where it had been – a patch of flattened flowers at the edge of the grove.

Walking at the front of the procession, Luis carried a telescope mounted upon a tripod, which he would stop every few minutes to set up and point towards a tree or into a dense patch of foliage, picking out birds and lizards so small that Stevie was astonished by his ability to find them.

For much of the way she walked side by side with Miley, speaking about school, sports and cartoons. As they spoke, her heart ached at how much Miley seemed to have grown since they'd last seen each other. She loved her niece so much it hurt, and she knew that Miley loved her back. But, desperate as she was to play the role of doting aunt, she also felt the need to keep a safe distance. Regardless of what Humphrey or even Miley herself might say, Stevie was well aware of how their bond infuriated Abi. Much like her name, her home and even the love she had received from their parents, as far as Abi was concerned, Miley was a treasure to which Stevie had no right.

At one point during their conversation, Miley pulled a face at Stevie's suggestion that folks in the UK didn't watch baseball.

'So what do they watch?'

'Most people watch football. It's not like our football, though. We'd call it soccer.'

Miley thought about this for a moment, a sceptical look on her face. Then, as casually as if they were discussing the weather, she asked, 'Are you going to come home someday?'

'Home?'

'Yeah. Back to Concord.'

Caught entirely off guard, Stevie found she had no idea how to reply. She was permitted to see her niece so infrequently these days that she'd forgotten the whiplash that could so often punctuate a conversation with a kid her age.

'Would you like me to?' she asked.

Miley nodded. 'I miss you a lot.'

Stevie had to concentrate to hold it together. She knew exactly what she wanted to say, of course. She wanted to say yes. That she, too, was desperate for them to spend more time together. Instead, she felt her heart break as she searched for the words to explain that Abi preferred for there to be an ocean between them.

'Well,' she said, 'I'm really not sure. I miss you too. But I've been offered a new job. If I decide to take it, I would need to stay in London.'

'Is it a big job?'

'Pretty big, yeah.'

'Would they pay you more money?'

'Yeah, I think they would.'

Miley considered this. 'You should probably take it then. Mom says the reason we don't see you is because flights are too expensive, and you don't make a lot of money.'

'Is that really what she says?'

'Yeah. So if you made more money, I could see you more.'

Again, Stevie had to bite her lip, trying hard not to think of the grandeur of the Blythe family home, the private schools they had each attended, the Jaguar that Frank had driven when Stevie was a teenager. And yet Miley had said it so brightly. So matter-of-factly. For a second, Stevie found herself bizarrely envious of the way a child could accept a certain view of the world.

'I think my mom has a boyfriend.'

Stevie blinked, Miley having tossed this so abruptly into the air that she wondered if she'd misheard.

'A boyfriend?' she repeated.

'Yeah. I haven't seen him yet. But I've heard her talking about him on the phone a couple times.'

'You don't think she was talking *to* him?'

'No. Definitely about him.'

'So what makes you think he's a boyfriend?'

'I don't think she wants me to know about him. Both times she took the phone into the other room so I wouldn't hear.'

Stevie took a breath, trying to determine how far Abi would permit her to enquire.

'And how would you feel,' she said, 'about your mom having a boyfriend?'

'I'm not sure.' Miley wrinkled her nose. 'I guess it would be nice for her if someone took her out on dates. My friend Brooke's mom has a boyfriend and she seems pretty happy.'

Before Stevie could press any further, Humphrey called out to them from up ahead.

'Hey, Miley! Come check this out! Luis has found something cool!'

Immediately, Miley broke into a run, scampering to catch him up.

Stevie watched her go, mind spinning with the sudden

revelation that Abi might be seeing someone. Assuming it was true, it would be the first time, to Stevie's knowledge, that Abi had been in a relationship since Miley had been born.

She cast her mind back, trying to determine if that could really be correct. She supposed there might have been some casual relationships over the years – guys who Abi hadn't thought serious enough to introduce to the family. There was no way Abi would have told her about those. But Stevie was fairly certain that she was right. To put it simply, Abi had always seemed far too busy for a guy, first with her role as a mother to Miley and then within Conrad Blythe.

Thinking about it a little further, the last hint Stevie could recall that Abi was seeing someone had been over a decade ago, during her second year at York. Not that Abi was aware Stevie had learned of this potential relationship. It had been information gathered, rather than information shared.

It had been Thanksgiving. Abi had come home for a few days to New Hampshire, and one evening, long after darkness had fallen, Stevie had gone into the kitchen to make a turkey sandwich. All had been quiet, Abi and Humphrey watching a movie with Frank in the lounge. Abi's phone had been sitting on the kitchen counter, though, plugged into a charger. And as Stevie had assembled her sandwich, the device had pinged, a message coming through.

Stevie hadn't meant to look. It had been a reflex, rather than a conscious effort to snoop. But in the split second her head had been tilted towards the phone, she'd seen the preview of a message flash up on the screen.

Miss you, babe. Can't wait until you're back here.

Immediately Stevie had tried to put it out of her mind. Sure, it was interesting. It had seemed almost certainly to be from a guy. But she'd been well aware of how furious Abi would have been at her for reading her messages. Likewise, with no name appearing alongside the preview, there'd been no way of determining who the sender might even have been.

A moment later, though, a second had come through.

This time, Stevie hadn't been able to help herself. After all, if Abi was seeing someone in York then there was a chance she might extend her stay in the UK after finishing her studies. To Stevie, who'd been enjoying Abi's absence immensely, this prospect had been too tantalising to ignore. And so, glancing quickly at the screen, she'd read:

I'll do it soon. Promise. I just need the time to be right. You know it would break her if I did it now.

This time, Stevie really had tried to forget about it. The first message had been innocent. Intriguing, even. But there'd been something darker lurking within the second. Whatever Abi and this guy were involved in — whatever was going to break someone if the time wasn't right – Stevie had quickly decided she wanted nothing to do with it.

Hauling herself back to the present, Stevie put the question from her mind, watching Miley as she looked excitedly through the telescope. She stood there for a moment, thinking about all the things she would like to say to her little niece. All of the ways she wished their family could be different.

Sighing, she took out her phone to check the time, but was instead surprised to find a message from Abi flashing up on the screen:

Need to discuss the deer you and Olive found by the waterfall. Can you come to my hut? No time today. Too much on with the party. Come tomorrow morning.

Stevie frowned, wondering why Abi needed to discuss the deer. There hadn't, from what she'd seen, been anything particularly unusual about it.

But before she could puzzle over it any further, Olive came to stand beside her.

'Hi,' she said.

'Hey,' Stevie replied, quickly putting her phone away.

'Enjoying yourself?'

'Sure. I only wish I'd brought a little more water. I'm not used to this kind of humidity.'

'Take some of mine, if you like. I brought some for Zach, but quite frankly he can look after himself.'

Reaching into the beach bag she was carrying on her

shoulder, she fetched out a full bottle of water. Stevie took it cautiously. She had already clocked the way Zach had walked on ahead with the other boys, Olive bringing up the rear of their little procession with Alana. But now she also noted the frustration in Olive's tone.

'Is everything OK?' she asked. 'With Zach?'

'Yes,' Olive replied, although she seemed to realise that she had done so too quickly. 'It's fine. We just had a bit of a tiff this morning about being so far away from our son. Zach wanted to fly home and things got pretty heated. It'll be OK.'

As Stevie took a sip of the water she couldn't help but think that Olive didn't sound convinced. She decided not to press her, though.

'Stevie,' Olive said. 'I hope you don't mind, but I need to ask. Last night, before we noticed Mike going into the jungle. You asked if Abi had ever mentioned someone called Joel. Was he . . . I mean, the answer is no. Abi's never mentioned him either. Not once. Was he a brother of yours?'

Stevie hesitated. 'Yeah,' she said. 'Yeah, he was our brother.'

'And why has Abi never brought him up? Was he another . . .'

She tailed off, clearly unsure of how to phrase her question.

'It's OK,' said Stevie. 'No. Joel wasn't adopted. He was actually the eldest sibling. Mom and Dad had him a couple years before Humphrey.'

'And did he . . . ?' Again Olive paused, clearly desperate to ask but once more unsure of how to do so.

'He died,' said Stevie. 'There was an accident. Just a few weeks before I came to live with the Blythes. They'd gone on a camping trip in the White Mountains. Mom and Dad, Joel, Humphrey and Abi. The way I've been told it, on the last morning of the trip the three kids went off to play by a waterfall while Mom and Dad packed up the tents. I don't know exactly what happened. Whether they got too close or if he was being stupid or something. All I know is that Abi and Humphrey came running back through the forest, screaming about how Joel had gone over the edge.'

Stevie looked down at the ground. 'I've seen that waterfall a couple times for myself. Mom and Dad never took us back, but I went with some guys from school. Growing up where we did, you do a lot of hiking.' She shook her head, eyes glazed. 'A hundred and fifty feet. Sheer rock at the bottom. There was never going to be any helping him after a fall like that.'

Olive winced. 'I'm so sorry, Stevie. Your poor family.'

Stevie gave a weak smile. 'Humphrey likes to say that we're the last Blythes standing. First there was Joel's accident. Then Mom got sick. And then last year Dad had his heart attack. Now it's just the three of us.'

'And Miley,' said Olive.

'Of course. And Miley.'

They walked in silence for a short while. Then, Olive said, 'What was he like? Joel, I mean.'

'From what I've heard it sounds like he was a special

kid. Kind. Brave. The way our folks used to talk about him it was as if he was the golden boy of the family.'

Olive looked like she wanted to say something.

'What is it?' said Stevie.

'It's nothing,' said Olive.

'It's OK,' said Stevie. 'Say what you want to say.'

'It's just . . . I thought Abi was my best friend. I told her everything about myself when we were at uni. To make it out here and learn that all that time she had not one but two siblings she never told me about . . . And now, of course, to learn that she's since had Miley, too . . . Honestly, it's a little difficult to take in. I can't help but wonder if I did something wrong. Or if maybe I misunderstood our friendship.'

Before Stevie could reply, up ahead Humphrey laughed at something on Seth's phone. Then he tapped the screen to watch it again. Stevie watched them for a moment, before returning her attention to Olive.

'Don't take it personally,' she said. 'Abi's never spoken about Joel. Not to anyone. You have to remember that she was just seven when he fell. And she *saw* him go over the waterfall. It's got to be a traumatic thing for her to recall. And as for me . . .' Stevie winced. 'We've never had a good relationship. From day one Abi's wanted me gone.'

'What do you mean?'

'Exactly that. I can remember, as kids, how she would beg our parents to send me back. How she'd steal things and hide them in my room to make me look like a thief. She wouldn't even let Humphrey and me go on a hike.'

Clocking the confusion on Olive's face, Stevie withheld a sigh.

'As I say, after Joel's accident Mom and Dad didn't often want to go back into the national parks. I think the memory of it all was just too much. But there was a time when I would sometimes go with Humphrey. When he was eighteen our folks bought him this truck, and on the weekends or during summer break he would sometimes say, "Come on. Let's go on a hike." I would grab my boots, fill a pack with water and snacks, jump in Humphrey's truck . . . And every time, without fail, Abi would be there too.

'For a while I couldn't understand why she insisted on coming. It wasn't as if she ever seemed to want to be there. She would always hang a few feet behind, trailing us like an angry shadow. Eventually, though, it dawned on me – Abi didn't want me to be alone with Humphrey. All of those days spent watching us . . . It had been a warning. *Don't get ideas,* she seemed to be saying. *He isn't your brother. You don't belong here.'*

Stevie shook her head. 'I know that I wasn't adopted as a replacement for Joel. Mom had always wanted a big family, and after having Abi, she and Dad learned that they couldn't have any more kids themselves. So they started thinking about adopting. When Joel died, they'd already gone through the paperwork and background checks. They were just waiting for me to arrive. So I know I wasn't intended as a replacement. But by the time I got there . . .'

She thought carefully about what her next words would be, aware of how closely Olive was watching her.

'By the time I got there, I think that was how I was seen. From the day I arrived our mom *clung* to me. *Showered* me with love. Obviously I'll never know how things might have been had Joel not died. But I do remember it bothering Abi. Enough that while Mom and Dad refused to entertain the idea of sending me back, they abandoned any plans to adopt again. Because while she's never said as much, I think Abi saw me as a replacement for Joel. She hated that idea. Not just the thought that she and Humphrey could be replaced, but that Mom could love the replacement as much as she seemed to love me.' She turned, looking Olive in the eye. 'So you see. It's not you. It's all me.'

For a few moments, Olive simply looked back at her, eyes wide with the disbelief. Finally, she let out a sigh.

'You know,' she said, 'I always wondered if, in a slightly morbid sort of way, it was our mums that brought us together. I never understood why Abi wanted to be my friend. She was so beautiful, so confident, so clever . . . When I first brought her back to the flat to meet the others, I couldn't believe that she wanted to stay with us. To stay with *me*. But I think that when your mother is sick . . . I think that when two of you have supported each other through that it creates a bond. It's not really something anyone else can understand, if they haven't been through it themselves.'

She paused for a second, apparently gathering herself. 'I know that in the end my mum pulled through,' she said.

'I know that. But we didn't know she would at the time. And I sometimes think that Abi, having already been through that experience with Jane, saw what I was going through. And that's what brought us together. That's what bonded us.'

'It must have been so difficult,' said Stevie. 'Being away from home while she was ill.'

'It was,' Olive agreed. 'But Mum encouraged me to go. We only got her diagnosis about a month before the start of my first term. She knew how badly I wanted to go. But I had Jazz there with me. I met Zach and the others . . . And I went home a lot to be with her. Every holiday and reading week. We made it work.' She took a shuddering breath. 'Your mum's illness . . . It took your grandmother as well?'

'That's right. Although that was a long time ago. Before Frank and Jane adopted me. Before I'd even been born.'

Olive opened her mouth to say something, but before she could Miley called out from up ahead.

'Aunt Stevie! Come see this! We found a sloth!'

Stevie looked at Olive, sensing that there were still a thousand questions she wanted to ask.

'Stevie!' Miley called again. 'Come see!'

'Coming!' Stevie called back.

She met Olive's eye.

'Stevie,' said Olive. 'I—'

She didn't finish. At that moment, they heard Humphrey laughing again up ahead of them. And then the sound of Mike roaring.

14

A few minutes earlier, Mike had been watching as Humphrey fixed Seth with an uncharacteristically serious expression.

'So what do you think?' he asked. 'Would you say there's anything in it?'

Seth frowned. 'I don't know, dude. Don't get me wrong, I like exotic plants. But I'm hardly enough of an expert to tell you with any certainty whether this blue flower of yours might actually be poisonous.'

'What about the tests Abi's running?' Humphrey pressed. 'You said at dinner that you're an environmental consultant. Should she be taking the results at face value or should she push ahead with doing some further tests?'

Seth laughed. 'Bloody hell, Humphrey, I don't know. Yes, I'm an environmental consultant. But I work for a construction company. In the UK, of all places. I can't say I've ever had to deal with an undiscovered species of poisonous plant.'

'You must have a hunch,' said Mike. 'You used to keep poisonous stuff back at uni, didn't you?'

He had been trailing a few feet behind them. Deliberately so, having been uninterested in joining in with Seth and Humphrey's conversation. As a result, they seemed almost to have forgotten that he was even there. At this comment, though, Seth turned, throwing an unpleasant look over his shoulder.

'Are you talking about the ivy I had during first year?' he asked. 'The plant that you definitely didn't report to the warden?' He turned to Zach, who was keeping pace beside him. 'Do you remember that? He reported me. For growing some ivy on my windowsill!'

Zach winced. 'To be fair, mate, the warden did agree that it would be toxic.'

'If you ate it! Were you planning on eating it, Mikey?'

Mike scowled. 'Should you even be discussing this? If Abi thinks the flower is sensitive information, then surely we should be—'

Humphrey waved a hand. 'It's fine. I don't mind you guys knowing.'

'But this place isn't yours any more.'

At this, Humphrey, Seth and Zach all stopped, Mike feeling a glimmer of satisfaction at their shocked expressions. Before any of them could respond, though, Luis, who had been walking a few metres ahead, stopped and set up the tripod, pointing the telescope towards the top of a nearby tree. Pressing his eye to the lens, he spent a few seconds adjusting a dial, before inviting them over.

'Here,' he said. 'Please. Look!'

He grinned at them, clearly oblivious to the tone of their conversation.

Shaking his head at Mike, Seth went to the telescope and put his eye to the lens.

'What have we got?' asked Zach.

'Sloth,' Seth replied.

'Hey, Miley!' Humphrey called out. 'Come check this out! Luis has found something cool!'

Mike tried hard not to look as Miley hurried to catch them up. When he'd learned that she would be joining them for the hike he had considered dropping out. The question of whether she might be his – of why Abi might not have told him about her sooner – was turning over and over in his mind. Now he was finding that whenever he saw Miley he couldn't help but look for traces of himself in her. A feature. An expression. Anything at all.

He turned away as she went running past, looking back to find that Zach had come to stand beside him.

'Mate . . .' he said. 'That was brutal.'

Mike scowled. 'It's true though, isn't it? Humphrey got himself kicked out of Conrad Blythe.'

'I know. But you shouldn't . . .' Zach adopted a grim expression. 'Look, do you need to head back?'

'No.'

'Are you sure? You're clearly feeling rough. And if this Miley situation's bothering you that much—'

'I said no,' Mike snapped. 'I'm not having him see me leave.'

He glared at Seth, who was now showing Humphrey something on his phone. But his expression softened when he saw Miley looking through the telescope. He watched her for a little while, searching her face as she broke into an enormous grin.

'That's so cool!' She turned, Mike's heart suddenly beating a little quicker as she looked in his direction. 'Aunt Stevie! Come see this! We found a sloth!'

Mike looked down at the ground, his heart racing.

Perhaps it *was* too much for him to be around Miley. Maybe he wasn't ready just yet. Or at least, he wouldn't be until he'd spoken to Abi.

He wasn't sure how long he stood there, his eyes fixed on the ground. But when, finally, he managed to lift his head, he looked into Zach's eyes and gave a small nod.

'OK,' he said quietly. 'Let's go back.'

He began to walk in the direction they'd come, Zach at his side. He could barely have taken two steps, though, before he heard the tinny sound of a video being played on a phone. Mike knew this particular piece of footage all too well, hearing the now-familiar sound of Alana offering to help him out of the pool, followed by a yelp of surprise and then a loud splash.

He stopped, turning back just in time to see Humphrey howling with laughter, eyes glued to Seth's phone.

'*Oh my God!*' he cried out. 'Play that again. Play it again!'

Grinning, Seth did just that, tapping at his screen to start the footage again.

'I'll send it to you,' he said. 'I'm thinking about freeze-framing the moment he hits the water. I might make it my lock-screen photo.'

Mike's blood suddenly ran hot.

He heard Zach say something softly by his side, but the words didn't compute. His anger rising, Mike did something he had never done before in his life. Something he must have thought about a thousand times as a student but had always managed to resist.

Before he could stop himself, he gritted his teeth, clenched his fist and strode towards Seth.

15

Jazz found Abi on the terrace, locked in an argument with an American in a smart shirt and a pair of clear-rimmed glasses.

'I don't understand,' the guy was saying, a slightly nasal quality to his voice. 'Why am I even here? What is the point of hiring an event planner if you're going to insist on doing my job for me?'

'I'm not doing your—'

'You are!' The planner threw up his arms, an iPad clutched in one hand. 'Every suggestion I've made you've overruled. Every task I have for today you've already actioned yourself. I just don't get why you brought me all the way out here when you so clearly want to manage this event yourself.'

Abi, who was sitting at a table, her laptop in front of her, scowled at him.

'So what if I've picked up a few things? You're still getting paid. You'll still get to put this on your portfolio. What have you got to complain about?'

Keeping at a distance, Jazz stood by the restaurant door, watching as the planner's face began to steadily turn red.

'I'm a professional,' he said. 'I turned down other work for this. Good work. And I'm not putting something on my portfolio when a client can't even—' He stopped, forcing himself to take a breath. 'You know what? I'm not doing this. If you want to manage this event yourself, you go right ahead.'

He turned before Abi could protest, his fury written plainly across his face as he barged past Jazz on his way back into the restaurant.

For a few seconds Jazz just stood there, watching Abi closely. If she seemed fazed by the encounter she didn't show it. The planner barely had time to leave the terrace before she had returned her attention to the laptop.

'How's it going?' Jazz called out.

Abi didn't look up, her fingers tapping furiously at the keys. 'I thought you guys were going on a hike?' she said.

'I stayed behind.'

'Why?'

'Because I heard that you weren't joining us.'

Abi turned from the screen, eyes narrowing. 'Am I meant to be flattered or something?'

'Not particularly. I stayed because I wanted to speak to you. Alone. And this seemed a good opportunity.'

They both remained silent, eyes locked. Jazz could see the loathing in Abi's expression. The distrust.

Good, she thought. We might as well be on the same page.

Jazz watched as Abi picked up a bottle of water and took a large swig. Then, after seemingly thinking for a moment, she snapped her laptop shut.

'OK,' she said. 'I'm incredibly busy, Jazz. As you can see. So just tell me what you want and then we can all get on. In fact, tell me why you're here at all. I invited you in the spirit of the reunion, but you never liked me back at York. I don't think you liked any of the guys either. Not really. So tell me why. Why come all this way for a trip you clearly don't want to be a part of?'

Jazz took a deep breath. 'I came because I don't trust you. Because when Olive told me how excited she was about this out-of-the blue reunion, I knew someone would need to watch over her.'

'Watch over her?'

'That's right. Olive never understood you. The pretty American who wanted to spend every day with her. She would have done anything for your approval. Over-looked any flaw. But *I* understand you. I know you can't be trusted. And that's why I came. Because when you're around, someone needs to look out for Olive.'

Abi laughed. 'You're crazy, Jazz. You know that?'

'I'll tell you what I do know.' Jazz looked Abi square in the eye. 'I know what you did. To Olive. When we were last here.'

'I didn't do *anything* to Olive—'

'The bus,' Jazz cut across her. 'I know what you did on the bus.'

She felt a flicker of satisfaction as, for a few short seconds, Abi looked genuinely shocked.

'I've never told her,' Jazz said. 'And I don't plan to. You ruined her life. And if she ever found out how, it would destroy her. But understand this.' She took a step closer, lowering her voice as she closed the distance between them. 'I don't know why you've set this up. I don't know what your game is or what you want, but I sure as hell don't believe this is a harmless reunion. So just remember, when you try to do whatever it is you've brought us here for, that you might have fooled the others but you haven't fooled me. I know what you did. I know what you are. And I am watching you.'

She didn't wait for a reply. The message was delivered, and from the look on Abi's face she knew it had been understood.

Turning on the spot, Jazz strode back into the restaurant.

16

As the afternoon drew to a close, the beginning of the party now just a few short hours away, Stevie sat out on the restaurant terrace.

The hike had ended at around three, with Zach and Mike turning back after the confrontation with Seth, while the rest of them carried on through the jungle for another few hours. Upon their return, Stevie had mostly clung to Humphrey, getting some food and spending an hour together by the pool before he'd gone to his hut to shower. She had then come to the restaurant, where she had the terrace almost entirely to herself. The place was beginning to hum with anticipation for the evening ahead. Down in the garden, she could see that the party area was laid out, and guests were beginning to trail from the pool back to their huts in order to get ready.

Sipping on a smoothie, she had propped her phone up on the table, Max's face filling the screen. It was almost midnight back in London, but it looked very much to

Stevie as if Max was out, a glass of rosé in her hand and the outdoor seating area of a bar just about visible behind her.

'Mike *hit* him? Like, actually hit him?'

'Sure did,' Stevie replied. 'Right on the mouth.'

'God. What did the other guy say to deserve that?'

'No idea. But after he'd done it Mike shouted, "Screw you, Seth! You were a waster when we were students and you're a waster now!"'

'And you didn't ask someone what that was all about?'

'No! It was awkward enough already. Whatever they're falling out over is between them. I was just glad to keep the hike going. It meant I still had eyes on Humphrey.'

Max rolled her eyes. 'This is *wasted* on you, Stevie. If I'd been there I would have grilled *everyone*.'

Stevie smiled. She didn't doubt for a second that of the two of them her friend would make a far better sleuth.

'What are those people all doing there?' Max continued. 'Seriously, why have they have turned up? Because from what you've described they all seem to hate each other.'

'I've been thinking the same thing,' said Stevie, sipping her smoothie. 'Well, Olive clearly adores Abi. To a point that, if I'm honest, feels a little delusional. She told me that after she and Zach got engaged, she wanted Abi to be a bridesmaid at their wedding, but Abi didn't so much as respond to her message asking if she would do it. Of course she would have had other things on her mind, having just found out that she was pregnant with Miley, but Olive didn't know that when Abi suggested a reunion.

Abi's friends only found out that Miley existed when they arrived here.'

'Poor girl,' said Max.

'Poor girl indeed,' Stevie agreed. 'Then there's Mike. He *is* in love with Abi. No doubt about it. And I'm pretty sure he's single, so I'd say he's come in the hope of rekindling something.'

'You don't think he's just happy to be with his friends again?'

'No way. Even before their scrap this afternoon, you could see at yesterday's dinner that he *hates* Seth. Total personality clash, I'd be amazed if those two had spent any time alone back when they were students. And the only other member of the group he seems to be interested in talking to is Zach. So yeah. He's clearly here for Abi. Maybe he's hoping they'll get together again, like they did by the waterfall.

'As for Seth, he just seems to be here for a good time. I bumped into him this morning on the beach, out for a walk by himself with a book on the local plantlife. So my best guess there is that he's genuinely here for the party and the free accommodation.'

'What about Olive's cousin?'

'Jazz?'

'Yeah. What's her deal?'

'I'm not quite sure. She didn't come out on the hike today, and at dinner last night I didn't see her smile once. She barely even spoke. Spent most of the evening just glaring at Abi, watching her as if she was expecting her to do something.'

'Do what?'

'I have no idea.'

'Weird. And Olive's husband? Is he just here because Olive wanted to come?'

'I think so. To be honest, he seems a little disengaged. He hardly said a word over dinner, and then afterwards, when Olive asked him to join her for a walk around the grounds, he told her he was going back to their hut instead.'

Max grinned, clearly enjoying this more than Stevie was. 'OK,' she said. 'So the golden question. Why do you think Abi's invited them all over there? Because this clearly isn't just a reunion. Why's she brought them back together?'

'Your guess is as good as mine.'

'You've got no idea?'

'None at all.' Stevie took another sip. 'Tell you what, though. Miley mentioned this afternoon that she thinks Abi might have a new boyfriend. Apparently she's noticed her taking the phone out of the room to talk to someone about a guy.'

'You think that might have something to do with the reunion?'

'I'm not sure. Mike and Seth are the only available guys, and I can't see her being interested in either of them.'

At this point, Max's eyes narrowed, her expression becoming a fraction more serious. 'What about Humphrey?

Tonight's Abi's big moment. If he was going to try upstaging her, I guess now would be the time.'

Stevie winced. 'There's been nothing today to suggest that he's planning anything. But then I suppose there wouldn't be, would there? He'd hardly let it show.' She shook her head. 'I just don't know. Humphrey can be jealous, sure. But I've never thought of him as malicious. Abi was always more likely to tick that box. I do agree, though. If he's going to do something, tonight would be the night. I'll just have to keep an eye on him until it's all over.'

'And I'm guessing you haven't spoken with him about the promotion?'

'Not yet. Although I did mention it to Miley earlier. She asked about me coming home, so I thought I'd best float the idea that I might not be.'

'How did she take it?'

'She said that if the new job pays more money, I should take it. Apparently Abi's told her the reason we don't see each other often is that flights between New Hampshire and London are too expensive.'

'Well, that's heartbreaking.'

'Right?'

Max shook her head. 'You realise she's a psychopath, don't you? Abi, I mean.'

'She isn't as bad as that.'

'No, I mean she's an actual psychopath. I read an article about it, Stevie. And Abi ticks just about every box. She's manipulative, she's prone to jealousy, she has a complete lack of empathy or remorse. Just look at the way she's treated you all your life. She's a textbook case.'

'You can't just diagnose Abi as a psychopath because you read a *Buzzfeed* article.'

'It was *Huffington Post*, actually. And it doesn't matter where I read it. I'm telling you, Stevie, you grew up with a psychopath for a sibling.'

Stevie said nothing, so taken aback by this assessment that she found herself without a reply.

Eventually, Max sighed. 'Have you seen her at all today?'

'Not yet. She's messaged me, though. Wants me to go to her hut tomorrow so she can ask about the deer by the waterfall.'

'What do you think that's about?'

'Who can say? Guess I'll find out in the morning.'

Max nodded. 'And when do you need to think about getting ready for this party?'

'Around about now, probably.'

'You going with the green dress?'

'I think so.'

'Nice.' Max made an approving sound, then she drained what remained of her rosé. 'Listen, Stevie, I've got to go. They're about to call last orders and my pals are going to be wondering where I've got to. Go and get ready for your party. Keep an eye on your brother. And you'd better let me know as soon as you find out anything new.'

Stevie promised that she would, and a moment later they ended the call. Setting her phone down, Stevie leaned back in her seat, her mind spinning from Max's assessment that Abi was a psychopath.

Of course she had heard of psychopathy. Likewise, she understood that it wasn't necessarily as portrayed in Hollywood movies about bloodthirsty serial killers. It was more nuanced. More subtle. But in all the years since her adoption, the prospect of Abi fitting this particular prognosis – of being an actual, bona-fide psychopath – wasn't something that Stevie had ever considered.

Reaching again for her phone, she googled *signs of psychopathy*, quickly finding herself on an article by *Psychology Matters*. Near the top of the piece, a paragraph read:

Psychopathy is a personality disorder characterized by a distinctive pattern of interpersonal, affective and behavioral traits. Signs include superficial charm, manipulative behavior, and a lack of remorse or guilt. Other key indicators include jealousy, impulsivity or fearlessness, a disregard for rules or consequences, and a lack of interest in long-term goals.

Some of the criteria certainly rang true. Abi could be charming, she could be manipulative, and she certainly seemed to have felt no guilt or remorse for the tireless campaign she had mounted to have Stevie removed from the Blythe family. Likewise, she was prone to jealousy. Stevie had long ago concluded that while Abi's initial dislike for her had been the sense that she was there to replace Joel – that she and Humphrey were, by implication, just as replaceable – it was her jealousy of the love that had been showered upon her by Jane Blythe that caused Abi to truly hate her.

But there were just as many characteristics that did not, in fact, ring true. Abi was rarely impulsive, and while she was undoubtedly confident, Stevie didn't know if she would say *fearless* was quite the right word. Hadn't it been fear, after all, that had prompted Abi to invite Stevie to The Midnight Orchid? Fear of what Humphrey might do to derail her big moment? A disregard for rules or consequences didn't feel quite right, either. Nor did a lack of interest in long-term goals. Had Abi not decided, at the age of twenty-two, to step up to the challenge of raising Miley as a single mother? Had she not worked hard at Conrad Blythe, supposedly launching The Midnight Orchid almost single-handedly?

She closed the article, Max's words ringing once more in her mind.

I'm telling you, Stevie, you grew up with a psychopath.

'No, Max,' she murmured. 'I don't think I did.' Then, shaking herself back into focus, she looked up to see a waiter standing over her. 'I'm sorry?' she said.

The waiter gave her a kind smile. 'Would you like another smoothie?'

She looked at the empty glass, considering his question for a moment before shaking her head. 'No, thank you. I should get back to my hut.'

The waiter nodded and moved along. As he did so, Stevie stretched and then climbed to her feet. She would need a little time to get ready for the party. And she was eager for a shower after their hike through the jungle.

But just as she was about to head back into the restaurant, something in the garden caught her attention. Looking down, she saw Humphrey making his way into the forest. She watched him go, aware of the troubled expression that she could feel upon her face as he disappeared into the trees.

'Humphrey . . .' she murmured. 'What are you doing here?'

Part Four: The Party

17

As the evening drew in, the DJ took to the stage, music pulsing from the garden. The hotel's launch party – the moment for which they had all convened – was beginning.

Spotlights began to move over the rapidly gathering crowd, while fairy lights twinkled in the trees and flame-lit torches lined the paths. With all fifty of The Midnight Orchid's huts now full, a congregation of a hundred or so people filled the garden. Dressed in glittering gowns and light linen suits, they danced to Elvis Presley, posed as photographers did the rounds, and gladly accepted the champagne and canapés that were being proffered by a small army of staff.

It was exactly as Olive had imagined. The location beautiful. The atmosphere electric. The party itself the most glamorous that she'd ever had the opportunity to attend. She was there with her friends, and soon, Abi would be giving a speech. At midnight there would even be fireworks.

And yet, she found that she couldn't enjoy it.

She was in the crowd, watching the DJ at work on stage. At her side, Jazz shook her head. 'I still can't believe Mike hit Seth. God, I wish I'd been there now.'

'It isn't funny, Jazz.'

'It sounds pretty funny.'

'Well, it isn't!'

They were both silent for a moment. Then, Olive sighed, her shoulders sinking.

'I'm sorry,' she said. 'I just . . . I was so excited for this reunion. I wanted it to be perfect, but none of it's going right. First Abi springs Miley and Stevie on us. Now Seth and Mike have fallen out. And even Zach—'

'Where *is* Zach?' Jazz cut across her.

'I don't know! He went running off about ten minutes ago. Didn't tell me where. Just said that he was going for a walk.'

Jazz watched her carefully. 'I'm guessing you haven't made up since this morning?'

Olive shook her head. 'We've barely spoken. I don't know why he's so desperate to go home, but whatever's on his mind is really bothering him.'

Jazz studied her cousin for a moment longer.

'All right,' she said. 'Tell you what. We don't need the boys for the two of us to enjoy this. Let them deal with whatever's upset them. We're in a beautiful place. You're looking fabulous . . .'

Olive gave an unconvincing smile. 'I just want to understand,' she said. 'I want Abi to explain . . . Why didn't she tell us about Stevie and Joel when we were all at York?

Why has she gone *ten years* without telling us about Miley?
What did we do wrong?'

'Nothing. No one did anything wrong, Olive—'

'We must have. *I* must have . . .'

She didn't finish, terrified that if she said much more she
wouldn't be able to do so without crying.

'Listen to me,' Jazz said sternly. 'You didn't do anything
wrong. Whatever reasons Abi had are hers alone. They're
nothing to do with you.'

'But—'

'But nothing, Olive. Now here's what's going to happen.
I'm going to get us some more drinks. Then we're going
to have a dance. And when that husband of yours turns up
I am going to kick his arse until he tells us why he's acting
so strangely. How does that sound?'

Olive nodded, her lower lip trembling. 'OK,' she managed. 'Yeah. That sounds good.'

Jazz pulled her in for a hug. 'Don't let Abi get you
down,' she said. 'Or Zach. Let's just make the most of
where we are.'

Olive smiled, but she couldn't manage a reply this time.
After Jazz had gone off in search of drinks, she looked
around at the crowd, searching for Abi. There was no sign
of her. Presumably she was off somewhere else, preparing
to give her speech or entertaining guests in another part of
the hotel.

Olive chewed her lip. She knew, on some level, that
Jazz was right. There might well be no point dwelling
on Abi's reasons for going quiet. Nor for holding back

about Stevie and Joel. There might not even *be* a rational explanation. But that wasn't good enough for Olive. She had to know. In that moment, she knew for a fact that she wouldn't sleep that night unless Abi told her what she'd done wrong.

18

On the other side of the garden, Mike moved slowly among the crowd.

He felt painfully out of place, a drink in his hand that he hadn't touched and a gloomy expression on his face that he couldn't shake. There was no helping it, though. The day's events had left him not just despondent but outright despairing.

For one thing, punching Seth hadn't been half as satisfying as he'd imagined. He'd never punched anyone before and he was fairly certain he'd done it wrong. His hand throbbed every time he flexed his fingers, and yet Seth barely seemed to have suffered a split lip.

He scowled, trying hard not to think of the way this would undoubtedly be spun into yet another anecdote at his expense. *And then,* he pictured Seth saying, *he tried to punch me, but he ended up spraining his own stupid hand!*

But troubling him even more than the thought of Seth's amusement was Miley. Of all the times to finally lash out at Seth, he couldn't believe that he'd done it while she had been there to see. The look on her face . . . The shock. The fear. It had been enough to break his heart.

Feeling movement on his arm, he glanced down to see a mosquito sitting on his wrist. Without thinking, he slapped the palm of his hand down on top of it, remembering his sunburn just a second too late.

He winced, the place where the mosquito had been now stinging as if he'd rubbed it against a nettle.

This place, he thought to himself. This *fucking* place.

His phone buzzed in his pocket. Taking it out, he saw that Seth had put yet another message on the WhatsApp group, asking when someone would be joining him for a drink. Apparently he was sitting at the poolside bar.

Mike put the phone away again. He wasn't interested in replying. If he was completely honest, he wasn't interested in seeing any of the group. Leave Zach and Olive to their tiff, and Jazz to whatever it was that she was up to. All he cared about was Miley, and the question of whether she might be his.

As if on cue, she darted across the path in front of him. He started at the sight of her. At nine o'clock he'd assumed she would be in bed, but it seemed Abi must have decided she could stay up for the party.

For a second she looked wildly around, apparently deciding which direction she was going to shoot off in next. It was then that she noticed Mike. Locking eyes, he saw a look of recognition in her expression, followed swiftly by fear.

He felt a lump rise in his throat, his heart breaking anew

at the thought that this could be his daughter's first impression of her father.

He thought about saying something – about calling out to her – but before he had a chance she was gone, vanishing into the crowd with Alana in pursuit.

Mike screwed his eyes shut.

He couldn't do this. He'd told himself that he would be patient. That he would speak to Abi once the party was over. But seeing Miley now, he knew that it couldn't wait. He had to know. And he had to know right now.

Tipping back his champagne in one go, he put the glass on a passing tray and began to move – eager, now, to find Abi.

19

Though she was trying hard not to admit it, Stevie was becoming increasingly nervous at the difficulty she was having locating Humphrey.

She had knocked for him at his hut on her way over, only to find that he hadn't been there. She'd then done two loops of the garden, nodding and smiling at the occasional Conrad Blythe board member she'd recognised, but again had found no sign of him. She'd even checked the pool-side bar, still to no avail. It wasn't until she decided to try inside the restaurant that she finally tracked him down.

Immediately, as she stepped inside and saw him sitting there at the bar, she felt a rush of relief.

The place was surprisingly quiet, compared to the previous evening's dinner service, with just a few tables occupied out on the terrace and a couple of other patrons at the bar. Stevie figured no one would be interested in dining right now. Instead, the guests were mostly gathered down in the garden, dancing to the DJ as they worked their way through the canapés. Had Stevie not known about the crowd down on the lawn the empty restaurant would have been a strange sight, with the music surging in through the open terrace doors. Like a lavish birthday party that no one had turned up for.

If she was honest, the lack of people in the restaurant only added to her relief. Although it was tempered slightly by the question of how many drinks Humphrey had consumed in the time she'd been searching for him. Watching him from the door, she observed silently as he drained half a cocktail in one go before waving for the bartender to make him another.

'Humphrey . . .'

At the sound of her voice he turned, the lazy smile plastered across his face confirming that the cocktail she'd just seen had not been his first.

'Stevie!' he called out. 'Where've you been, little sis? Come on, let's get you a drink. What're you having?'

'Maybe it's a good idea to slow down a little on the drink—'

'*No!* Come on. Sit with me! We haven't caught up yet just the two of us, and I want to know all about London.'

He swayed precariously on his bar stool, his voice rising to a shout. Stevie wondered if she should try to get him back to his hut, fearful of what Abi might do if he made a scene. Quite how she would do that, though, she had no idea. He was unlikely to go willingly, and while she could probably convince some of the hotel staff to help her escort him away from the bar, she doubted that such an approach would go down well.

She sat down on the neighbouring bar stool, asking for a daiquiri when the bartender came over.

'So come on,' said Humphrey, after the bartender had set down their drinks. 'How's London? Any guys on the scene?'

'Nope,' she replied. 'No guys.'

'Any *girls*?'

'No.'

He seemed to think about this for a second. 'You must be screwing someone. Everyone's screwing *someone*. And if you aren't, maybe you should be. It's good for you.'

'Humphrey!'

He laughed. Then, he pointed towards a tray of champagne flutes that a waiter was preparing to carry down to the garden.

'I chose that,' he said. 'That champagne. I chose it. Why don't we see how many of our friends on the board are drinking it? See if they'll still agree that I didn't do anything for this place.' He shook his head. 'I did so much. I chose loads of the booze. I helped furnish the huts.' He frowned suddenly. 'Which hut are you in? Where did Abi put you?'

'Number fifty, I think.'

Humphrey raised his eyebrows. 'Damn. She literally put you in the furthest one from the lodge.'

Stevie forced a laugh. 'You can't tell me you're surprised. Isn't that exactly where she'd want me? As far away as possible?'

'It's still a shitty thing to do.' He shook his head. 'I'd

offer to swap, but I don't think you'd want mine. I'm right next door to Abi.' He laughed to himself. Then, he asked, 'Has she really brought you all the way out here just to keep an eye on me?'

'What makes you say that?'

'Well, when I last suggested inviting you to this thing, she said no. Then, suddenly, I'm kicked out of the company and she wants you along. Doesn't take a genius to see the correlation there.'

Stevie gave a weak smile. 'Can you blame her for being suspicious? You stormed off to Thailand, posting videos of yourself ranting about the people on the board.'

'I took those videos down.'

'I know.'

'And I went home to apologise.'

'I know. And that's all good stuff, Humphrey. But Abi has every right to be wary.'

He sighed. 'Maybe you're right. But I do wish she'd give me the benefit of the doubt. I worked hard on this place, no matter what those fuckers on the board might say. I feel like I've at least earned the right to attend the party.' He looked her in the eye, offering a sad smile. 'You should go enjoy yourself, Stevie. I promise I'm not planning some evil scheme. You don't need to keep an eye on me.'

Again, she watched him, searching his face for any sign that he might be lying to her. It was no good, though. His expression was unreadable.

'Maybe I just want to hang out with you,' she said.

He laughed. 'I don't see why you would. I'm hardly going to be any fun this evening.' He sighed again. 'I screwed this up,' he said. 'Didn't I? I got myself kicked out of the company. Ruined the best thing I had going for me. I threw away what Dad left for me . . .' He propped his elbows on the bar, dropping his head into his hands. 'What am I gonna do?'

Stevie thought for a moment. Then, after a pause, she managed a grin. 'What about your surf school?' she said. 'The one you used to talk about opening when you were sixteen?'

Humphrey raised his head again, eyes widening. 'You remember that?'

'Of course. I think it was the same year you experimented with highlights.'

Humphrey smiled. A small smile, but it was something.

'And you could spend some more time with Miley,' said Stevie. 'That would be good, wouldn't it? She loves you so much.'

Once more, Humphrey's expression turned suddenly sombre. 'I can't see that happening. Abi doesn't like me hanging out with Miley.'

'What do you mean?'

'She doesn't let me take her out on my own. I've said I could take her hiking, take her to hockey games . . . But Abi always says no.'

'Why?'

Humphrey shrugged. 'She says I'm too irresponsible. Can't be trusted to take proper care of her. Guess I've only myself to blame for that.' He took a swig of his drink. Then, seemingly eager to change the subject, he asked, 'What were you and Olive talking about on the hike? It looked like you were really getting into it.'

Stevie hesitated, wondering if she should try to lie.

'She was asking about Joel.'

Humphrey's eyes narrowed. 'And what did you tell her?'

'I guess everything Mom and Dad told *me*. How great he was. How special.'

Humphrey grimaced.

'What?' said Stevie.

'Nothing.'

'No, what? What is it?'

'Just . . . You shouldn't believe everything Mom and Dad told you about Joel.'

'Why not?'

Humphrey was silent. After a long pause, though, he sighed.

'Look,' he said. 'It was awful when Joel died. Of course it was. If a kid goes over a waterfall that's always going to be tragic. But he wasn't the golden boy Mom and Dad made him out to be.'

'What was he then?'

Humphrey screwed up his face. 'You want the truth, Stevie? He was a little shit. I know you shouldn't speak ill of the dead, and I'm not saying he deserved what happened. But he wasn't a good kid. He was clever about it, though. Never let Mom and Dad see it. He was the sort to say his prayers and do his homework when the adults were looking, but the moment their heads were turned the other way he'd put a rock through the neighbour's window and say that it was you. Just for the hell of it. He was always pulling shit like that. And no one ever saw.'

Stevie stared at him. She was sure that he wouldn't be saying this out loud if he hadn't been drinking. Still, she'd never heard anyone speak about Joel this way. She found herself caught completely off guard.

'Are you really not going to go enjoy the party?' he asked.

She shook her head.

'Why not?'

'Because . . .' She was unsure of her answer and the word hung uselessly in the air.

'Because you don't believe me.'

Stevie stared at him, searching his face.

'Humphrey,' she said, 'please just tell me the truth. Tell me why you're actually here.'

For several moments he didn't reply. But eventually, he relented. He took a long sip of his cocktail. Sat a little straighter on his bar stool. And then he began to speak.

20

At the poolside bar, Seth sat alone with a beer.

He took a swig, massaging his jaw as he set the bottle back down. For an hour or two it had throbbed a little, but by now the feeling had mostly subsided. If he was completely honest, it hadn't been a very good punch. He'd been more surprised than wounded. Three years Seth had spent winding up Mike while they were students. Three years and the most he'd ever got back in terms of resistance was the occasional snide remark. Maybe even a *get lost*. A punch was the last thing he'd expected. On some level he thought he might even be impressed.

He took out his phone, hoping to see if anyone had responded to his request for a drinking buddy. But the reunion WhatsApp group remained silent. It seemed the day's events really had taken their toll.

Then, as if on cue, he saw movement from the corner of his eye, turning just in time to see Mike looking round the corner of the bar.

'Whoa!' Seth threw up his hands to cover his face. 'It's

Mikey Tyson, back for round two! Go easy on me, Mikey! Don't sock me again!'

Mike scowled, turning abruptly to leave.

'Wait!' Seth laughed, calling after him. 'Mikey, wait. Please. Have a drink with me.'

Mike paused, glaring at him.

'Come on, dude,' Seth pressed. 'I've been alone here for forty minutes. What kind of reunion is this? If someone doesn't come join me soon I'm going to have to start making friends with strangers.'

'I don't want a drink.'

'OK. What do you want, then?'

'Have you seen Abi?'

'Abi? No, not yet. I suppose she'll be busy hosting. Mingling with her guests.'

'That's what I thought, but I can't find her anywhere. I've just done three laps of the garden and no one seems to have seen her. Not even any of the staff know where's she's got to.'

Seth frowned. 'I'm sure she'll turn up. She's supposed to be giving a speech soon, isn't she?' His eyes narrowed. 'Why do you need to find her so badly?'

Mike didn't reply. Instead, he hovered on the spot, deliberating, before turning away and striding back towards the garden.

'Mikey?' Seth called after him. '*Mikey?*'

No reply came.

Muttering to himself, Seth snatched up his bottle, draining what remained of the beer, before springing from his bar stool and hurrying to follow.

21

Jazz found Zach in the lobby. He was coming from the direction of the huts, a distinctly unhappy look on his face. At the sight of Jazz, there seemed to be a flicker of panic in his eyes, and he made a quick change of direction.

'Where have you been?' she demanded.

'Nowhere.'

He tried to sidestep her, but she was too quick, darting to block his path.

'I just went for a walk.'

'Where?'

'Nowhere.'

'You've been *somewhere*.' Jazz glared at him. 'What's going on with you? Why are you being so weird?'

'I'm not being—'

'You *are* being weird, Zach. Olive's told me all about it. This morning you were trying to make her fly home. Now you're running off by yourself without so much as telling her where you're going. Get it together. She's upset. She's confused. You know better than anyone what she's like when Abi's around. She needs her husband watching out for her. Not me.'

For the majority of this speech, there had been defiance in Zach's eyes. But at the mention of Abi's name, something changed. He looked suddenly rattled. Frightened, even.

Jazz, in turn, felt her own expression soften. 'What?' she said. 'What is it?'

'Nothing,' he said. 'It's nothing. I need to go . . .'

He tried a second time to sidestep her, more determinedly this time, but Jazz remained steadfastly in his path.

'Stop,' she said sternly, grabbing his wrists so that she could hold him in place.

She stared into his eyes. She could see in his face that he was lying. Something had clearly happened.

'Just stop,' she said. 'Drop the bullshit, Zach. And just tell me where you've been.'

22

'So the truth . . .' said Humphrey. 'The truth is that I came out here because I'm worried about Abi.'

Stevie raised an eyebrow. 'You're worried about her?'

'That's right. If I'm totally honest, she's been acting a little weird recently.'

'Weird how?'

Humphrey grimaced. 'She's been having meetings with Pete.'

'Pete?'

'Pete Wozniak.'

Stevie thought for a second. 'Dad's old friend? The attorney?'

Humphrey nodded. 'When I got back from Bangkok, and I went to the house to apologise for flying off the handle, Abi was on the phone to Pete. I overheard her say she was going to *tell the family* something after the launch was done.'

'The family? As in you and me?'

'I guess so. Maybe Miley, too.'

At that moment, the music that was rising from the garden abruptly came to a halt, drawing a playful groan from the crowd.

'Sorry, folks!' the DJ called out, voice amplified by the PA system. 'Sorry to interrupt. We'll have the music back on real soon, but if I could have your attention for a moment. It's just gone nine o'clock and I believe our glamorous host has a few words she'd like to say to us. So could you please put your hands together and welcome Miss Abigail Blythe to the stage.'

The audience quickly broke into applause, a few even giving a cheer and a whoop. Stevie ignored it, though, her eyes fixed on Humphrey.

'What was it?' she asked. 'What do you think Abi was going to tell us?'

'I don't know. She hung up after that. She sounded upset, though.'

'And how do you know she was talking to Pete?'

Humphrey ran a hand through his hair. 'Don't judge me, OK? I was worried about her and . . . Well. After I'd apologised, she went into the kitchen to fix Miley some lunch. I stayed in the living room, and I noticed she'd left her phone on the coffee table.'

'Oh, Humphrey . . .'

'I didn't just *look* at it. She had an email come through, so I took a glance. I could only read the first line, but I could see that it was from Pete and that it mentioned a meeting they'd had that morning.' He shook his head. 'I had no idea what it was all about. But I can't help wondering, now that we're here . . . Could whatever it is have something to do with these guys from her university days?'

Stevie said nothing.

'Miss Blythe?' The DJ laughed. 'Where are you, Miss Blythe? Don't tell me I've misread the call sheet.'

The audience laughed, the applause now beginning to fade. Once it had ended completely, Stevie heard the DJ speak once more.

'Tell you what, folks – it's opening night. I'm sure Miss Blythe's been held up somewhere and will be with us soon. Let's get the music back on and when she makes her grand entrance we'll try this thing again.'

As the music started up again, with the opening bars of an old Chaka Khan classic drifting up to the terrace, Stevie and Humphrey locked eyes.

'Missing her own speech?' said Humphrey.

Stevie swallowed back a lump, suddenly nervous. They sat in silence for a moment, and she felt certain that her brother was pondering the same question as her. Abi had organised this party to a tee. What could have happened for her to miss her speech?

Draining his drink, Humphrey rose to his feet. 'I'm gonna check on her.'

Stevie nodded. 'I'll come too.'

23

'Mikey!' Seth called out. 'Mikey, come on. This is a really bad idea.'

Mike didn't reply, barging on ahead.

'Mikey,' Seth tried again. '*Mike!*' He grabbed him by the shoulder. 'Do you really think Abi's going to appreciate you doing this on her big night? Demanding to know if you're the father of her kid? I understand it's a conversation you want to have, but I'm telling you, this is *not* the time.'

Mike wrenched himself free. 'Piss off, Seth.'

'Piss off?' Seth repeated. 'You *punched* me earlier today, and yet here I am, trying to stop you from doing the stupidest thing you've ever done. But I'll just leave it, shall I? I'll just piss off?'

'I have to know!'

Mike's voice rose to a cry. Taken aback, Seth watched as he took a second to collect himself.

'I have to know,' he said quietly. 'I don't care if it's the right time. I don't care if it's stupid. If I ruin Abi's night and she wants me to leave then I'll get on a plane home tonight. But I need to know if that girl is my daughter.'

For a few moments Seth just stood there, unsure of what he was supposed to say. Mike even seemed to wait for him, hovering a while as if braced for further protest. When none came, he turned on the spot, striding in the opposite direction.

'Mike,' Seth groaned. '*Mike* . . .'

He didn't go any further. Because as they stepped into the lobby they both stopped in their tracks. A short distance away, Zach and Jazz were staring at one another, Jazz's hands locked around Zach's wrists.

It was Jazz who broke the silence, frowning at their arrival. 'What are you two doing?'

'I need to find Abi,' said Mike. 'I have to talk to her.'

'Why?'

'Because he's gone completely fucking mad,' Seth muttered.

'I have to talk to her!' Mike's voice rose again. 'I've been looking for her all around the party but she doesn't seem to be there. So I'm checking her hut.'

It was Zach who protested first.

'You shouldn't do that,' he said.

'Why not?'

'Because . . .' Zach's eyes were slightly manic. 'Because it's her opening night. Whatever you're wanting to talk to her about, she's surely going to be more receptive once the party's out of the way.'

'Thank you!' Seth chipped in. 'That's exactly what I—'

'Enough!' Mike took a deep breath. 'I'm going to find her. And when I do, I'm going to talk to her. This is happening. So please, all of you, just get out of my—'

'Are you looking for Abi?'

At the sound of Olive's voice, they all turned. She stood a short distance away, looking at them with wide, troubled eyes.

'That's right,' said Mike, voice shuddering slightly. 'No one seems to know where she is, so I'm seeing if she's in her hut.'

Olive nodded. 'I'll come with you.'

'Olive, no!'

Jazz tried to argue but Olive immediately shot her down.

'I have to know, Jazz. I have to know why she kept it all from us. And it can't wait until tomorrow. You can come with me if you like but please don't try to stop me. I need to speak to her. I need to ask these questions.'

Seth watched as she locked eyes with Mike.

'Now,' she breathed. 'Shall we go?'

24

The last thing Stevie expected, as she and Humphrey arrived at Abi's hut, was to find all five of her sister's friends arguing on the path outside her door.

Beside her, Stevie heard Humphrey murmur, 'What the hell is this . . . ?'

She shook her head. She had no idea. But from what she could tell, it looked as if Olive – and perhaps Mike, too – wanted to call on Abi, with Zach, Jazz and Seth all trying desperately to stop them.

'Hey,' Humphrey called out. 'Hey! What the fuck is this? What do you guys think you're doing?'

At the sound of Humphrey's voice the group paused, all five heads turning to look in their direction.

'We're looking for Abi,' said Olive.

'Well, she doesn't seem to be here, does she? The ruckus you're making on her doorstep . . . Don't you think she'd have come out by now just to see what's wrong with you all?'

Olive and Mike exchanged a look.

'Even so . . .' said Olive, voice suddenly wavering.

Stevie watched as she stepped around Zach, making her way towards Abi's front door.

'Olive . . .' Jazz reached out for her, but Olive shrugged her away. Stepping up to the door, she knocked gently.

'Abi?' she said. 'Abi, are you in there?'

When no reply came, she knocked again. A little harder this time.

'Abi . . . ?'

This time the door moved. Just a crack. But at Olive's touch a tell-tale sliver of light crept from the hut out into the jungle.

Exchanging a glance with Humphrey, Stevie felt her heart beat a little quicker. Looking at the group, she could see that they were thinking it too.

The door was open. Why was the door open?

Slowly, Olive reached out with a trembling hand and took the handle. The group was now completely silent, eyes wide. The music continued to drift from the garden, muffled, at this distance, to the extent that without their bickering they could now hear the sounds of the birds and the insects in the jungle around them. But as the door swung open, there came another sound. Joining the night-time chorus, just for a few seconds, was the sound of Olive's terrified scream.

Part Five: The Body

25

An hour later, Stevie sat alone at the restaurant bar. Her back was turned to the terrace, but she could still hear the party continuing in the garden below, guests laughing as music blared from the PA system.

In her mind, though, she was in her childhood bedroom, sitting beside a teenaged Humphrey on her Harry Potter bedspread. A floor below, in the dining room, their parents were berating Abi.

'It's OK,' Humphrey was saying. 'We all know it wasn't you.'

Stevie wasn't replying. It wasn't that she doubted him. This was the third time that Abi had hidden something in her room, in the hope of portraying her as a thief. First it had been Humphrey's Game Boy, then their father's watch. Now it was their mother's favourite earrings. Stevie felt more than just hurt. She was confused about why Abi seemed so desperate for their parents to send her back. And, she guessed, somewhere in the back of her mind she was worrying about whatever cunning ploy Abi might turn to next in her campaign to get rid of her.

The bedroom door opened, a familiar figure silhouetted against the landing light.

'Humphrey,' said Jane Blythe. 'Could I have a moment with your sister, please?'

Patting Stevie on the shoulder, Humphrey left without a word. As their mother stepped into the room, he flashed her one last supportive smile, before closing the door gently behind him.

Even now, so many years later, Stevie could still remember the smell of Jane's perfume as she crossed the room and sat beside her on the bed. That delicate fragrance that Frank always gave her on their anniversary.

'We've spoken to Abi,' she said. 'This isn't going to happen again.'

Stevie nodded glumly. Then she asked, 'Did you think it was me? At first?'

'No, my darling. I know you wouldn't steal. Believe it or not, your sister isn't the criminal mastermind she seems to think herself.'

Stevie felt her lip begin to quiver. 'Why does she hate me? Why does she—'

Her voice cracked, and as she began to cry Jane Blythe put an arm around her shoulder.

'Oh, my girl . . . Abi just finds it difficult to accept that you're as much her sister as Humphrey is her brother. But she will. I hope that one day she'll see you as we all do. It's tough now, but I think that in time you two will be great friends.'

But Jane Blythe had been wrong. Abi and Stevie had never become close. And now they never would. Because Abi was dead.

Abi was dead.

It didn't feel real. Didn't feel *possible*. And yet Stevie had seen her.

They all had.

Upon finding her on the floor of her hut, Seth had run to fetch the lodge's in-house doctor, who had quickly confirmed that there were no signs of life. He'd then ushered them outside, his phone to his ear as he'd called the police.

Standing together outside the hut, the jungle pressing in around them, Stevie had looked at each of Abi's friends in turn. None of them had made any effort to hide their distress at what they'd just seen. Olive had cried. Seth had gone pale. Even Jazz, who Stevie had taken to be fairly unshakeable, had looked rattled.

They all had good reason. The sight of a body was traumatic enough in its own right, but with a single glance it had been immediately clear that Abi's death had not been natural. No more so to any of them than Stevie. Because Stevie had seen death once before.

She could still vividly remember the day, when she was fourteen, that Jane Blythe had finally succumbed to her illness. It had been Stevie who found her, while taking her a fresh jug of water with which to wash down that morning's medication. Lying in bed, monitors and machines stationed around her, Stevie could easily have believed that her mother was asleep. Her skin was a little pale, her lips parted slightly. Her head was tilted slightly to one side, propped up by thick pillows.

Devastating as it had been, Stevie had taken comfort over the years in how peaceful her mother had looked. The sight of Abi's body, however, had been anything but.

'The flower,' Olive said between sobs. 'You all saw it, didn't you? The flower.'

She needn't have said it. They had all noticed the blue petals scattered on the floor around Abi's body. Just as they had noticed the water glass that lay beside her outstretched hand, the foam on her lips and the spider webs of little red veins that criss-crossed in each of her eyes.

Yes, they had all seen the signs. They'd all known what it had meant.

All of them but Stevie.

'Why would the flower be there?' she'd asked, unable to ignore the fear in each of their expressions. 'Why's that important?'

When no one answered, she'd turned to Humphrey. After a long moment he'd sighed. And then he'd described the warning they'd received from local experts about the orchid.

'But you aren't suggesting . . .' Stevie had stared at him, eyes bulging. 'Are you saying someone's poisoned her? That someone's done this deliberately?'

'I'm not suggesting anything.'

He'd managed just about to hold her gaze. But his tone had been far from convincing.

Standing there, in the jungle, Stevie had looked around the group, taking in each of Abi's friends one by one. She'd waited for someone to say something. To offer some alternative theory. No one had come forward.

'You knew?' she'd said. 'You all knew about this?'

Again, for several moments no one had replied.

'Abi told us,' Olive had said. 'Jazz and me.'

'And Humphrey told *us*,' Mike had said, looking to Zach and Seth.

Stevie hadn't replied. No one ventured anything further. But as they looked at one another, fear in their eyes, the silence had said it all. Abi, it appeared, had been poisoned. Poisoned by a flower that they alone had known to be deadly.

Up in the restaurant, Stevie listened as the party continued. No one in the garden had any idea what had just happened. They had no idea that their host lay dead with police on the way.

Hearing footsteps, she turned to see Humphrey approaching.

'The cops are here,' he said. 'Just two for now. It's going to take some time for more to arrive. There's only a tiny police force covering the entire peninsula, and we're about as remote out here as it's possible to be.'

Stevie nodded. 'What do they say we should do?'

'They've told us not to say anything until the others can get here. Abi's body is out of sight. We've got a couple

211

security guys standing outside the hut, so that nothing's disturbed.'

'But surely we can't just let the party carry on?'

'What else are we meant to do? We're going to need to arrange transport for any guests who want to leave. Mini-buses. Places for them to go. The manager's looking into all of that, but it's going to take time. And right now, no one knows that she's . . .' He closed his eyes. 'That she's *dead*. But once people do, they're going to have questions. They might even panic. If we let slip what's happened before we're able to deal with it, or before more police arrive to help keep everyone calm, then we risk making it all even worse.'

Stevie looked down at the bar.

'It won't be long before people realise something's wrong,' she said. 'They'll all have noticed that Abi didn't turn up to give a speech. Now there's a police car in the parking lot and security guards stationed out-side her hut. How long before people start asking what's going on?'

'I don't know.'

'And what if they start—'

'*I don't know.*'

Stevie looked at him, unused to the stress in his tone. He sighed, shoulders sinking.

'I'm sorry,' he said. 'I'm sorry, Stevie. But I just don't know.'

They fell into a long, uneasy silence.

'Do you really think one of her friends did it?' Stevie

asked. 'Do you think one of them actually poisoned her with the flower?'

'I don't know,' Humphrey said again. 'We all saw inside the hut. A water glass next to her hand. Blue petals all around her on the floor. The foam at her mouth . . . It seems pretty clear to me that it was somehow in her water. But no one else knew it was poisonous. Abi was so insistent that it had to be kept quiet until we could do more tests – until we knew for certain that it was dangerous. So if someone really has poisoned her . . .'

'It had to be one of them,' Stevie finished. She frowned. 'Why did you tell them about the flower? On the hike? How did it come up?'

'I wanted Seth's opinion on it. He grew some toxic plants in his room, back when they were students. Got in trouble over it with the warden in their dorm, apparently. And now he's an environmental consultant with a company in the UK. I wondered if he might be able to give some advice on what we should do.' Humphrey ran a hand through his hair. 'If we *are* entertaining the idea of someone killing her – if we're seriously going to consider that – then it has to be someone she knew. She wouldn't accept a glass of water from just anyone. I think her friends fit that bill.'

'She might have poured it herself,' said Stevie. 'Someone could have snuck in this afternoon and spiked the water in her fridge.'

'True,' Humphrey admitted. 'But what about the door? It was ajar when we found her, which suggests someone had been in there with her and left in a hurry. And there was no sign of the lock being forced, which means it must have been someone she knew. Someone she had allowed to come inside.'

He stared at the liquor shelf behind the bar, eyes wide. 'My money would be on one of the guys. If Abi told Olive and Jazz about the flower herself, she would have been more wary about accepting anything from them. But she didn't know I'd asked Seth, Zach and Mike about the flower on the hike. She'd have no reason to think that they would even know it was poisonous.'

'But why would she be wary of Olive and Jazz?' Stevie asked. 'What reason would she have to think they might kill her? Olive adored her, and Jazz might be a little grumpy but she doesn't strike me as a killer.' Her eyes narrowed. 'Could it have been one of the locals? One of the people who warned you about the flower? Like . . . what if you didn't *need* to tell the staff about the flower? You say it's local knowledge. Presumably you've hired people from the area to work here? And if so, Abi would have been happy letting one of those people into her hut. Maybe even accepting a glass of water from them.'

Humphrey considered this. 'I mean . . . maybe? Although Abi was eager to hire fluent English speakers, so there aren't actually that many locals on the roster. To be honest, most of the customer-facing staff have travelled from across the country to be here.'

'So then what reason would her *friends* have to do something like this?'

They fell once more into silence, Humphrey seemingly not having an answer.

After a few moments, Stevie said, 'What if it isn't what it looks like?'

'How so?'

'Well, what if someone found her dead and they put down the petals and the water glass to make it *look* like she'd been poisoned?'

'Why would someone do that? How would they even *know* to do that? Again, you'd have to know that the flower was poisonous, and the only ones here who do are her friends.' A grim expression settled upon his face. 'Stevie. We have to face facts. Someone went to see her. She welcomed them into her hut and they gave her a glass of water that had somehow been spiked with the flower. That's what we saw. It's what's happened. And it could only have been done by one of her friends.'

Stevie didn't reply, watching as Humphrey put his head in his hands. Then he asked the question she had been dreading.

'How are we going to tell Miley?'

Stevie's heart sank. One of the very first things they had done after finding Abi's body had been to seek out Alana, tell her the news and instruct her that Miley was to be taken to bed. Of course, no one knew yet that Abi was dead. That is, no one but her friends, Alana, the manager and the lodge's doctor. And until the police told them otherwise, they intended to keep it that way. They would tell Miley once they had more of a grasp on the situation.

But until that moment came, they couldn't risk her hearing someone speculating about where Abi might be.

'Put her to bed in Stevie's hut,' they had told Alana. 'She can't go back to Abi's. Not while the body's still in there. If she asks, tell her that their hut is too close to the party – she won't be able to sleep with the music playing.'

That had been nearly an hour ago, in which time they hadn't seen or heard anything from either Miley or Alana. The lie, it seemed, had worked. For now.

'Stevie,' Humphrey pressed. 'How are we going to tell her?'

Stevie shook her head. She had absolutely no idea.

26

Sitting alone on a wicker chair in the lobby, Olive watched, glassy-eyed, as the reception manager spoke with the police. There were two officers, each dressed in dark caps and white polo shirts bearing the words *Policía Turística*.

She didn't want to be there. But then again, there was nowhere else in that particular moment that she might prefer to be. She couldn't bear to return to the garden. Seeing people continue to drink and dance . . . Even now, with the music carrying up to her in the lobby, she wanted to scream at them to stop and throw their champagne flutes to the floor. It felt so wrong for them to keep partying while Abi lay dead. And yet she knew she wouldn't have been able to sit in her hut, the walls pressing in around her as the image of Abi's body filled her mind.

Abi's body.

It was the first time she had seen death up close. The first time she had ever even known someone truly close to her to die. And to think that a member of their group could somehow be responsible . . .

No. She refused to believe it. No one could actually have *murdered* Abi. And certainly not one of her friends.

She thought back to the moment when they had all stood outside Abi's hut, waiting as the doctor searched for signs of life. An hour had since passed, but she could picture the scene as clearly as if she were still there, the expressions on each of their faces seared into her mind.

No, she told herself. None of them could have done this.

She thought of Ryan, wishing she was home with him safe in her arms. She briefly wondered if she should call her parents, just to hear his voice. But ten o'clock at night in Costa Rica would be five in the morning back at home. How would she explain why she was phoning at such a time? How would she tell them why she looked so distressed? They would want to know, and she didn't think she could find the words if she tried.

Instead, her thoughts turned to Miley, and once more she felt despair wash over her. Right now, Abi's daughter was somewhere in the hotel. With luck she would be asleep somewhere, perhaps in Stevie's or Humphrey's huts, blissfully unaware of the news that would greet her when she awoke.

Ahead of her, one of the police officers said something in Spanish. She strained to hear what it was, wishing for more than the basic GCSE-level Spanish she had learned half a lifetime ago. It was no use, though. She

218

managed only to pick out the occasional word before the manager began to lead the officers in the direction of Abi's hut.

She looked away, hating the idea of them standing over Abi's body – of them discussing which of her friends might have killed her. It felt almost as insulting as their decision to let the party continue down in the garden, even if it was only for the time being.

The moment the officers had gone, Olive found herself hit by a wave of grief. She pressed both hands to her face, trying to hold back her tears. Only when she sensed movement beside her did she open her eyes again to see that Zach had sat down in the neighbouring seat.

'Hey,' he said weakly.

'Hey,' she replied.

She didn't quite know how she felt to have him there. She would have liked to think that having her husband beside her would bring some comfort, even in spite of the disagreements that their trip to The Midnight Orchid had caused. Instead, as she looked at him now she realised she felt nothing. No warmth. No relief. Not even any resentment. He was simply there, where a moment earlier he had not been.

Whatever she did or did not feel about him, though, she could see how badly he was affected by the evening's events. He stared into the distance, skin pale and eyes glazed.

They sat in silence for a while. Then, finally, he said, 'What do you think happened?'

When she didn't answer, he faced her, looking her straight in the eye.

'Who do you think it was?' he asked. 'The flowers. Who do you think—'

'No,' she said sharply.

He frowned at her. 'What do you mean, "No"?'

'Just no. We're not talking like that.'

'Olive,' he said sternly. 'We all saw the petals. Someone's clearly—'

'*We're not doing this,*' she cut across him. 'We're not. I won't start speculating about our friends being murderers.'

He turned away, a grim expression on his face. 'Mike took me aside,' he continued. 'He thinks—'

'I don't want to know.'

He fell silent again. This time for good.

For a few moments they sat there together, watching on as a couple of guests pointed towards the police car parked outside. Then, Zach rose to his feet and walked away. Olive didn't watch him go. She stared blankly ahead, tears starting to fall.

27

In need of a walk and a few minutes alone, Stevie left the restaurant and made her way to the garden.

The DJ couldn't know, of course, what was happening. But if anything the music seemed to have been turned up rather than down since Abi's body had been discovered. 'A Little Less Conversation' had been abandoned in favour of Rhianna's 'SOS'. The guests, likewise, were getting swept along, the party beginning to shift from canapés and small talk to shots and strobe lights. All the same, as Stevie skirted the edge of the crowd she couldn't help but over-hear whispers about the presence of two police officers in the lobby.

It had happened even quicker than she'd expected, the police having barely been there half an hour. But from what she could hear, the guests didn't seem to have connected the arrival of the officers with Abi's absence. Instead she heard one speculating about a break-in at one of the huts. She lingered just long enough to hear that something simi-lar had apparently happened at a resort down the coast, a wealthy tourist's Rolex stolen from the dresser while he'd been taking a shower.

She hoped against hope that it would be a while before they started to suspect what might actually be going on. At the very least that it would be after more officers had arrived. Because Humphrey had been right – the last thing they needed was a hundred inebriated guests panicking with no one there to contain the situation.

Pausing by the fountain at the centre of the garden, she closed her eyes, her mind going without warning to Humphrey's dark joke that she had shared with Olive during the hike. That the three siblings were the last Blythes standing.

It did, to his credit, seem bleakly accurate. First there had been Joel, going over the waterfall. Next it had been Jane, taken by the same disease that had claimed her own mother. Then, only last year, it had been Frank's turn, struck down in an instant by a heart attack.

And now Abi was gone too. Poisoned, supposedly, by one of her own friends.

At the same time, Stevie's head spun with the ramifications of what Humphrey had shared with her in the moments before they'd gone searching for their sister. Why, exactly, had she been organising secret meetings with the family attorney? And what was it that Humphrey had overheard her describing – the thing she had apparently intended to reveal to the family once the grand opening of The Midnight Orchid was dealt with?

At first these questions had been perplexing. But now, with Abi lying dead, they immediately felt more sinister.

Before she could stop herself, Stevie began to wonder . . . Had that been why Abi called the reunion? Could whatever she'd been planning to share with her family have been something that she, likewise, had wanted to share with her friends? If so, what was it? What could be so important after all these years? Why would it require meetings with the family attorney? And was it at all possible that one of Abi's friends had poisoned her in an effort to keep her from revealing it?

For a moment Stevie reflected on the irony of her being one of the last Blythes left. She, who – according to Abi, at least – should never have been a Blythe in the first place.

She felt a sudden surge of guilt. She wasn't sure if it was Abi's voice speaking or her own, but why, she asked herself, did *she* deserve to remain? Why did she deserve to go on, carrying the Blythe name, while her parents, Joel and now Abi had all fallen by the wayside?

At the same time, she felt a sense of hopelessness. This was the family that had taken her in. The family that had given her a name and a home – to which, though she sometimes struggled to admit it, she had hoped one day to return. But what was there to return to now? Could they still count as a family – she, Humphrey and Miley?

Quickly, before her feelings could escalate any further, she took a deep breath. Then, eager for a distraction of some kind, she opened Google and searched *Osa Peninsula poisonous flowers*.

The results weren't enlightening. Wiping her eyes with the back of her hand, she skimmed through a list of a few species local to the area that could irritate the skin, but nothing that would kill, and certainly nothing that resembled the midnight orchid.

She tried again, searching instead for *Osa Peninsula poisonous plants*. This time she was rewarded with something interesting. Not a flower, but a tree that was supposedly regarded as one of the deadliest in the world. Tapping on an article, she began to read:

The manchineel tree (*Hippomane mancinella*) is a poisonous tree found along the coastlines of Central America and the Caribbean.

Upon contact with the skin, the sap can cause blistering, burns and inflammation. Smoke from the burning wood can injure the eyes, while the juice from the fruit, if ingested, can cause oral and esophageal ulceration and severe edema. The fruit is commonly known as *manzanilla de la muerte* – the little apple of death.

Heart pounding, Stevie stared at the final paragraph.

The juice from the fruit, if ingested, can cause oral and oesophageal ulceration and severe edema.

Returning to Google, she began once more to type, this time searching *Can manchineel juice kill?*

The answer read:

There are no modern accounts of manchineel juice causing a fatality, largely as a result of increased aware-ness surrounding the danger that the tree may pose. However, there are historical records of indigenous warriors using the sap to poison enemy water supplies, as well as to coat arrowheads before combat.

If you were to bite into an apple, the taste would at first be sweet, with a burning sensation following soon after. The throat would then swell and begin to close up. Expect to be in severe pain for the next eight hours, although the swelling in your throat could last longer.

Stevie looked out at the jungle. At the countless number of trees that surrounded the lodge.

Could one of those be a manchineel? She had abso-lutely no idea. It seemed possible, though, if the species really did grow all over Central America. And if there was a manchineel tree here, what then? Could someone have used one of those apples to kill Abi, only to leave petals beside her body in a bid to pretend it had been the flower?

It was a possibility. She figured that someone could have collected an apple, with the intention of crushing it and giving Abi the juice. Or perhaps they had given her some of the sap from the tree itself. The text Stevie had just read did suggest that it had once been used to poison water sup-plies. In any case, the culprit could easily have scattered petals beside Abi's body, hoping it might appear as if she had been poisoned with the flower. They could have even hunted a deer or been lucky enough to stumble upon an already-deceased one, which they then thought to plant in the grove beside the waterfall in order to make the flower appear dangerous.

But none of this seemed likely.

For one thing, the culprit would have needed to know that the flower was considered poisonous in order to plan such a deception – known it, but crucially not believed it. If they believed the flower was deadly, they would surely have just used it. Likewise, they would presumably be aware that a post-mortem would be conducted. If juice or even sap from a manchineel tree had been used to kill Abi, it would undoubtedly be found. So while it was possible that a manchineel tree could have been used, Stevie found herself wondering what the point would be.

It occurred to her as well that the symptoms described in the article didn't match those she had seen in Abi's hut. There was no mention of foaming at the mouth or red veins visible in the victim's eyes. She figured that, given the lack of modern cases of manchineel poisoning, it was possible certain symptoms might simply not be as well known as others. But the information she had just read seemed comprehensive. If a manchineel tree could cause anything like the symptoms Abi had displayed, Stevie suspected they would at least have been mentioned.

Putting her phone away, Stevie looked at the guests, watching as they continued to dance and mingle. She both longed for and dreaded the moment more police would arrive, desperate for this morbid sense of being in limbo to end while also terrified of what would happen when the guests finally twigged what was going on.

Turning away from the party, she looked towards the swimming pool. Had she done so a second later, she would have missed it. But as it happened, she looked just in time to see Seth and Jazz disappearing together around the side of the poolside bar.

She blinked, the moment so fleeting she almost wondered if she'd imagined it.

There was no doubting it, though. She had absolutely seen them. More than that, it seemed immediately clear that they were going somewhere secluded. Somewhere they wouldn't be seen or heard.

Stevie deliberated over what to do. In any ordinary circumstance, she would leave them to it. Respect their privacy and try to pretend she hadn't seen anything. But these were not ordinary circumstances. Her sister was lying dead, and Humphrey certainly believed, even if Stevie herself was uncertain, that one of Abi's friends must be responsible.

She wondered whether she should run back up to the lodge and fetch one of the police officers. But she knew all too well that by the time she'd found them and brought them back they would have missed several minutes – if not all – of whatever Seth and Jazz had gone to discuss.

And so, taking a deep breath to steady her nerves, she rose to her feet and hurried after them. Arriving at the little wooden shack, she pressed her back to the wall, not daring to peek around the corner for fear of being caught. That was fine, though. She was close enough now that she could easily hear them.

'Tell me you didn't know about this,' Seth was saying. 'Tell me you didn't know it was going to happen.'

'Know about it?' Jazz snapped back at him. 'How could I have . . . ?' Something changed in her voice. 'Are you asking if I killed her? Is that what you're saying?'

'You know what, Jazz? Yeah. Maybe it is. We all know you hate Abi. You haven't shown a scrap of interest in talking to me or Mike in years. You have *no reason* to want to come on this reunion. And yet here you are, talking to me about how you think Abi ruined Olive's life on the last day we were here. Now she's been poisoned, and you're expecting me not to be suspicious?'

Jazz swore at him. 'What good would killing Abi do? How's it going to make what she did on that last day any better now? I told you, Seth. I came out here to watch over Olive. To *watch*. Not to get involved. All I wanted was to keep her close and make sure Abi didn't do anything else to screw up her life.'

Seth didn't reply.

'What?' said Jazz.

'Nothing.'

'*What?*'

'Well, that's exactly what you *would* say, isn't it? If you'd done it. You'd try to pretend you didn't care.'

'Piss off, Seth,' Jazz spat. 'Or, you know what? Why don't you tell me where *you* went running off to? See if *you* can't explain yourself?'

Seth made a nervous sound.

'Yeah,' Jazz pressed. 'Don't think I didn't notice. Just minutes after we'd found Abi you went running off on your own. What were you doing?'

'I went to my hut.'

'Why? What did you do? Because let me tell you, it's pretty fucking rich of you to accuse me of being shifty when you're the one pulling shit like that.'

For a long while, Seth was silent. Stevie, heart pounding, stood as still as if her feet had turned to stone.

'I had to go and check something,' he said. 'In my hut. I won't tell you what, so don't ask. But you must be able to see that I'd have no reason to hurt Abi.'

'Great,' said Jazz. 'Just great. Really helpful. And can I expect this kind of grilling from the others? I saw you having a chat with Zach before you came to fetch me. Does he suspect me too?'

'No,' Seth replied. 'I've never told Mike or Zach what you think we saw—'

'What we *did* see.'

'Fuck's sake, Jazz!' Seth's voice seemed to rise against his will, and he had to take a breath before continuing. 'Even if I *had* said something, I reckon you'd be safe. Mike's got his eye on Humphrey.'

At this, Stevie felt her blood run cold.

'Humphrey?' Jazz repeated. 'Mike thinks Humphrey did this? Why? Because he's been kicked out of the company?'

'Exactly. Mike's theory is that Humphrey believes Abi was involved in his being sacked. Orchestrated it in some way, so that she could eventually claim Conrad Blythe for herself.'

'That's bullshit,' said Jazz. 'Mike's biased. He was in love with Abi and he can't stand Humphrey. It's hardly surprising that he's jumped straight to pointing the finger. The way you've been winding him up since we arrived, you're lucky he isn't blaming you as well.'

'Yeah, well, he's got it all pretty neatly worked out. He seems to think it's a good enough reason for Humphrey to have killed her. And you have to admit, it's strange for Humphrey to even be here, when he's supposedly been given the boot. Plus, he's known about the flower for *way* longer than any of us. We only found out about it today. He's apparently known for months. Gives him much more opportunity to plan her murder, don't you think?'

'And what's Mike going to do with this theory?'

'He's gone back up to the lodge. Says he's going to talk to the police about it right now.'

Jazz said something in reply, but Stevie barely registered it. Her heart was thumping against her ribs, the image of Mike speaking to the police now filling her mind.

Could he really think Humphrey was a killer? That he would kill his own *sister*?

She felt a sudden urge to run back up to the lodge. She had to stop Mike. Try to talk him down. Or at the very least she had to find Humphrey and warn him. In any case, it didn't dawn on her until it was too late that she had stopped listening to Seth and Jazz's conversation. It was only when she heard Seth say something about going back to his hut that she realised she was about to be discovered.

Panic seizing her, she tried to run. But she wasn't quick enough. Before she could flee, Seth rounded the corner, the fear in his eyes instantaneous as he saw her standing there.

A second later Jazz appeared too, her own expression one of fury. 'What are you doing?' she demanded. 'Are you *spying* on us?'

'It's not . . .' Stevie tried. 'I just wanted to . . .'

But she couldn't find the words. Standing there, with the two of them glaring at her, panic turned to outright fear, and before she could stop herself she was running in the direction of the lodge.

28

Mike followed the two police officers back into the lobby, closing the door to the little office that the manager had provided for them to speak in.

'Thank you, Mr Bickler,' one said. 'We will make sure your statement is taken seriously.'

The officer's accent was strong, but he spoke perfect English. They both did. Mike imagined it was probably a requirement for anyone joining the designated tourist branch of the police. He nodded, his expression grim, and thanked them in return. He then turned out of the lobby, onto one of the gravel paths that snaked through the jungle, and began to walk in the direction of his hut.

To their credit, he did believe that the two officers would take what he'd had to say seriously. But he had to admit that he would be glad when more police arrived. These two had asked the right questions and made plenty of notes, all while looking suitably grave. But he'd felt the nerves radiating off them. The impression they'd given was of being out of their depth. Holding the fort until someone else took charge. Mike expected that he would probably need to give his statement again when the next group of police arrived. That was fine, though. So long as whoever came had the nerve to deal with a killer. Because that, as far as Mike was concerned, was exactly what Humphrey was.

He took a breath, trying to keep his anger from building any further. He'd let Abi down. That was the truth. He hadn't been there to raise Miley. And then he hadn't had the courage to go and speak to her before Humphrey made his move.

Well, he wouldn't let her down now.

Mike would tell the world how Humphrey had been humiliated by Conrad Blythe. How he had been removed by the board and thrust into Abi's shadow. He would make sure everyone knew that this was the moment Abi's fate had been sealed. And then, when all of this was over, he would step up. He would ask about a paternity test and, if it came back positive, he would move to the States.

Because he could see it now.

Miley was his. His daughter. His own flesh and blood.

Somehow, he hadn't sensed it before, but he knew it now. He could *feel* it. Abi had brought them out here to tell him the truth. But Humphrey's resentment – his jealousy – had robbed her of the chance.

He would need to prove it, of course. He didn't know how, but he would find out. There would be places you could go. People who could help.

233

And then it hit him. He already knew of someone. Someone who was right there at the hotel.

Gritting his teeth, he turned away from his hut and strode straight back in the direction he had come from.

29

Seth slammed the door to his hut, swearing repeatedly under his breath.

How had Jazz noticed? He'd only been gone a few minutes, and they should all have been thinking about Abi. How had she clocked him slipping away?

He let out a fresh string of expletives. Louder this time. Because of course it wasn't just Jazz who knew. Not now that Stevie had overheard them by the pool.

He sank onto the edge of the bed, putting his head in his hands as he tried to slow his thumping heart.

It was OK, he told himself. It was going to be all right. He hadn't done anything wrong. But then it wouldn't look like that, would it? Not if Stevie went to the police. Told them that he had been caught sneaking back to his hut just minutes after Abi's body had been found.

He cursed his own foolishness. Why hadn't he waited? Just a little longer, until the coast had actually been clear? The truth was that he'd panicked. He'd seen Abi's body and he'd feared what would happen if the little packet hidden inside his suitcase had somehow been unearthed.

He took a long shuddering breath. He supposed Abi had her answer, now. It seemed the plant was indeed dangerous.

In a morbid sort of way, he had to admit that he found it all quite interesting. A new species of poisonous plant – one that seemed to have been genuinely undocumented. For a second he wished he'd taken one of those, too.

But as quickly as that thought flashed into his mind, he ushered it away. Jazz, presumably, already suspected he'd had a flower in his hut. Stevie, too. The last thing he needed was for there to actually be tiny traces of the species in his room for a determined crime-scene investigator to root out.

Yes, he thought to himself, the flower was interesting. But did he really believe that it was one of their group who had used it?

He supposed someone must have. Either someone had genuinely killed Abi with the flower, or they had killed her with something else and dressed the body up to look as if the flower had been used. Each scenario required a culprit who had known that the flower was poisonous. And they were supposedly the only ones who fit that bill.

He couldn't see Humphrey doing it, though. Regardless of what Mike thought. More likely it had been Jazz, getting back at Abi for what she'd done to Olive ten years ago.

He rose to his feet, pacing back and forth.

What, exactly, had Jazz thought that confronting him was going to achieve? It had been years since he'd thought about what they'd seen. And in all those years he'd managed to pretend that there'd been nothing *to* see. He wasn't about to start changing his tune now.

He stopped pacing and forced himself to take a deep breath. It was going to be fine, he told himself. It wasn't ideal, of course. He might well have some difficult questions to answer. Especially if Jazz or Stevie told the police that he'd mysteriously disappeared just after Abi had been found. But he hadn't done anything wrong. And no one was going to work out what he had actually been up to. Not Jazz. Not Stevie. No one.

30

Stevie hurried back up to the lodge, the conversation she had overheard at the poolside bar still playing inside her head. Could Mike really believe that Humphrey had killed Abi? Could he seriously be considering it?

The knot in her stomach became tighter as she recalled what Mike had said the previous evening by the waterfall. He'd been in love with Abi. Was still in love with her. Stevie wondered how far she herself might go, if she thought someone she loved had been murdered. Someone who she believed could be the parent of her own child . . .

She rounded the corner, heading back into the lobby. As she did so, her heart leapt into her mouth at the sight of an officer already locked in conversation with Humphrey.

Dressed in his dark cap and white polo shirt, the officer looked young, his expression suggesting that he was just as intimidated by the situation as Stevie was. Still, he was speaking to Humphrey intently. They stood beside the reception desk, the space between them narrow so that they could talk in lowered voices.

For a few seconds Stevie stood and watched, terror gripping her as she wondered whether to intervene. To run over and leap to Humphrey's defence.

In the end, she didn't have the chance. The officer seemed to ask Humphrey one last question, to which he shook his head in reply. Then, the young man nodded, thanked Humphrey and walked away.

Immediately, Stevie hurried over.

'What was that?'

'Nothing,' said Humphrey. 'Don't worry about it.'

'Are they accusing you of something?'

'No!' He looked genuinely shocked. 'Stevie, no.'

'What, then?'

Humphrey hesitated. Then, eventually, he sighed.

'They can't find Abi's phone.'

She frowned. 'They what?'

'Abi's phone. They want to make sure it's safe, in case there's something on it that might explain what happened. But it's not in her hut. They wanted to know if I thought it strange for her to not have it.'

'And do you?'

'I do. Especially today. The amount of calls she's been getting from suppliers and people in the company . . . I can't think of any reason she'd be without it.'

Stevie watched him carefully, almost afraid to ask the question that had sprung immediately into her mind.

'Do you think . . .' she said. 'If someone really has

poisoned her, do you think they could also have taken her phone? That there might have been something on there that would have incriminated them?'

Humphrey looked pained. 'I really don't know,' he said. 'But I guess it would make sense.'

He fell silent, and for a few moments she just looked at him, feeling completely out of her depth. She had never met a killer – at least, not that she was aware of – but she wouldn't expect one to look as harrowed by their own actions as her brother did now. She'd never seen him so still. So sullen. So defeated.

She imagined what Mike might say, if he could see Humphrey now. The thought flitted across her mind that he would tell her she was looking at a picture of guilt, rather than grief.

'I need a drink.'

At this, Stevie snapped abruptly back into focus. 'Are you sure? I really don't know if it's wise to be drinking. We need to—'

'Water,' he said sharply. 'I just need some water.'

Stevie took a step back, caught off guard by his tone.

He sighed again. 'I'm sorry, Stevie. This is all . . .' He grimaced. 'I just need a minute, OK?'

She nodded. 'Sure. Of course.'

She watched him go into the restaurant, wondering what she should do. Should she warn him of Mike's theory? If Mike really had already spoken with the police then she didn't want him caught unawares. But at the same time she was just as worried about making the situation worse. Humphrey was already in a delicate state – to learn that someone was accusing *him* of murdering Abi would surely break him. Or perhaps it would go the other way. Perhaps he would storm off to confront Mike, a scenario which undoubtedly would not help.

Alternatively, she could speak to Mike, and try to impress upon him that Humphrey wouldn't have it in him to commit such a serious crime. Or she could go straight to the police and try to dissuade them of Mike's theory. But what would she say? That Humphrey couldn't be a murderer because he was her brother? That she *just knew* it wasn't him? It was hardly a convincing argument.

So what, then, was she meant to do?

'Stevie.'

She turned to face the voice, her heart beating a little quicker as she found the last person she wanted to see standing just a few feet away.

Mike cleared his throat, his expression sheepish.

'Could I talk to you for a minute?'

She stared at him, feeling a sudden mix of fear and revulsion. What did he want? Had Seth or Jazz tipped him off that she'd overheard them? Had he come to confront her?

'Please,' he said. 'It's important.'

Stevie thought for just a little longer, before eventually nodding and motioning towards the wicker chairs.

'I'm so sorry,' he said as they sat down. 'I get the sense that you and Abi didn't have a brilliant relationship. But I—'

'He didn't do it, Mike.'

She'd blurted it out before she could stop herself. Mike frowned at her.

'Sorry,' he said. 'Who didn't—'

'Humphrey. He didn't kill Abi.'

Mike's expression changed ever so slightly, a hint of panic mingling with the confusion.

'I overheard Seth and Jazz,' Stevie explained. 'A few minutes ago. They were speaking by the poolside bar. Seth was saying that you think Humphrey poisoned Abi.'

'How does Seth know that?'

'Zach told him.'

This time, genuine anger flashed across Mike's face. He might even have gone a little red, although he was so sunburnt it was difficult to tell.

'I know my brother,' Stevie insisted. 'He's a lot of things, not all of them good. But he isn't a killer.'

'You can't deny he has a motive, Stevie.'

'You bet I can. What good would killing Abi do him? What's the logic? The board is hardly going to ask him to come back into the company and fill her shoes.'

'I didn't say the motive was logical. He probably did it on the spur of the moment. He couldn't bear to see her climbing the ladder at Conrad Blythe without him, and he jumped on the opportunity while they were both here.' He looked Stevie in the eye. 'Are you really telling me you can't imagine it? He'd been drinking . . . He's sitting in this lodge that he believes should be half his . . . I don't doubt that he might regret it now. But you can't tell me the theory doesn't add up.'

Stevie studied Mike's face, realising without doubt that there was nothing she could say to dissuade him.

'Seth said that you've already shared this theory with the police.'

Mike nodded, failing, this time, to meet her eye. 'I thought they should know.'

Stevie looked away, her mind swimming with questions that all terrified her. Should she warn Humphrey? Would the police even believe Mike's theory?

'Listen,' said Mike, 'this isn't what I wanted to talk about. I came to find you because . . . Because I'd like to ask for your help.'

Stevie wondered what help this man could possibly think she might offer him after what he'd just told her.

'How much,' he continued, 'of what I said last night by the waterfall do you remember?'

'All of it.'

Mike winced.

'I believe . . .' he started, before tailing off to take a steadying breath. 'I believe that Abi brought us here to reveal that I'm Miley's father.'

Stevie felt her eyes widen. 'You really think that?'

'Yes,' he said. 'I do. And while I know it's probably too soon to think about what will happen to Miley when this is all over, I wanted to say that, if I'm right, and she really is my daughter, then as her surviving parent I'm ready to step up.'

Stevie stared at him, scarcely able to believe what she was hearing.

'Are you saying you want to *adopt* her?'

Mike shuffled uncomfortably. 'Perhaps. In time. If that's something she might want. For starters I thought I could look at moving to the States. So that we can get to know each other.'

'Mike . . .' Stevie shook her head. 'How can you believe this?'

'What do you mean?'

'I mean how can you think Abi brought you here to introduce you to Miley? If you were Miley's father – and that's a big if – why would Abi decide to share that with you now, after keeping it from you all these years? And why stage the reunion in order to do it? Surely, if I've understood your feelings for her correctly, she would have known that all she had to do was tell you.'

Mike puffed out his cheeks, his face turning a little red. 'Well,' he huffed, 'we may never know. Your brother's seen to that.'

This time, it was Stevie's turn to wince.

'Look,' Mike continued, 'I wanted to speak to you about a DNA test.'

'A DNA test?'

'That's right. It came up at dinner that you work for a genealogy agency. I thought you must know how this sort of thing works. Where to go. How to sort it all out.'

Stevie stared at him, wondering once more if she could really be hearing this.

'Mike . . .' she said. 'I don't think . . . I'm just not sure

I can . . .' She tailed off, no idea how that sentence was going to end.

For a few moments Mike waited to hear her answer. When it became clear that he wasn't going to receive one, his expression darkened.

'Will you help me or not?'

Stevie stared at him, a hundred unsettling images flashing through her mind. Mike disembarking from a plane in New Hampshire. Mike shaking Miley's hand, introducing himself as her father . . .

But before she could reply, she heard footsteps. Looking over her shoulder, she saw Humphrey coming back towards them, a bottle of water in his hand.

'Stevie?' he said. 'Is everything OK?'

She told him it was, but that didn't stop him fixing Mike with a suspicious look, the two men locking eyes for several uncomfortable seconds.

For a while there was silence. Then, at last, Mike rose to his feet.

'I'll leave you to it,' he told Stevie. 'Please think about it, though.'

They waited for him to leave, Stevie's heart pounding in her chest.

'What was that?' said Humphrey.

'Nothing,' Stevie replied.

'You sure?'

'Yeah.'

She could see in his eyes that he didn't believe her. But he didn't question it either.

'Shall we . . .' He looked down at the ground. 'Shall we go find somewhere to wait? For the rest of these cops, that is.'

Stevie nodded. 'Yeah,' she said. 'Yeah, let's do that.'

She was quietly glad that it seemed he wasn't going to challenge her. But her relief didn't last long. Because at that moment, as they turned to walk in the direction of the huts, she found Miley standing behind them, dressed in her pyjamas.

How long she had been there Stevie couldn't say. She could tell, though, even before her little niece had said a word, that Miley knew. From the desperate look in her eye, Stevie could see that she had found out. She saw the fear etched across her face before the question tumbled from her mouth.

'Where's my mom?'

31

Jazz found Olive in the lobby, sitting in a wicker chair as she looked blankly into space. She didn't pause to wonder what might be running through her cousin's head. Instead she made her way briskly over, her phone clutched in her hand.

'OK,' she said. 'There's a driver who can be here in just over two hours. He'll take us to a hotel down the coast.'

'We're leaving?' Olive asked.

'Too right we are. We don't want to be here while the police are sweeping the place. And they'll probably have no choice but to send us somewhere else anyway. I say let's go before everyone learns what's happened and they start scrambling to book up all the drivers and other hotel rooms in the area.'

'Won't we need to stay, though?' said Olive. 'We found her, Jazz. Surely the police will want to speak to us?'

'Well, if they do then they can do it in another hotel. Or better yet, they can do it over the phone once we're back in the UK.' Jazz tapped at her screen. 'I'll book this driver now. He won't have enough seats for all of us, but Seth and Mike can sort themselves out.' She looked up, noticing for the first time that Olive was alone. 'Where's Zach?'

'I don't know.'

'You don't know?'

'He went off to clear his head. About an hour ago.'

Jazz's eyes narrowed.

'I really don't think we should leave,' said Olive. 'It doesn't feel right. We need to be here for Abi.'

'*Be here* for her?'

'Yes! We can't run away. Not with her body just lying on the floor.'

Jazz had to fight to contain her frustration.

'And what good do you think our being here is going to do her? Because I'll tell you what's going to happen. When more police arrive they're going to set up a crime scene in her hut. They're going to take statements from people and they're going to need to arrange emergency accommodation for everyone. What's so wrong with trying to get ahead of that process?'

Olive looked less certain. 'All the same. I'm . . . I'm going to stay. She deserves for us to stay with her.'

'She doesn't deserve anything from you, Olive.'

'Of course she does. She was our friend—'

'She wasn't your friend!' Finally, Jazz's frustration got the better of her. 'I'm sorry, Olive, but she wasn't. You never had any idea what she—'

She just about managed to stop herself, but she could see all too clearly that the damage was done. Never before had she lost her temper with Olive. Now her cousin looked up at her with wide, glassy eyes.

'Look,' said Jazz, teeth gritted. 'I'm booking this driver. And when he gets here I'm going to another hotel. Are you coming with me or not?'

Olive shook her head, the movement so small it was almost imperceptible. 'No,' she said quietly. 'I'm staying.'

Jazz stared at her. Then, after a few moments, she sighed.

'You know what, Olive?' she said. 'I'm done with looking after you. You can do what you like.'

32

It was difficult to know exactly how Miley was handling the news that Abi was gone. There had been tears. There had been disbelief. Now, as her world crumbled around her, there was just stony, red-eyed silence.

That was the worst part, Stevie thought. The silence. The complete inability to know what was happening inside her niece's head.

Sitting with Miley, Humphrey and Alana at a table on the terrace, it was almost eleven o'clock. Two hours since they'd found Abi's body. One since the police had arrived.

Stevie looked around. From what she could see and hear of the other guests, it seemed not only that everyone now knew the police were there, but also that the connection to Abi's absence was slowly starting to do the rounds. The DJ was still playing, a decent number of determined partygoers still enjoying themselves in the garden. But as the speakers buzzed out the ominous opening bars of Billie Eilish's 'bad guy', a crowd was starting to slowly gather inside the restaurant. One group was huddled by the bar, speaking intently in quiet tones. When they thought she wasn't looking, they threw quizzical glances at Miley. Stevie wanted to scream at them. To get in their faces and tell them to leave her be. She settled instead for glaring across the restaurant floor, knowing all too well that such an outburst would hardly help.

After half an hour or so she went to the bar, telling the others that she wanted a glass of water because she was too ashamed to admit that in fact she just needed a moment alone.

As she sipped her water, she thought about Mike's request that she help him determine if he really was related to Miley. Likewise, she found herself thinking about Abi's phone. It seemed almost inevitable that there was something on there her killer wanted to hide. Humphrey was right – for her to have simply lost it or been without it seemed too unlikely. But what that something might be she was struggling to imagine.

After a short while, her thoughts were interrupted by Humphrey pulling up alongside her.

'Well, that was brutal,' he said. 'Not exactly how I imagined breaking the news to her.' He shook his head, his expression bereft. 'How could we have let this happen? Seriously, how?'

Stevie grimaced. Before telling Miley anything about Abi, they had asked her to explain what she already knew. It quickly became clear that she had slipped out of Stevie's hut while Alana had been in the bathroom. Unhappy at being sent to bed and eager to rejoin the party, she had pretended to be asleep, waiting for her opportunity to escape. Once out in the open air, she'd kept to the bushes and the trees, making a game out of hiding from Alana and spying on various groups of partygoers. It had been during this time that she'd overheard some of the other guests speculating on the arrival of the police, as well as the presence of two security personnel standing guard outside Abi's hut.

Look, one guy had apparently said. *I obviously don't know anything. But for the police to have turned up and a pair of security guys to suddenly start standing guard outside Abi's hut doesn't look great, does it? Especially when no one's seen her all night.*

It had been at this point that the terrified Miley had gone running through the lodge, searching frantically for Humphrey and Stevie.

In the end, neither of them had needed to say it. Catching them completely off guard, Miley had seen the truth in the panicked glances that they had instinctively exchanged. Something had happened. Her mother was gone.

Stevie sighed, looking back towards the terrace. Miley was still sitting with Alana, staring into space, an untouched milkshake on the table in front of her.

'What are we going to do?' she said. 'What would Abi want us to do?'

Humphrey shook his head. 'I've no idea.'

'She never said anything to you? Never mentioned

where she would want Miley to go if something happened to her?'

Again, Humphrey shook his head. 'Never,' he said. 'It never came up.'

Stevie looked down at the bar, the sudden knowledge that it might be up to them to determine what happened to Miley threatening to overwhelm her.

'We've got to find Abi's phone,' said Humphrey. 'There's got to be something on it. Something that tells us what happened.'

Stevie nodded. 'We will.'

'How?'

'I don't know. But you hear about what police can do these days . . . I'm sure it's only a matter of time.'

Humphrey didn't reply. Instead he let out a long sigh, the stress written all over his face.

'What did Mike want?' he asked. 'When I went for my water. I know you said it was nothing, but he clearly had something on his mind.'

'He wants me to help sort out a DNA test,' Stevie replied. 'To prove if Miley is his daughter.'

Humphrey's eyes widened. 'And what's he planning to do if it comes back positive?'

'I'm not sure. He said he wants to *step up*, whatever that means.'

'Are you going to help him?'

Stevie grimaced. 'I haven't decided. He doesn't know Miley. He lives on the other side of the Atlantic. Part of

253

me wants to help him organise a test just to prove that he *isn't* related.'

'So you don't think he's her dad? You don't think there's even a chance?'

'I don't. There's no resemblance there. Not even a bit. But then . . . I guess stranger things have happened. He and Abi got together twice on the last day of that trip. Once by the waterfall and then, according to Seth, again in Abi's tent once they thought the others were asleep. That's two separate opportunities for her to fall pregnant. If she did, then I could imagine her making up the story about the guy in the bar just to save involving Mike.'

'OK,' said Humphrey. 'Yeah. I could imagine that too. And are we saying that this is related to her death? Like . . . would someone really go so far just to stop her from telling Mike the truth?'

Stevie thought once more of the conversation she'd overheard at the poolside bar.

'Humphrey,' she said, 'do you know of anything that Abi might have *done* to Olive? When they were all here ten years ago?'

'Done to her? Like what?'

'I don't know. But I heard Seth and Jazz talking. Just a few minutes before I spoke to Mike. Jazz seems pretty convinced that they saw Abi do something to Olive the night she and Zach got engaged.'

'But they didn't say what?'

'No. And Seth denied pretty adamantly that they saw anything at all. But whatever Jazz claims they saw, it must have been serious. Seth thought it might be motive enough for Jazz to have poisoned Abi.'

'*Shit.*' Humphrey shook his head. 'No,' he said. 'No, Abi's never mentioned anything. I'm sure she hasn't.'

'And you haven't ever . . . I don't know. You haven't ever *suspected* that she did anything?'

'No. Never. I mean . . . what sort of thing are we even talking about here?'

Stevie grimaced. 'I've no idea. Something bad enough that Jazz apparently felt the need to travel all this way, just so she could make sure Abi didn't do it again. And bad enough, in Seth's mind, at least, that he thinks Jazz could have killed Abi for it.'

Humphrey thought for a moment. 'OK,' he said. 'Try this on for size. What if Abi's meetings with Pete the attorney have been about preparing to tell Mike that he's Miley's father. Maybe she's been getting advice on the legal implications, or something like that. She suggests a reunion in order to get Mike here, but before she can tell him the news, Jazz poisons her in return for whatever she did to Olive.'

Stevie winced. 'I guess it works. Some of it, at least. But I'd have a lot of questions.'

'Such as?'

'Well, why would Abi need to stage the reunion? I think that Mike was so besotted he would happily have come on his own if Abi had told him she wanted to talk. And why do it now? What's changed after ten years that means she would suddenly want him to know?

255

Then there's Jazz. She told Seth she wasn't interested in getting any kind of revenge on Abi. She said she just wanted to keep an eye on Olive. Make sure Abi didn't do anything else to her.'

'And you believe her?'

'I think so. She said she doesn't want to dig up the past. Apparently it wouldn't achieve anything.'

'But you don't think Seth bought that.'

'I don't know. Although, for what it's worth, she accused *him* of acting strangely. Apparently, after we'd all found Abi's body, she noticed him slip away by himself. He says he went back to his hut but he wouldn't tell her what for.'

Humphrey let out a long breath. 'Jeez,' he said. 'This sounds like one hell of a conversation to have overheard.'

Stevie watched him, thinking about the other element to have come from Seth and Jazz's conversation.

She swallowed back a lump. 'There's something else, Humphrey. Something that Seth told Jazz.'

She hesitated, aware of the sudden expression on her brother's face. She had to tell him, she told herself. She couldn't have him caught off guard by the police.

She took a deep breath, forcing as much confidence into her voice as she could manage.

'They think . . .' she said. 'Or rather, *Mike* thinks you might have had something to do with what's happened to Abi.'

Humphrey's eyes widened. 'He *what*?'

'He thinks that the board removing you from Conrad Blythe . . . well, he seems to think it might be a motive.'

'Motive? He thinks I *killed* her?'

'He isn't thinking clearly. He was in love with Abi. He thinks he might be Miley's *dad*—'

'What if he goes to the police about this? What happens then?'

Stevie could barely meet his eye.

'Humphrey . . .' she said. 'I think he *has* spoken to the police.'

'Fuck,' Humprey spat. '*Fuck!*' He looked around wildly, panic in his eyes.

'Humphrey!' Stevie urged. 'Please. The police will understand that you couldn't have done this. They'll see that Mike isn't thinking clearly.'

'And what if they don't? What if they agree with him – if they think I had motive?'

Stevie raised her hands in an attempt to calm him, wary that Miley wasn't far away.

'I can't stay here,' he said. 'I've got to . . . I need some . . .'

He turned away, striding off so suddenly in the direction of the lobby that Stevie had to scramble to follow him.

'Humphrey . . .' she said. 'Humphrey! Where are you even going?'

'I don't know.'

'Humphrey, please—'

'*I don't know!*' He raised his voice, although she could see immediately that he regretted it. He stopped in his tracks, his eyes falling to the ground. 'I'm sorry, Stevie. I just . . . I need some space. A little time to think.'

She didn't try to stop him this time. She just watched, despairing, as he stalked from the restaurant and into the lobby.

33

Inside the hut he shared with Olive, Zach sat on the edge of the bed, heart thumping as he looked down at Abi's phone.

It lay in the palm of his hand, the screen giving little away.

He tried to compose himself. He had to get inside it. He *had* to. But unlocking the phone required a fingerprint. Abi's fingerprint. And that fingerprint was now inaccessible, on account of Abi's body being in a hut guarded by two members of the lodge's security team.

Dropping the phone onto the bed, Zach swore loudly. He pressed his hands to his eyes, fear turning to outright despair.

After several long moments, he forced himself to think. To focus.

If he couldn't get into the phone, then he had to get rid of it. But was that even possible? Without unlocking it he couldn't so much as switch it off, and he was sure he'd heard somewhere that police could track a phone while it was still on.

He stood, mind racing as he tried to cobble together a plan. Then, moving quickly, he went into the en-suite bathroom and filled a glass with water. Placing it beside the sink, he dropped the phone inside, making sure it was fully submerged. He watched impatiently, staring as the screen flickered before finally going dark.

After waiting another minute or two for good measure, he snatched the phone from the glass and scrubbed it with a towel, trying, as he'd seen in movies, to ensure there were no fingerprints for anyone to find. Then he hurried to the glass doors at the back of the hut, which he threw open. Stepping into the night air, he drew back his arm and hurled the phone with as much force as he could muster into the jungle.

He watched it fly for a couple of seconds, sailing over the treetops before the inky darkness swallowed it whole.

He took a deep breath. Then another, listening to the distant sounds of the party as he breathed in the night air. When, finally, he felt a little steadier, he turned and went back inside.

It was gone. Lost in the jungle. He had done what he could, but even with the phone out of sight, he didn't feel safe. He wouldn't permit himself that until he was back in the UK. Far from this place, and far from the truth he was so desperate to ensure would stay buried.

34

Back in the restaurant, Stevie was doing her best to stay calm.

Had she done the right thing by telling Humphrey about Mike's theory? She thought she had at the time, but now she was less sure. And where exactly had he stormed off to? Several troubling possibilities ran through her head. By far the most frightening, though, was the thought of him seeking Mike out in order to confront him. That would hardly help his case, should the police decide to take Mike's accusation seriously.

Miley, at least, didn't seem to have noticed Humphrey's outburst at the bar. Or if she had, she didn't ask where he'd gone. Stevie was glad of that. She couldn't bear the thought of lying to her little niece. But how she would even begin to explain what had upset Humphrey – to describe Mike's accusation – she had absolutely no idea.

They sat together at their table on the terrace, Miley staring off into space while Stevie searched helplessly for something useful that she could say – something even vaguely comforting. Every so often, she would meet Alana's eye. She could tell from the other woman's expression that she didn't have anything to offer either.

Eventually, Miley asked, seemingly from nowhere, 'Who's the guy you were talking to?'

Stevie blinked at her.

'The guy,' said Miley. 'When I came to find you. Who was he?'

'Do you mean Mike?'

'Is he British?'

'He is, yeah.'

Miley nodded. 'He came to our hut. Last night.'

Stevie stared at her. 'Why did Mike come to your hut?'

'He wanted to talk to Mom.'

'About what?'

'I couldn't hear. She thought I was asleep so she made him go into the garden.'

'And you're sure it was him?'

Miley nodded again. 'I didn't see his face. I was in bed. But I heard his voice. He definitely sounded British.'

Stevie's mind raced. Why had Mike not said anything about visiting Abi? When would it even have been? Once she and Olive had ushered him from the jungle he'd gone straight back to his hut. So it must have been sometime between dinner ending and his walk to the waterfall. But again, if he had come straight from Abi's hut when Stevie and Olive had seen him tottering into the jungle, that raised the question – why hadn't he mentioned it?

'Miley,' said Stevie, 'I think this might be important. Could you really not hear anything that they said? Was there nothing before your mom took him out into the garden?'

Miley looked down at the table. 'He said they needed to talk. That's when Mom told him I was asleep and that they'd have to go outside. He didn't sound very happy. They were in the garden for a while, then he came back into the hut and ran straight to the door. Like he was mad or upset or something. Mom tried to run after him, but she couldn't get him to stop.'

Stevie thought for a moment, turning Miley's words over in her mind.

Why had Mike gone to speak with Abi? What had she told him to prompt such a reaction? And why hadn't he mentioned it when, just a short while later, Stevie and Olive had followed him to the waterfall?

But before Stevie could come up with answers to any of these questions, Miley asked in a trembling voice, 'Who am I going to live with?'

The question snapped Stevie so abruptly from her thoughts that for a second she wondered if she'd imagined it. As she looked at her niece, though, and saw the heartbreak in her eyes, she knew that she hadn't. Just as she had no idea how to reply. She looked at Miley, her heart shattering into a thousand pieces.

At that moment, she heard footsteps behind her. Turning, Stevie saw Olive approaching their table.

'Hey,' she said.

'Hey,' Stevie replied.

Silence hung heavily in the air, Stevie seeing clearly in Olive's face that she wanted to talk.

'Miley,' she said, looking her niece directly in the eye, 'we'll work all of that out. I don't have the answers yet, but I promise everything will be OK. As for right now . . .' She looked across the table, meeting Alana's eye. 'Right now, would it be OK if you sat with Alana for a few minutes? Just while I speak to Olive?'

Miley nodded.

'Do you want anything from the kitchen? Some ice cream or something? Or maybe some fries?'

Miley shook her head. 'No.'

Stevie hesitated, gazing at her little niece as she longed once more for something she could do to help. Something that would make everything OK. Eventually, though, she admitted defeat, rising to her feet and walking with Olive to the bar.

'I'm sorry,' Olive said. 'I didn't mean to drag you away. I just wasn't sure what to . . .'

'It's OK.' Stevie watched as Olive fought back tears. 'Are you on your own?'

Olive nodded. 'For now. We've . . . Well, I'm not sure where any of the guys are. Mike and Seth have both gone off by themselves. Zach's clearing his head somewhere. And I've . . . Well, I think I've had a fight with Jazz. She wanted to book a driver to take us to another hotel down the coast. But I told her I couldn't leave, and now she's . . .'

She paused, apparently unsure of where Jazz had now gone. Stevie watched her carefully, wondering exactly how much suspicion to cast on the idea that Jazz wanted to make a quick escape from The Midnight Orchid.

'I just . . .' Olive continued. 'I can't imagine someone doing this. Let alone it being one of our *friends*. It has to be an accident, doesn't it? Or a misunderstanding. The fact that there were petals next to Abi's body doesn't necessarily mean that someone *killed* her—' She stopped abruptly, her face tightening as she fought back tears. 'I'm sorry,' she said again. 'I'm so sorry.' She cleared her throat, working hard to compose herself. 'How is she? Miley, I mean. Does she . . . Does she know?'

Stevie nodded. 'Yeah,' she said gently. 'She knows.'

'That poor girl . . . Is there anything I can do?'

'I'm not sure. We've been doing our best to reassure her, but I think she must still be in shock.'

'Who will she live with?' Olive asked. 'Humphrey?'

Stevie shook her head. 'I don't know that either.'

'Surely Abi would have named someone? A godparent or something?'

'She may have done. But I don't know of any godparents. And if she did decide to name someone else, she wouldn't have told me. You're probably right, though. I'm sure she'll have left instructions. Maybe some kind of a . . .'

She tailed off, the thought suddenly perplexing her, although she couldn't say why.

Then it hit her.

Without so much as a word of explanation to Olive, Stevie turned and hurried back to the table.

'Miley,' she said, dropping to one knee. 'Miley, please. I have to ask you a question. It's really important.' She paused, making sure that Miley was listening. 'Your mom's new boyfriend. The one you heard her talking about on the phone. Do you know what his name was?'

A confused look spread across Miley's face. After a moment's pause, though, she nodded.

'Could you tell me, please?'

Miley told her. And as she did so, Stevie felt her heart drop.

35

Mike couldn't say exactly what had drawn him, once more, to the waterfall. He supposed he just needed some space. Somewhere alone to think about what would happen next.

Stevie would help him. He understood his request might have come as a shock, but she'd come around eventually. She would have to. And then? Once the DNA test was done?

He supposed he would need to look at visas. Places to live in New Hampshire. If he was honest with himself, it was a frightening prospect, the thought of how much his life was about to change. Becoming a dad wasn't something he'd ever imagined in much detail. He'd never had reason to.

But that was about to change. He was going to be there for Miley. Because that was what Abi had wanted. It was what she'd brought them out there for. He knew it in his bones.

He emerged into the clearing, moonlight shining on the surface of the pool, illuminating the ripples as the water cascaded down. As he took in the scene he felt tears in the corners of his eyes. If only Abi had told him. If only he'd known that Miley was out there.

Before he could follow this train of thought any further, he stopped, his gaze settling on a figure crouching a short distance away. Whoever it was, their back was turned, the night too dark to make out any distinguishing features.

'Hey!' Mike called out. 'What are you doing?'

The stranger leapt up, jumping at the sound of his voice. As they turned, meeting Mike's eye, his breath caught in his chest. After several long moments, he managed to look away, his gaze straying to the patch of ground beside which his unexpected companion had been crouching.

It was then that he realised what they had been doing. Where, specifically, he had caught them.

They had been crouching over the blue flowers.

'Listen,' said Mike. 'This doesn't need to—'

But before he could go any further, the interloper ran at him, clearing the distance between them in seconds.

Mike didn't have time to think about how he should react. He barely had time to cry out before his attacker was upon him.

36

Stevie held her phone to her ear, body tense as she listened to the dial tone.

'Come on,' she murmured. 'Please pick up. *Please pick up.*'

But she was to have no such luck, her heart sinking as the call went to voicemail. She took a breath as the automated message played out, the attorney's voice bright as he asked her to leave a message.

'Hi, Pete,' she said. 'It's Stevie Blythe here. I'm sorry to call so late, but could you please get back to me as soon as you get this? It's urgent.'

She ended the call, trying and failing to subdue her disappointment.

She should have known he wouldn't pick up. It would be almost two in the morning in Concord. Hardly office hours. Pete would no doubt have long since gone to bed. She believed, though, that when he got her message he would do as she asked. Not that it made the thought of having to wait until the morning any less frustrating. She had a theory. One she was confident in. She just needed Pete to confirm it.

Will.

The calls that Miley had heard Abi making – the calls that she had apparently been careful to take into another room – had been to discuss a guy called Will.

Only . . . what if Will wasn't a guy? What if Miley, who would presumably have no knowledge of wills and attorneys, had misinterpreted, assuming her mother was talking about a new boyfriend, when in reality she had been speaking to Pete about *making a will*?

Stevie's head spun. If Pete could confirm this then what would it mean? Was it pure coincidence that Abi had made a will just weeks before being murdered? Or was there something else going on? Had she known, somehow, that something was going to happen?

Infuriating as it might be, she had no way of knowing. There was nothing to be done with this theory until Pete called her back and confirmed her suspicions.

Admitting temporary defeat, Stevie put her phone away. She had run into the lobby to make the call, leaving Olive standing confused at the bar. Now, as she peered through the restaurant doors, Stevie could see that she was still there, a lost look in her eyes.

She knew she should go back in. But she didn't move. Instead, she stood, watching Olive closely as another troubling question played in her mind.

At the poolside bar, she had overheard Seth and Jazz speaking about something Abi had done to Olive.

Something so terrible that Seth had thought it could be motive for Jazz to have killed Abi. But now Stevie was wondering – whatever this terrible slight had been, why did Olive herself seem so unfazed by it? Surely *she* should be the one that Seth was accusing? Not Jazz. And yet Olive seemed utterly bereft by Abi's death.

Had she forgiven Abi for whatever had been done? Did Jazz simply hold the grudge on her behalf? Or, Stevie thought to herself, was it an act? Was Olive perhaps not the gentle, grieving soul that she appeared?

She turned this thought over in her head. But before she could pursue it any further, Seth appeared in the lobby, stopping dead in his tracks as he rounded the corner and locked eyes with Stevie.

For a few moments, neither of them moved. They simply looked at one another, Stevie's mind suddenly swimming with all the questions she wanted to ask him. What had Abi done to Olive? Was it really terrible enough to accuse someone of murder? And why did Olive herself seem so unaffected by it?

She had to know. Had to ask him.

But, as if hearing her thoughts, Seth retreated, panic sparking in his eyes as he began to quickly walk away.

'Seth,' she called after him. 'Seth, wait!'

He didn't reply, only increasing his pace.

'Seth!' She tried calling once more, but he rounded the corner again and disappeared as quickly as he'd arrived.

For a second Stevie thought about running after him, but she didn't know what it would achieve. He clearly wasn't going to speak to her. And she doubted that Jazz would either. If she wanted answers, she would have to get them another way.

'Stevie!'

Hearing her brother's voice behind her, she breathed a sigh of relief.

'Humphrey . . .' She turned to face him. 'Where have you been?'

'Sorry,' he said. 'I went to my hut. Needed to clear my head.'

'And are you OK?'

He looked her in the eye. 'I'm frightened, Stevie. Look . . .' He raised his hand. It was trembling slightly. 'What if they believe him? The police. What if they believe Mike's theory—'

'They won't.' Stevie's voice was level, her tone firm. 'I promise, Humphrey. They just won't.'

But Humphrey didn't look convinced. 'We've got to find Abi's phone,' he said.

'They will. You know what the police can do these days. They'll track it or trace it or something. But listen,' she said. 'There's something else. Something you need to hear. I think I might know why Abi had been meeting Pete—'

She didn't finish. Because it was then that they heard a cry on the air. A voice calling out for help.

Her blood turning cold, Stevie turned her head towards the sound. It was coming from the restaurant, she realised, her mind going immediately to Miley.

No, she thought quickly. Not from the restaurant itself. It was too distant. It was coming from the garden.

Together with Humphrey, she ran from the lobby into the restaurant and then out onto the terrace. Gripping the top of the glass barrier, she looked down, where she saw a couple come running out of the jungle.

'There's a body!' the woman cried out. 'By the waterfall. Someone's dead!'

37

Stevie tore through the jungle, moving as quickly as she dared. A couple of times she stumbled in the darkness, catching her foot on a root or a stone, but she just managed to stay upright. Humphrey ran beside her, eager to keep up.

When, finally, the trees parted and they found themselves at the waterfall, she could see that a crowd of perhaps twenty people had already gathered there. They seemed to form a human wall, backs towards her as they shielded something from view.

Stevie felt sick, heart pounding at the thought of who it might be as she pushed through to the front. She had to know. She didn't want to be confronted with yet more death, but she had to see who it was.

When, at last, she managed to fight her way through, she recognised the figure immediately. Lying face-down beside the flowers, in the torchlight of three or four different phones, she could clearly make out the checked shirt. The sunburnt arms. The sensible haircut.

It was Mike.

Part Six: The Arrest

38

Twenty minutes later, Stevie and Humphrey sat across from one another in the lobby, silently attempting to process what they had just seen.

Within moments of joining the crowd in the clearing, two members of the lodge's security team had arrived. Lighting up the body with powerful torches, they had immediately stepped in, shepherding people back towards the garden.

It hadn't been an easy task. For perhaps an hour now, there had been a sense of the party winding down, the mood among the crowd turning from anticipation to puzzlement. Where was Abi, people had been asking. Why hadn't she given her speech and why were the staff all claiming not to know anything? Likewise, with over two hours having now passed since the police had arrived, every guest had either seen or heard that there were two officers onsite. They'd wanted to know what was wrong. They'd wanted answers. So when two partygoers had come running from the jungle, screaming about a dead body, few had hesitated in running to investigate, the crowd beside the waterfall steadily growing as more and more craned their necks to see.

Eventually, the security team had managed to take control. It had felt like a bleak sort of exodus as the guests trudged through the jungle back to the lodge in their finery. Around her, Stevie had heard people speculating about who the victim might have been. What he might have been doing there. How he might have died.

Emerging into the garden, they'd found that the spotlights were now still, the DJ having finally fallen silent. The party was well and truly over.

One small mercy, Stevie figured, was that at last more police had arrived. She and Humphrey had returned to the lobby just in time to see a dozen officers in dark uniforms moving into the hotel, nervous-looking guests parting to let them through. They'd swept through the building like a fog, quietly extinguishing whatever hope there might have been of keeping the festivities going.

From what Stevie could tell, their commanding officer was a woman of around forty. Dark hair tied tightly back and her mouth set in a thin line, as she'd stepped into the lobby her eyes had swept the place, taking in every detail. Now she was by the reception desk, speaking quickly in Spanish with the lodge's manager and in-house doctor. Stevie watched her for a while. She didn't have the nervous look of the *policía turística* who had been holding the fort for the past two hours. She meant business. If Stevie was honest, the cop made her nervous, although she tried to tell herself that was a good thing. Surely that was exactly the kind of person you'd want to be dealing with a double murder.

'What d'you suppose Mike was doing down there?'

At the sound of Humphrey's voice, she turned to face her brother.

'Do you think he'd followed someone?' he pressed. 'Had someone followed *him*?'

Stevie shook her head. She had no idea.

'I heard some people talking,' Humphrey continued. 'In the garden. Turns out the couple who found him had been looking for somewhere to smoke a joint. They followed the footpath into the jungle, heard the sound of the water-fall and decided to go check it out.'

Stevie winced, imagining how horrifying that first sight of Mike's body must have been. The shock and fear they would undoubtedly have felt.

At that moment, a shadow fell over them. Turning, Stevie saw that the cop had come to stand beside them.

'Excuse me,' she said. 'Humphrey Blythe? My name is Inspector Rojas. I'm leading the investigation here. I need to ask you some questions.'

39

Olive couldn't say how. She had no way of explaining it. But as she'd stood on the terrace, watching the guests who had gone running into the jungle being shepherded back out again, she'd known it would be Mike by the waterfall. Somehow it had just fitted. It was as if this had always been how his time at The Midnight Orchid would come to an end.

Sitting at a table with Jazz, Zach and Seth, she had barely spoken a word since Mike had been found. But the others were deep in hushed conversation, a grim look etched across each of their faces.

'Are you sure?' said Jazz. 'You're sure it couldn't have been an accident or something?'

Seth shook his head. 'No. I can't be sure. I only heard some people talking after they came back from the waterfall. But they were definitely saying that it looked like he'd been attacked. Like he'd been hit with a . . . I don't know. With a rock or something.' He swallowed hard, his expression grave. 'All that time . . .' he said. 'All that time I spent taking the piss out of him. Trying to wind him up. I never thought . . .'

At this point, words seemed to fail him. Olive could see the disbelief in his eyes, though. The guilt.

'Olive?' said Jazz. 'Are you OK?'

She didn't reply. If she was honest, she didn't know what there was to say.

Silently, she met Jazz's eye. Not a word had been uttered about their earlier spat. It seemed so trivial now, with another of their friends lying dead. In that moment she saw only warmth in Jazz's expression. Concern, even.

She looked at Zach, sitting beside her. He had been the last of them to appear from the jungle, and from the look on his face he seemed to be the most severely affected by Mike's death. He was staring into space, eyes glazed, skin pale.

'It's true,' she said at last. 'Isn't it? Someone's . . . Someone's killed them both.'

She looked at the three of them in turn, hands clasped tightly together on the table. Her husband. Her cousin. Her friend.

'I don't believe it,' she said. 'I don't care if we're the only ones who knew about the flower. I won't accept that any of you are killers.'

'I don't think you'll have to,' said Jazz. 'You're forgetting that there's someone else who knew about the flower

281

way before we did. Someone who Mike had been accusing of murder to anyone who would listen.'

Olive met her eye. No one spoke, but she could see a consensus in the group.

There, was unquestionably, one other candidate.

40

'Mr Blythe,' said Rojas. 'Are you aware that Mike Bickler had shared concerns about you with a police officer this evening?'

She spoke confidently, her English clearly well honed.

Humphrey nodded in response.

'And do you know what those concerns were?'

'He thought that I might have killed Abi.'

'How do you know this?'

'He came to speak with Stevie. Stevie then told me.'

Rojas gave Stevie a look that made her want to disappear into her seat. It wasn't aggressive, as such. It wasn't even outright unpleasant. There was just something in her eyes. Something that gave her the feeling of being examined, like a cell under a microscope.

Stevie forced a straight face. She didn't like this. Not a bit. She could guess easily enough where Rojas was going with these questions. And from his expression, Humphrey seemed to know it too.

'When did this happen?' Rojas asked. 'Mr Bickler's conversation with your sister?'

'I'm not sure.' Humphrey looked to Stevie. 'When would that have been? About an hour ago? Hour and a half?'

'Yeah,' said Stevie. 'About that.'

'And was that the last time either of you saw him?'

Stevie and Humphrey both nodded.

He looked frightened. Stevie felt it too.

'And where have you been,' Rojas asked, 'in that hour?'

Humphrey let out a long breath. 'I was with Stevie for a little while. Abi's daughter had just found out what had happened, so we were trying to look after her. Then I went back to my hut. I had to clear my head. Spend some time on my own.'

'Can anyone confirm that?'

'No. I'm staying by myself.'

'No one went with you?'

'No. As I say, I needed some space.'

'So you spent the half-hour or so before Mr Bickler was found dead completely alone.'

'That's right.'

Rojas gave him a hard stare. Then, she motioned for two officers who were standing nearby to come forward.

'Mr Blythe,' she said, 'please come with us.'

Humphrey's eyes widened. 'Why?'

'These officers will take you back to the station. There you will need to—'

'No!' Humphrey leapt to his feet. 'No, you don't understand.'

'Mr Blythe—'

'Get away from me!'

He backed away hurriedly, eyes filled with fear as the two officers pursued him. It was only when Stevie leapt to her feet, putting a hand on his arm, that he stopped.

'Humphrey,' she said. 'Humphrey, please. This is only going to make things worse.'

'I can't go with them, Stevie. They think I did it!'

'I know. But fighting them won't help.' She looked him in the eye, pleading with him. 'Please, Humphrey,' she said. 'Just go with them. Answer their questions. Everything will be OK.'

She could see the fear in his eyes.

'I didn't do this.'

'I know. But please just go. I'll call Pete. He'll know what to do.'

Humphrey said nothing. He didn't even move. Stevie knew he'd been in trouble before. That with his hedonistic lifestyle, this wouldn't be the first time he'd had to speak to the police. But he'd never been in trouble like this.

Finally, he gave a single tiny nod. 'Find Abi's phone,' he said. 'They *have* to find her phone. It wouldn't be missing if there wasn't something on there that could tell us who did this.'

'I know,' said Stevie. 'I'll make sure they do.'

Humphrey nodded again. Then, reluctantly, he approached the officers, the two men leading him quietly in the direction of the parking lot.

'Uncle Hump!'

Whipping around to face the voice, Stevie felt her heart sink as she saw Miley come running into the lobby. She looked terrified, staring at the glass doors as one of the officers pushed Humphrey roughly into a police car.

'What are they doing?' Miley asked, voice rising. 'Where are they taking him?'

'Nowhere,' Stevie said quickly. 'It's OK, Miley. They just need to speak to him.'

'Is he in trouble?'

She could so clearly see the fear in her poor niece's eyes. She searched for something reassuring to say. Something that wouldn't be a lie. But nothing came.

As the car's engine began, Miley let out a terrified shout. 'No!'

She ran out of the doors, seemingly intent on following the car into the jungle. Scrambling to follow her, Stevie just managed to catch her wrist.

'It's OK,' she said. 'Miley, it's OK!'

She knew it was pointless, her attempts being drowned out by the sound of Miley's howls. In the lobby, a crowd of guests had gathered to see the commotion. Among them she recognised Abi's friends.

She dropped onto one knee, holding Miley close so that she could look her squarely in the eye.

'Miley,' she urged. 'Listen to me, Miley. I'm going to

help him. I don't know how, but I promise. I'm going to help him. I'm going to bring him back.'

Miley said nothing, tears on her cheeks.

Pulling her into a hug, Stevie held her niece tightly, and together they stood on the steps of The Midnight Orchid, watching as the police car disappeared into the jungle, tail-lights swallowed by the darkness.

41

Though Stevie had managed to sound resolute when she promised Miley she would get Humphrey back, she quickly felt any confidence that she had managed to exhibit start to wane.

She held fast to the idea that Humphrey was innocent. She knew in her bones that her brother wasn't a killer. But the reality was rapidly dawning on her that while she had promised Miley that she would save him, she had absolutely no idea how she might do that.

Having returned Miley temporarily to Alana, she sat down in one of the wicker chairs opposite the reception desk, watching as a large group of guests frantically asked a police officer about minibuses to take them from the hotel. She couldn't hear the reply. There were too many all speaking at once. But she could guess from the officer's stern expression what it must be. If not an outright *no*, then it was certainly a *not yet*.

She let out a long, shuddering breath.

Just how much trouble was Humphrey actually in?

She didn't believe that he could have killed Mike, but she could absolutely see how it looked. Mike had been adamant that Humphrey killed Abi. Now Mike himself was dead – attacked, it would seem – and Humphrey had no solid alibi.

She felt sick, a weight settling in her stomach as she realised that Humphrey couldn't even claim to be oblivious of Mike's theory. She had told him about it. *She* had given him the reason for which he was now accused of being Mike's killer. Hell, it was her warning that had sent him storming off on his own. And she had just let him go.

She tried not to think of how things would be different if she'd just said nothing. Of how, had she kept it to herself, he would have had not only an alibi, but would have had no idea that Mike even suspected him of killing Abi.

She pictured him now, frightened and in shock, being whisked towards a foreign police station for God-knew-how-many hours of questioning.

'He didn't do it,' she told herself. 'He didn't.'

But who had?

If their assumption was correct – that it could only have been one of the small number of people at the hotel who had known the flower was poisonous – then it left just Abi's friends. Abi's *remaining* friends.

Olive. Zach. Seth. Jazz.

Could she imagine one of them being capable of killing two people? Killing two of their own friends?

Her immediate answer – her instinct – was no. But then she still had no idea what awful wrong Abi had supposedly done to Olive ten years earlier. She thought as well about how Mike had apparently gone to Abi's hut the previous evening. The conversation they'd had in the garden, before Miley had heard him storming away. What, exactly, had he been so eager to speak with her about? Why had he fled in such a hurry? And could that conversation have been the reason they were now both dead?

Stevie shut her eyes, thinking of everyone she was letting down. Humphrey, soon to be questioned by the police. Miley, confused and alone. Even, on some level, her adoptive parents . . . Frank and Jane. The people who had taken her in. The people who had *wanted* her. The family they had left behind was falling apart, and despite her best efforts, Stevie was failing to hold it together.

Before her despair had a chance to carry her any further, her phone began to ring in her hand. She glanced at the screen. Immediately recognising the number, she scrambled to answer, moving with such urgency that she almost dropped it.

'Hello?' she said, thrusting the phone against her ear. 'Hello? Pete?'

She waited for the reply, imagining in the silence that he was standing in his office, overlooking Main Street in Concord. The place was bright and airy, filled with the same oak furniture and old books that had been there when Stevie had been a kid. Somewhere in his desk, she imagined there was still a box of candy for when Frank came to visit with one of the Blythe children in tow.

'Stevie?' she heard him say. 'I just got out of bed for a

glass of water and I picked up your message. Is everything all right?'

Stevie put a hand to her face.

'Sorry,' she said. 'I'm so sorry to have called. But no. Things aren't all right. Something's . . .' Her voice began to tremble. 'Pete, something terrible has happened.'

She told him everything. Abi's death, Humphrey's arrest . . . It was only now, as she described it all out loud, that she realised how unbelievable it must sound for so much to have happened in a single night. As she laid everything out, she realised it had only been four hours since she and Humphrey had stood outside Abi's hut, Olive pushing the door open to reveal her body upon the ground.

Pete listened in silence. Then, when Stevie was finished, he said, 'Everything's going to be OK. I'll go to the airport now and catch the first flight down there. I'll be with Humphrey in the morning.'

'You will?'

'Of course. Your old man was my best pal. You kids can depend on me for anything. Now, I'll call the local police station, let them know that I'm coming and get a message to Humphrey not to answer any questions until I arrive.'

Stevie felt tears well in her eyes.

'Try not to worry, Stevie. Is there anything else you need from me before I call a cab to the airport?'

Stevie cleared her throat. 'Yes,' she said. 'Yes, there is. I need to know . . . I need to ask you, Pete . . . Did Abi recently ask you to help her make a will?'

He didn't reply, a deafening silence on the other end of the line.

'Please,' she urged him. 'Please just tell me if I'm right. Miley's heard her a couple of times on the phone to someone, talking about a will. She assumed it was to do with a new boyfriend – a guy called Will. But Humphrey knows that she's been meeting with you. I'm guessing that was to draw something up.'

'Stevie,' Pete said gently. 'I'm sure you know I can't discuss a client's—'

'Please, Pete. Just . . . Please.'

Once again, there was silence on the line. Then, at last, the attorney spoke.

'OK,' he said. 'Yes. I helped your sister draw up a will. But you need to understand that I can't tell you what's in it. Not until we can arrange an official reading.'

Stevie nodded. 'I understand. But you can at least tell me how she seemed? When she asked you to help her with it, was she OK? There was nothing strange or . . . ?'

She tailed off, not quite sure how that sentence might end.

'I guess,' Pete said, 'I could tell you that.' He sighed. 'I couldn't find any reason to feel suspicious or concerned. Abi had a senior role in a large company. She was a single mother with a young child to think about. All she told me of her motives was that she wanted to get her affairs in order, should anything . . .' Stevie could almost hear him grimacing. 'Should anything *happen*.'

She closed her eyes.

'And I suppose,' Pete continued, though she could hear

the reluctance in his voice, 'as it's you. And given the circumstances . . . I can't tell you anything specific, but I can say that there was nothing in the will that gives me cause for concern. You might disagree, of course, when it comes to the reading. There might be things that would mean something to you but which I would miss. But nothing, as far as I could see, that gave cause for alarm.'

Stevie nodded. 'Thank you,' she said. 'Thank you, Pete.'

'You're welcome. Now is there anything else before I get ready to leave?'

'There is actually,' said Stevie. 'One more thing. Abi told you during a phone call that she was going to share something with the family after the launch. Was she just talking about the will? Was she going to tell us that she'd had one made?'

Pete hesitated. 'I'm sorry, Stevie. I'm a little lost. When did Abi and I have this conversation?'

'About six weeks ago. It was the day Humphrey came back from Bangkok. He went to the house, to apologise for how he reacted to being removed from the company, and while he was there he heard Abi on the phone to you.'

The attorney paused again. 'Stevie, I don't know who Abi was speaking to, but it wasn't me.'

Stevie frowned. 'But Humphrey said he saw an email from you arrive on Abi's phone. It mentioned a meeting you'd had that morning.'

'That's right. I remember the meeting, but we didn't speak on the phone after that. Whatever Humphrey heard, Abi must have been speaking with someone else.'

Stevie stared into space, mind suddenly racing.

'Do you know,' she said feebly, 'what Abi might have meant? What it was, exactly, that she was planning to tell the family after the launch was out of the way?'

'I'm afraid not.'

Stevie didn't question him further. She felt certain he was telling the truth.

They spoke for perhaps another minute before he told her that he would set off soon for the airport. He promised to call her again with an update after he'd seen Humphrey. Then he rang off, leaving Stevie feeling more lost than before she'd called.

What, exactly, had Abi planned to tell the family after The Midnight Orchid had opened? And if it hadn't been Pete on the phone, to whom had she been speaking?

Stevie's heart sank. It was reassuring that Pete was on his way. But she couldn't sit around doing nothing in the meantime. Not with Humphrey about to be questioned for killing two people. She couldn't sit and wait in the hope that Pete alone would clear everything up. The question was what – *what* could she do?

'Stevie . . .'

Turning to face the voice, she saw that Olive was standing a few feet away.

'I . . . I want to talk.'

42

At Olive's request, she and Stevie went down to the garden, where they sat together beside the fountain.

'The others are in the restaurant,' she explained. 'I don't know how long we might have before they come looking for me. I told them I'd gone to the loo. They wouldn't like that I'm talking to you. They think . . .' She grimaced. 'They think that Humphrey's guilty. They think he killed Abi and Mike.'

'Don't you agree?' asked Stevie.

'I don't know. I struggle to imagine it. But then I don't believe that any of my friends are capable of doing it either. And if we really were the only ones who knew that the plant was dangerous . . .' She clasped her hands, foot tapping with nervous energy. 'To be honest, I've only just accepted that it could be murder at all. With Abi I thought there must be a misunderstanding. That she'd had an accident or something, and the petals by her body were just there by coincidence. But now with Mike . . .' She had to pause for a beat and take a steadying breath. 'Did you see him, by the waterfall?'

Stevie nodded.

'I heard that it looked as though he'd been attacked.'

'That's right.'

Olive looked pained. 'So if someone attacked Mike then it seems I have to accept it. There is a murderer here. And if I accept that, then I suppose I also have to consider that the same person might have killed Abi.' She took a deep breath. 'How can you be so sure Humphrey's innocent? I heard you speaking to Miley when they took him away. You promised you'd get him back. But the police must think it could be him if they've taken him for questioning.'

'Because I know my brother. And I know that he wouldn't kill someone. Let alone his own sister.'

'What about Mike?'

'What would killing him achieve? Surely, if Humphrey's motive for killing Mike was to keep him quiet – to keep him from telling everyone that he must be Abi's murderer – he'd have needed to do it *before* Mike started talking. Doing it after the fact isn't going to help. If anything it would only incriminate him further. Just look at what happened. Within minutes of Mike's body being found, Humphrey was loaded into a police car. He would surely have been able to predict that.'

'Unless Mike's death wasn't planned.'

'It wasn't Humphrey.' Stevie was aware of the cold tone that had slipped into her voice. She made no attempt to hide it, though.

Olive thought for a moment. 'OK,' she said. 'So you must think it was one of us.'

Stevie didn't reply, watching her closely.

'Why are we speaking, Olive?'

'Because I wanted to understand why you think Humphrey might be innocent. And I suppose . . .' She chewed her lip. 'You seemed to hit on something. When we were talking about what might happen to Miley.' Her eyes suddenly widened. 'Where *is* Miley?'

'She's with Alana. The woman Abi appointed to look after her. They've gone to my hut.'

Stevie felt a sudden rush of shame, like a punch in the gut, as she thought of her niece being watched by a stranger at such a traumatic moment. It couldn't be helped, though. Stevie had promised that she would bring Humphrey back. If she could somehow achieve that – find something that would convince the police he was innocent – then her little niece would surely forgive a few hours of neglect.

An awkward silence hung between them.

'Well . . .' Olive cleared her throat. 'As I was saying. You seemed to make some kind of connection while we were talking. I wanted to ask – if I'm really going to start thinking about Abi being murdered – what it was that you'd thought of.'

For a short while, Stevie said nothing. Even if she hadn't been suspicious of Olive, she would have thought twice about discussing Abi's will with her. With anyone, for that matter. It felt wrong. Like sharing something that wasn't hers to offer.

297

But then, what choice did she have? She had no idea why Abi had drawn up the will. Nor any way of determining if it really was just an innocent bit of housekeeping or if it was rooted in something altogether more sinister — that is, if Abi had somehow known that she was going to die. What if Olive knew something? What if she'd heard or seen something that could help answer those questions?

Trying hard to ignore the feeling of being boxed into a corner, she sighed.

'Quite recently,' she said, 'Humphrey noticed that Abi had been having meetings with our family attorney. An old friend of our dad's. And apparently she wanted these meetings to be kept quiet. It occurred to me that she might have been going to draw up a . . .' Stevie hesitated, knowing that if she said it there'd be no taking it back. 'To draw up a will.'

Olive's eyes widened. 'A will?'

'That's right. I've spoken to Pete, the attorney, and he's confirmed it. Abi drew it up about two months ago.'

'What did it say?'

'Nothing unusual, apparently. Nothing weird or out of the ordinary. But I can't help wondering. Especially when we know, for a fact, that there's a killer here tonight.'

Olive stared at her. 'You think she knew something was going to happen.'

'Maybe. Or perhaps she was worried something *might*.'

Olive thought for a moment. 'Have you told the police about this?'

'Not yet.'

'Why not?'

Stevie didn't reply.

'You're worried it'll further implicate Humphrey.'

Again, Stevie didn't reply.

Olive nodded. 'OK. So what do we have, besides the will, that might suggest Abi thought someone was going to cause her harm?'

'You mean other than the fact that someone has killed her?'

'You know what I mean, Stevie. Is there more security around here than you would expect? Did she seem nervous or on edge about anything?'

Stevie paused, thinking about the request that had brought her to The Midnight Orchid.

Humphrey can't do anything about the board's decision, Abi had said. *He's out. Non-negotiable. But he's insisting he still wants to come to the launch party. I'm terrified he's going to try something.*

She shook her head. 'No. Nothing that I can think of.'

Olive closed her eyes, as if her next question was too painful even to contemplate.

'Do you think . . .' she said. 'Do you think she might have done this herself? Did she know the flower would kill her, and her insistence it was harmless was an act?'

'You think she could have taken her own life?' Stevie's eyes went wide, this horrifying possibility having not even occurred to her.

Olive looked unsure, clearly just as uncomfortable with the idea. 'I don't know. I can't imagine why she would.

But is it really harder to fathom than the idea of it being someone we know?'

Stevie turned Olive's words over in her mind. Then she scrambled for her phone, a sudden thought occurring to her.

'No,' she said. 'Look. Look at this. She messaged me while we were hiking this afternoon. Asked me to come to her hut tomorrow. Who asks someone to visit them the day after they're planning to take their own life?'

She showed Olive the WhatsApp message Abi had sent her during the hike, asking to discuss the deer by the waterfall.

'So she can't have done it herself,' said Olive.

'Or if she did, then at the point when she messaged me she can't have been planning to do it tonight.'

They fell into gloomy silence, Stevie feeling that they were drifting further from a resolution. After a minute or two, she took a breath, deciding to try a different approach.

'Olive,' she said. 'Last night. After the waterfall. When we parted ways and you took Mike back to his hut . . . Did he say anything to you about visiting Abi?'

'Visiting her?'

'That's right. Before we saw him going into the jungle.'

Olive shook her head. 'No. He didn't say anything like that. Why?'

'Miley heard Mike turning up at their hut last night, looking for Abi,' Stevie said. 'It must have happened before he went to the waterfall, but I can't think why he wouldn't mention it. Apparently he went inside and the two of them spoke for a little bit.'

'Spoke about what?'

'Miley isn't sure. Abi thought she was asleep, so she took Mike out into the garden so as not to disturb her. She said that Mike sounded unhappy, though. Apparently after they'd spoken for a couple minutes in the garden she heard him storming off in a rage.'

Olive frowned. 'Strange. He didn't seem angry by the waterfall. If anything he just seemed sad.'

'I agree. But it just seems too much of a coincidence, doesn't it? They have a secret conversation in Abi's hut and then they both end up dead.'

Olive nodded. 'Yeah,' she said quietly. 'Yeah, it's odd.'

They fell once more into silence, an intense look on Olive's face. After a while, she said, 'You know, the more I think about it, the more I agree. I don't think Abi can have done it herself.'

Stevie raised an eyebrow. 'No?'

'No. When I went to her hut this morning, I saw what looked like a bag of prescription medicine in the bathroom. She was clearly taking it, too – there was a strip of tablets out on the coffee table. She picked it up and dropped it back into the bag before we talked. I'm no expert, of course, but if you were so certain you were going to end your own life that you went to the trouble of drawing up a will, I struggle to imagine you would worry about keeping up with a prescription.'

Stevie frowned. What would Abi need a prescription

for? Humphrey hadn't mentioned anything about her being ill. Nor, to Stevie's knowledge, did she have any long-term health conditions that would need managing.

She thought about it a moment longer. And then it came. Like a blindfold being removed, she saw what she had so far missed. She understood why Abi had drawn up the will. And with that realisation there immediately came an entirely new perspective on what Abi had been engineering for the launch of The Midnight Orchid.

43

'Do you think they've found it?' asked Olive.

Stevie didn't reply, her eyes glued to the door.

They stood together a few metres away from Abi's hut, watching as two cops stood guard outside. The police didn't look best pleased to see them, but Stevie refused to be sent away. She needed to know if her theory was right.

'Come on,' she had pleaded with Inspector Rojas fifteen minutes earlier. 'All I'm asking you to do is take another look inside the hut. You're going to have to do that anyway, right? Well, if you look, right now, and you find what I think you're going to find, then wouldn't that just save you time later?'

Rojas hadn't been happy. But she had, at least, agreed. She'd gone into Abi's hut. Then, she'd sent for the lodge's in-house doctor, with whom she'd spoken in Spanish before ushering him inside. It had been a few minutes now and neither of them had come back out.

Stevie turned to Olive, wondering once more about the

possibility of this being an act. Of the chance that Olive had killed Abi and was now just using Stevie to gather information.

As quickly as she'd thought it, though, a second notion crossed her mind.

What if nothing had happened all those years ago? What if it was Seth, rather than Jazz, who had been correct by the poolside bar? He'd been adamant that Jazz was wrong – that in reality they had seen nothing. Had it been Stevie's history with Abi that caused her to side with Jazz? To believe, without even knowing what, that she had done something terrible?

It was possible, Stevie figured. But then, as she thought of the way Seth had fled from her when they'd locked eyes across the lobby, she found it difficult to believe. If he truly thought Jazz was wrong, surely he would answer Stevie's questions?

'Olive . . .' said Stevie. 'What was she like?'

'Who?'

'Abi.'

She saw the confusion in Olive's expression. Heard the sorrow in her own voice.

'She liked you,' Stevie continued. 'You were friends. What was that . . . What was she like? As a friend?'

Olive stared at her, with seemingly no idea of how to reply. After a long pause, she took a breath. But before she could speak, the door to Abi's hut opened, Rojas and the doctor stepping outside.

Stevie could see immediately that she had been right.

She could see it in the doctor's severe expression. In the way Rojas now looked at her so suspiciously.

Abi had known she was going to die.

But it hadn't been murder that was on her mind.

44

They returned to the plaza in the middle of the garden, Olive sitting on the edge of the fountain while Stevie paced back and forth.

In an ideal world, Stevie would have spoken with Rojas – asked exactly what pills and tablets had been in Abi's hut. She remembered all of their names. Unless the treatment plan had changed since Jane Blythe received it, she was sure she would recognise the medication.

But she had decided against this, noting the look of suspicion on Rojas's face after she had emerged from Abi's hut. The inspector was never going to give Stevie her answers. If anything, she would more than likely find herself on the receiving end of some difficult questions herself.

Olive shivered, her arms clutched across her middle. Neither of them had checked the time in a few minutes, but Stevie knew it must be getting on for two o'clock in the morning. With the DJ silent, she heard the chirping of some unseen insect. Over their heads, in the dim light cast from a nearby lantern, she could just make out the outline of a bat darting through the inky darkness.

'So you really think you were right?' said Olive. 'You think there was more medication in there than I saw yesterday?'

Stevie nodded. 'If the looks on the doctor and Rojas's faces were anything to go by then yes. I think Abi knew she was going to die. That's why she drew up the will. But I don't think she expected to be murdered. I think she could have been diagnosed with the same illness as our mom. And our grandmother before her.'

Olive's eyes widened. 'And what does that mean for us? Are you saying Abi might not have been murdered?'

Stevie shook her head. 'I remember seeing our mom deteriorate. It was rapid, once it kicked in, but it was visible. By the end she couldn't even get out of bed. Abi definitely wasn't in that kind of condition. And then there were her symptoms when we found her body. The foam around her mouth. The veins in her eyes.' Stevie grimaced. 'No. I don't think it was the illness that killed her. I think she would have had some time before it really took effect.'

Olive nodded. 'So whoever killed her didn't know that she was ill. If they'd known she was dying already, they could have just waited for the illness to do its work.'

'Unless they couldn't afford to wait.' Stevie stopped pacing, screwing her eyes shut. 'Is that why they took her phone? Was there something on there that she was planning to show someone? The thing she was going to "tell

307

the family after the launch"? Was all of this just to keep her quiet?'

'I'd have thought she was planning to tell you that she was ill.'

'So would I. I'll bet anything that the person Humphrey overheard her speaking with was a doctor or a consultant. But you have to wonder . . . what if it wasn't? What if she's got something on someone? Something she wanted to reveal before the illness took hold? What if that's why she set up your reunion?'

Olive was silent. Stevie, meanwhile, began to pace again.

'So someone goes to Abi's hut before the party,' she said. 'Whether they've been invited or they've turned up unannounced, we can't say. But we do know that whoever it is, she lets them inside and accepts a glass of water that they've poisoned with the flower. After she's dead, they take her phone, leaving in such a hurry that they don't even think to close the door properly on their way out.' She shook her head. 'It must be to do with this conversation Miley overheard last night. It *has* to be. Mike pays Abi a secret visit. They have a heated conversation and now they're both dead. That can't be a coincidence.'

She glanced at Olive, who looked equally deep in thought. 'What?' she asked. 'What is it?'

'It's nothing,' said Olive. 'It's just . . .' She paused for a moment. 'How did the petals get there?'

Stevie's eyes narrowed.

'The petals,' Olive continued. 'That were on the

floor around Abi's body. What were they doing there? Because you're right – whoever did this must have brought some water to Abi's that had been spiked with the flower. But it wouldn't have been visible, would it? Abi surely wouldn't have drunk a glass of water that had petals in it. So what were they doing there? It doesn't make sense.'

Stevie stood, her mind racing.

'So someone scattered those petals beside Abi's body after she was dead,' she said. 'What if they wanted whoever found her to see them? To see, immediately, that she'd been murdered? Perhaps that's even why they left the door open a crack. They wanted to make sure we could get inside and find her.'

'Why would they want that, though?' said Olive. 'Surely if you were going to kill someone and you wanted to get away with it, you'd try to make it look like an accident. You wouldn't reinforce to whoever found the body that they'd been murdered.'

At that moment, Olive's phone buzzed. Looking at the screen, her eyes widened.

'Oh, God,' she murmured.

'What?' said Stevie. 'Everything OK?'

'Yeah,' said Olive. 'Sorry. It's Jazz. She's looking for me.' She hurried to her feet. 'I'm sorry, Stevie. I have to go. I only said I was going to the loo. It sounds like they're worried. I need to . . .' She looked panicked. 'I'm sorry,' she said again. Then she turned and began to hurry in the direction of the lodge.

Stevie said nothing, watching as Olive half-jogged away.

She hadn't asked. She'd wanted to. She was desperate to understand. But somehow she hadn't managed to ask the one question that had perhaps been burning most fervently in her mind over the past few hours. Now, as Olive rushed back to her friends, Stevie felt an overpowering sense of a window closing. An opportunity drifting away.

She closed her eyes, took a deep breath then began to run. 'Olive!' she called out. 'Olive, wait!'

Olive stopped, a frown on her face as she turned back.

'Sorry,' said Stevie. 'I know you need to go. But there's something I have to ask you. Something I need to know. You and Jazz . . . You two are close, right?'

'Of course. We're cousins.'

'And I'd be right in saying that Jazz wasn't Abi's biggest fan?'

'I mean . . . they weren't particularly close. It was definitely me that brought them together.' Olive's eyes narrowed. 'Why? What's this got to do with anything?'

'You wouldn't say that Jazz resented Abi? Or had any kind of a grudge against her?'

'No. Stevie, what is this? Why are you asking these questions?'

Stevie sighed. 'I know this is probably an awful thing to consider. But is there any world in which you could see Jazz being the one to do this?'

Olive's eyes went wide. 'No! Stevie, no!'

'OK.' Stevie put up her hands. 'OK. Just . . . Just let me explain why I'm asking. Will you let me do that?'

Olive said nothing, glaring with such intensity that Stevie suspected she was about to storm off. But eventually she gave a single stiff nod.

'Thank you,' said Stevie. 'So the reason I ask . . .' She took a deep breath. 'Olive, did Abi do something to you last time you were all here?'

'Did she *do something*?'

'That's right. Something to . . . I don't know. Something to hurt you or upset you—'

'No.'

'You're sure?'

'Yes, I'm sure. Stevie, what are you talking about?'

'I overheard Jazz and Seth talking. About an hour after we found Abi. I wasn't trying to eavesdrop as such, but with everything that's going on . . .' Stevie stopped, aware that she was rambling. 'I heard them talking about something that Abi did when you guys were all here before. To you.'

Olive looked puzzled. 'And what was it?'

'I don't know. They didn't say.'

'But it was definitely something Abi had done to *me*?'

'Definitely. Something they'd seen. Or rather, something *Jazz* believed they had seen.'

'But not Seth?'

'Seth denied all of it. Which, from what I heard, really pissed off Jazz. But that's not why I'm asking you about it. The point is . . . whatever it was that they supposedly saw

Abi do to you, Seth thought it was bad enough to accuse Jazz of killing her.'

Stevie held her breath, watching Olive closely for any sign that she might be lying. That she might have known.

'I have no idea what that could have been.'

'No idea?'

'Literally none.'

Stevie thought about pressing her. Saying that she *knew* Abi had done something. Something so terrible that Seth had asked Jazz if she had been involved in Abi's murder, and that Jazz had seen fit to travel halfway around the world simply to watch over her cousin.

But at that moment, a voice carried over to them.

'Olive! Where the fuck have you been?'

Turning in unison, Stevie and Olive both saw Jazz storming towards them through the garden.

'You can't just wander off,' Jazz continued. 'Christ, Olive, we've been looking all over for you. We thought something might have happened!'

She came to a stop, looking at her cousin.

'What?' she said. 'What is it? Why aren't you saying anything?'

Stevie, too, saw now what was perplexing Jazz. It was Olive. She seemed to be staring at Jazz in disbelief.

'What did Abi do?' Olive asked.

'What?'

'What did she do? Ten years ago? What did Stevie hear you and Seth talking about?'

Jazz threw Stevie a scowl so vicious it could have rivalled one of Abi's.

'Olive,' she said. 'Listen to me. Stevie doesn't know what she heard. She listened in on a conversation that she didn't understand—'

'Did you kill Abi?' Olive asked. 'Is that why you came here?'

'No! Olive, no. I came to be with you. To make sure you were OK.'

Olive shook her head, tears in her eyes. 'Just tell me, Jazz. Tell me what happened.'

'Nothing happened.'

'Jazz, please.'

'*Nothing happened.*'

Olive looked at her cousin, her heart visibly breaking. Then, she barged past Jazz and walked quickly away.

'Olive,' Jazz called after her. 'Olive!' She moved to follow, before suddenly stopping, as if just remembering that Stevie was there too. 'You!' she snapped. 'You stay away from her. Your family's already done enough damage. And now you're back for more. Finishing your sister's work. Well, you just stay away. Or I won't be held responsible for what happens to you.'

Jazz didn't stop to see Stevie's reaction. Instead, she hurried to catch up with Olive, taking with her whatever hope Stevie had left of learning what Abi had done.

45

As Stevie arrived back at her hut, she felt despondent, weighed down by each of the mysteries she had so far failed to unravel.

The theory that Abi had been dying, diagnosed with the same rare illness that had taken Jane Blythe before her, did at least answer a few questions. It explained the will and it certainly explained the collection of pills that Stevie believed Rojas had found in Abi's hut.

But did Olive truly not know what Seth and Jazz had been speaking about by the poolside bar? Or was she simply protecting her friends? Did she know full well what Abi had done, and had she approached Stevie only to gather information?

Likewise, what had Mike discussed with Abi before he'd gone to the waterfall? What had been so important about Abi's phone and why had her killer wanted so badly to draw their attention to the flower that they'd taken the time to scatter petals around the body? And why, exactly, had Abi arranged the reunion with Olive and the others to begin with? Why fly a group of people she'd made no effort to see in nearly ten years halfway around the world? Did her diagnosis answer this question? Was it simply to see her friends one last time before the disease took hold? It was possible, Stevie supposed, although she struggled to believe it. Instead, it seemed much more likely that Abi might want something from them. Something that had required them to be there in person.

Taking a soda from the fridge, she went over to the coffee table and sank into one of the wicker chairs.

She wondered if Humphrey had arrived at the police station. If not, he must be getting close. How frightened was he feeling? How alone? She tried not to dwell on those questions, reminding herself instead that Pete was on his way.

Taking out her phone, she fetched up Olive's Facebook page once more, heading straight for the album from the summer the group had spent backpacking. She scrolled idly through the pictures, not really knowing what she was looking for. It was only when she reached the end of the album – the photos from the group's last night at the campsite – that she slowed, pausing on the shot of the others gathered around Zach and Olive in the minutes after they'd got engaged.

She imagined the scene. Zach reaching into his rucksack for the ring. Olive, having found it earlier that afternoon, crying out 'Yes!' before he could even pop the question. Olive then phoning her mum in the hospital to deliver the news, the sound of nurses giving a little cheer in the background.

Stevie smiled at the image. It was a cute story. The kind people fantasised about one day telling to their grandkids. And yet, with all she had learned over the past few hours, as she looked at this photo Stevie couldn't help but feel unsettled.

What had Abi done to Olive on the last day of that trip? What was this terrible thing that Jazz and Seth had apparently witnessed? And had she already done it when this photo was taken? Or had it still been yet to come?

She stared at the photo, yearning for answers. Pleading with it, even. In the end she looked at it so intently that when a knock sounded on her door she jumped half out of her skin.

Heart thumping, she rose from the wicker chair and crossed the hut. For a second she wondered if it was Olive. Or perhaps even Jazz. Maybe they had cooled off, she thought, and were coming to give her the answers she so desperately needed.

Her hopes were quickly dashed, though, when she opened the door to find Rojas standing on the porch.

'Miss Blythe,' she said. 'May I come inside?'

Stevie hesitated, searching for a good enough reason to say no. When none came to mind, she stepped begrudgingly aside.

'I would like to know,' said the inspector, 'what you think I found in your sister's hut.'

As she closed the door behind her, Stevie felt a sudden

rush of panic. Why was Rojas asking her this? Had she been wrong about Abi's health? Had Rojas and the doctor found something else?

'Medicine,' she said cautiously. 'A few different kinds. But pills, mostly. Prescribed by a doctor from New Hampshire.'

Rojas hummed in acknowledgement, prompting Stevie to relax just a little. She was being tested, she realised. Rojas had wanted to hear her say what was in Abi's hut before describing it out loud herself.

Without asking if she may, Rojas sat in one of the wicker chairs. 'And how,' she said, 'did you know to look for this medicine?'

'Just a hunch.'

'A hunch?'

'Yeah. A hunch. Olive was in Abi's hut yesterday. She saw a bag of what looked like prescribed pills, and I knew of a disease that runs in the women in our family. When Olive told me about the pills, I . . .'

Stevie stopped. Should she tell Rojas about the will? A voice in her head said that yes, she absolutely should. Rojas, after all, was the one leading the investigation into Abi's and Mike's deaths. But the thought of Humphrey sitting in a police interview room caused her to hold back. Would she, by telling Rojas that Abi had drawn up a will shortly before she died, only be providing more fuel with which to accuse Humphrey of her murder?

She swallowed back a lump. 'I guess I just put two and two together.'

'That's an impressive leap.'

Stevie chewed her lip, a loaded silence hanging in the air.

'Do you think my brother's guilty?'

'I think he has motive. And I think he had the opportunity.'

'What motive?'

'He was removed from your father's company. Your sister was not.'

'But if that was his motive, what good would killing Abi do him? What would it achieve? It won't change the board members' minds.'

Rojas made a small motion with her hands, almost like a shrug, before locking her fingers together in her lap.

'For many people, revenge is a powerful motive. You would be amazed how often murder is committed without a . . .' She paused, searching for the correct word. 'Without a *logical* reason.'

Stevie clenched her fists, determined not to give in.

'What if it wasn't the flower that killed Abi?' she said. 'I get that only a small number of people know it's poisonous. And I know that, of those people, you think Humphrey had the strongest motive. But I read earlier tonight about a tree. The world's *most poisonous* tree, apparently. If the autopsy shows that one of those was used to kill Abi, then it could have been anyone. I mean, just look at the size of that jungle out there. There must be one nearby, for anyone who knows to look for it.'

Rojas looked unconvinced. 'If a manchineel tree — assuming this is the tree you are referring to — has been used then yes, we will find it in the autopsy. But you should know, Miss Blythe, that while the manchineel is dangerous, there are no modern cases of it killing anyone. Only historical.' She leaned forward in the wicker chair. 'Now I will ask you one last time. What really made you ask me to search your sister's hut for those pills?'

Stevie met her gaze. Just.

'I told you,' she said. 'It was a hunch.'

For a long while, Rojas looked at her. Then, finally, she nodded and stood up.

'There are things you aren't telling me, Miss Blythe. Perhaps you think that staying quiet will help your brother. Let me tell you that you are wrong. If whatever you are hiding is important, things will be much worse for him.'

Stevie said nothing, working hard to suppress her fear as the inspector rose to her feet.

'When you decide you're ready to tell the truth, come and find me.' Rojas paused at the door. 'And you should also know,' she added, 'if you're going to continue with your theory, that manchineels don't grow in the jungle. They grow on the beach.'

Without another word, Rojas slipped back out into the night, closing the door carefully behind her.

46

'Olive,' Jazz called out. 'Olive, please.'

But her cousin didn't reply. She stormed on ahead, huts flying by on either side.

'Olive, wait!' Jazz grabbed her wrist, forcing her to stop. 'Where are you even going?'

'To talk to Zach. To see if *he* knows about—'

'No!' Jazz blurted the word out before she could stop her herself, fight-or-flight mode taking over. Immediately, she realised her mistake, the horror in Olive's expression confirming it.

Olive looked down at the ground, tears welling in the corners of her eyes.

'How can I not know about it? This terrible thing? How can I be the only one who doesn't know what she did? How can my own *husband . . .*'

Jazz looked at her cousin, searching desperately for the right thing to say. *Because we decided you shouldn't? Because we were too scared to tell you?* For ten years those answers had made sense. They'd seemed enough. But now, with

Olive on the cusp of learning the truth, they felt woefully inadequate.

'Please,' said Olive. 'Just tell me, Jazz. I want to know.'

'No, you don't.'

'Why not?'

'Because it's done. Nothing's going to change it. And if you found out now, I worry it would break you.'

Olive was silent as she worked to hold back more tears. Then, she said quietly, 'I can't believe you're betraying me like this.'

'Betraying you?' Jazz heard the disbelief in her own voice. 'In what way am I betraying you? I came all this way to protect you. To keep you safe from Abi, because you could never see for yourself what she was—'

'Enough!' Olive snapped at her. 'Just . . . enough.' She took a deep breath. 'Are you going to tell me or not? I want to know.'

Jazz shook her head. 'I can't. I won't.'

Olive nodded, not making any further reply. It seemed there was nothing left to say. She began walking back in the direction they had come, towards the lodge.

Her heart breaking, Jazz watched her go, wondering if, for all these years, she had done the right thing.

47

Stevie paced back and forth inside her hut, fighting the urge to panic.

She had to think of something. Had to find something that would help prove Humphrey's innocence. There was no shortage of unanswered questions to choose from. The disappearance of Abi's phone. Her conversation with Mike before he'd gone to the waterfall. The reason for the petals beside her body.

But the question Stevie kept coming back to was that of what Abi had done to Olive.

In part this was because it seemed like the only question she stood a chance of answering. There were, after all, people at the hotel who knew what had happened, even if they'd made it clear that they weren't going to tell her.

Perhaps she was kidding herself. Clutching desperately at the only straw that felt within reach. But she was convinced that all of this – everything that had transpired since arriving at The Midnight Orchid – came back to that one transgression. If she could just determine what had happened . . . If she could make either Seth or Jazz talk, then perhaps everything else would fall into place.

She stopped pacing, taking a breath as she tried to recall the conversation she'd overheard by the pool. Combing Seth's and Jazz's words for a clue she could somehow have missed.

She found nothing.

The only scrap that seemed of note was the question of why Seth had slipped away to his hut after Abi had been found. But Stevie saw no way of solving that particular mystery. Not, at least, while Seth refused to speak with her.

She screwed her eyes shut, trying not to think of the way Rojas had looked at her. Like she was small. Insignificant. In her mind, she replayed the snide comment the inspector had made on her way out of the hut.

If you're going to continue with your theory, manchineels don't grow in the jungle. They grow on the beach.

And it was then that it hit her.

Eyes widening, Stevie let out a laugh of disbelief.

Because Rojas had given her the key. Without meaning to – without so much as realising it – she had given Stevie exactly what she needed to make Seth talk.

48

The hostility in Seth's eyes, when he opened the door to his hut and found Stevie standing outside, was instant.

'Please, Seth,' she said. 'I just want to—'

He didn't let her finish, moving instead to slam the door shut. Panicking, Stevie did the one thing that she thought would catch his attention. Before the door could close on her, she shouted a single word.

'Manchineel!'

It had the desired effect. The door remained open. Just a crack.

Heart pounding, she stood, waiting to see what Seth would do next. Slowly, the door opened again. Seth looked out at her, the hostility in his expression turning to fury.

'I know you didn't kill Abi,' said Stevie. 'Or Mike.' She took a breath, hoping Seth wouldn't hear the nervousness in her voice. 'I just want to talk,' she said. 'I want to know what you and Jazz meant at the poolside bar. What, exactly, Abi did to Olive when you were here ten years ago.'

'It's nothing,' Seth spat. 'Nothing happened. Jazz is wrong.'

'Tell me what she *thinks* you saw then—'

'Nothing fucking happened.' Seth hissed at her, teeth gritted. 'And sharing Jazz's insane suspicions with you isn't going to make anything better.'

Stevie took another breath. 'Please, Seth. Just tell me what Jazz thinks you saw. Tell me and I'll . . .' She swallowed back a lump. 'Tell me what happened and then I won't tell anyone about the manchineel apples you had in your hut when Abi was killed.'

She saw the resentment in his eyes.

'I was doing some googling,' she continued. 'Trying to find something about the flower. I didn't, of course. But I did read something about a tree. The world's most poisonous. I suppose I assumed that a tree like that would naturally grow in the jungle. But I was wrong. A manchineel is different. Because a manchineel tree is coastal. It grows on the beach.'

She struggled to hold his gaze, nails digging into her palms.

'That's what you were doing,' she said. 'Isn't it? When I bumped into you yesterday morning on the beach. You went down there to pick manchineel apples, presumably so you could take them back to the UK. You even had a book with you. What was it? *The Flora and Fauna of Costa Rica*?'

'You can't prove that.'

'Maybe not. I guess you'll have got rid of them now.

325

That's presumably what Jazz saw you slipping away to do after we all found Abi's body. But here's what I'll bet *can* be done. I can identify the shoes you were wearing. If I went and suggested to one of these police officers that they come seize them, they could probably find traces of sand on the soles. From there, I'll bet all of your friends could confirm that they didn't go with you to the beach – that you went on your own.'

'So?' said Seth. 'I went to the beach. What does it matter?'

'Sure. You, Seth, who once got in trouble for keeping a toxic plant in your student accommodation and who brought a book on this trip about the flora and fauna of Central America, just happened to go walking by yourself on the beach. I'm willing to bet there's a manchineel tree on that beach. And I'll bet that if they felt the need, the police could probably call in some kind of expert to confirm whether any apples had recently been picked from that tree.'

If she were to be completely honest, Stevie had absolutely no idea whether it was possible to tell whether apples had recently been picked from a manchineel tree. Her bluff had the intended effect, though, a note of panic creeping into Seth's voice.

'But Abi hasn't died of manchineel poisoning!'

'No,' Stevie agreed. 'No, it doesn't appear as if she has. And a post-mortem will show that. But it still doesn't look great for you to be sneaking off on your own to collect apples. Regardless of how Abi died, I'm sure the police would be curious to know what you were planning to do with them. Unless, of course, I decide not to tell them.'

'So you're blackmailing me.'

She looked him in the eye. 'Please, Seth. I know you didn't kill anyone. So save yourself being put under the microscope and just tell me what I need to know. What did Jazz mean earlier? What does she think the two of you saw when you were last all here?'

For a long while, Seth was silent. Then, at last, he sighed.

'If I tell you, you'll keep schtum about the manchineel apples?'

'Yes.'

'You promise?'

'I promise.'

He scowled. 'Fine. But you didn't hear this from me. If anyone asks, I'll say that Jazz told you and you'll have her to deal with. Not a position I'd want to be in if I were you.'

'I understand.'

Seth nodded. 'OK,' he said. 'Here it is then. On the final day of our trip, the coach we were riding in stopped for about half an hour at a petrol station. It was an enormous place. More of a supermarket, really. They sold food, souvenirs, toiletries . . . So we all got off and went into the shop to buy some stuff that we might want that night at the campsite. Jazz and I happened to be done at about the same time, so we went back to the coach together. The others were still inside the shop. Or, at least, we thought they were. Zach, Olive and Mike certainly were. But as we got back to the coach, we saw that Abi was getting off.'

Stevie frowned. 'I thought you all went into the store together?'

'We did. We absolutely did. So for some reason she had broken away from the group and gone back onto the coach.' Seth grimaced. 'I didn't think anything of it at the time. But Jazz came to me the following day, when we were on our way to the airport. She pointed out that we'd left our rucksacks on the coach while we'd gone into the shop. Didn't fancy carrying them, so we'd just left them on our seats. We'd *all* left them. Unattended.'

He let this final detail hang in the air, holding Stevie's gaze as if willing her to understand.

She considered it for a moment, following this train of thought to its end.

She felt her eyes widen.

'Oh, God . . .'

'We didn't see her do anything,' said Seth. 'That's important. All we saw was Abi getting off the coach.'

'But presumably you think . . . You think she put the—'

'Jazz does. That's why she came out here this week. To keep an eye on Abi and make sure she didn't try anything else. But I'm not so sure.' He looked at her nervously. 'So we're done?' he said. 'You won't tell anyone about the apples?'

Stevie barely heard him. 'Yeah,' she whispered. 'Yeah, we're done.'

49

Sitting alone at the poolside bar, Jazz put her head in her hands.

Ten years Olive had gone without knowing the truth of what Abi had done to her. She'd built a life in that time. A family. Now that was all in danger of crashing down.

Despairing, Jazz let out a long breath, trying hard to dwell on how different their lives could have been had Olive never met Abi. If only she had gone to the students' union on a different night, would she have been spared? Would Abi have chosen someone else?

And what about Jazz, herself? Was Olive right? Had she betrayed her cousin by not saying anything? She didn't think so. What good would it have achieved when the truth would have broken Olive's heart?

She looked down at her phone, sitting in front of her on the bar.

Things had changed now. Protecting Olive from the truth had been one thing. Keeping it from her, when she wanted to hear it, was another entirely. Perhaps it was finally time for her to know.

Slowly, Jazz reached for her phone. Opening Whats-App, she found her chat with Olive, typing out just three words and hitting send before she could think long enough to stop herself.

I'll tell you.

50

With a heavy heart, Stevie raised her hand and knocked on the door to Olive's hut.

No answer came. She tried again. Still there was only silence.

For a second, she thought about turning away. She knew she needed to share what she had just learned with Rojas. But she wanted to speak to Olive first. She wanted to give her a chance to explain.

With a trembling hand, she reached for the door handle. To her surprise, she found that it didn't resist. Opening the door a crack, she poked her head inside the hut.

'Olive?' she said. 'Are you here?'

No answer came.

Stevie lingered in the doorway. She knew she should go to Rojas now. But she couldn't bring herself to turn back. Not after what she'd just learned from Seth. So she stepped inside, closing the door gently behind her.

She cast a quick look around the hut. Two suitcases stood open by the bed, a few clothes discarded on the wicker chairs. A couple of sun-bleached paperbacks and a glossy magazine sat on the coffee table. All looked perfectly normal.

Crossing the lounge area, her sneakers padding on the wooden floorboards, Stevie ventured deeper inside.

She had to test her theory. Had to hear it from Olive herself. Because she could see so clearly now how it might happen. And perhaps most importantly, she could see why.

Abi had set up the reunion so that she could come clean to Olive. Tell her face-to-face what she'd done on the coach and offer to make amends before her illness took hold. That was what Stevie believed. But the question that remained unanswered was whether Olive would be capable of murdering her in response.

On the dresser, a phone pinged. Jumping a little at the sound inside the otherwise-silent hut, Stevie shot it a glance. The screen lit up for a few seconds, displaying a photo of a young boy. Ryan, she assumed. Zach and Olive's son.

The screen went dark again, the hut falling once more into silence.

Stevie knew that she should leave. Olive wasn't there. She should go to Rojas.

And yet, she couldn't move. Instead, she stared at the phone, her mind seemingly stuck on something that she couldn't quite place.

Slowly, she reached out for it. Touching a button on the side, she stared as the picture of Ryan appeared once more.

Sometimes when Stevie was researching a long-lost

family member for a client, she would see a resemblance immediately. The shape of their faces, a particular shared feature . . . Often it would be unmistakeable. In other instances, she would need to really search for something, only finding it in a particular facial expression or in a photo taken from a certain angle. It would be harder to recognise. But once it had been spotted, it could never be unseen.

As she looked at the picture of Ryan, she knew that this was an example of the former. A resemblance she would never have thought to look for, but to someone with her trained eye was unmistakeable.

The truth hit her like a wave, the answer suddenly so clear that it felt almost laughable. Her mind began to race, her pulse rising as she considered how perilously wrong she had been up to now.

She was so distracted by what she had just seen that she didn't hear the footsteps behind her. Nor did she consider why Zach's phone might be there but not Zach himself. It was only when she felt a hand on her shoulder that it dawned on her she hadn't checked the en-suite bathroom.

51

Jumping half out of her skin, Stevie spun around, wrenching her shoulder away from the presence behind her.

Zach took a step back too.

'Whoa,' he said, raising his hands. 'It's OK. It's OK!'

Stevie retreated as far as she could, only coming to a stop when she backed into the glass doors to the hut's private garden.

'I'm sorry,' said Zach. 'I didn't mean to scare you.'

Stevie didn't reply. Her heart was pounding, breath coming in hurried gasps.

Zach looked confused. 'Where's Olive? Is she not with you?'

Eager to escape, Stevie tried to dart around him. To make for the door. But Zach moved faster, planting himself in her path.

'What's going on?' he said. 'Did you break in here? What were you doing with my phone?'

'Please,' said Stevie. 'Please just let me go. I won't tell anyone. I promise.'

'Tell anyone what? What is it you think I've done?'

'You killed them! Abi and Mike. You killed them both.'

She could hear her own terror, her voice quivering. Zach, meanwhile, stared at her, mouth falling open.

'Why?' he said. 'Why would I do that? They were my friends.'

Stevie looked over his shoulder, her eyes on the door.

'I want to leave.'

'So that you can tell everyone I'm a murderer?'

'If isn't true, you'll let me leave.'

He looked at her. 'Please, Stevie. Just talk to me. I don't know what you think you've learned, but if you'll just tell me I'm sure I can clear it up.'

He wasn't going to let her go. That much was frighteningly clear. She had no way of fighting him off and no way out.

And yet, Stevie found that her thoughts were only half-committed to the question of how she might escape from Zach. At the same time – almost against her will – she was rapidly piecing things together. Now that she had the solution it was as if her mind was running away with itself, hauling her along as it forged connections and answered questions that she hadn't previously even known to ask.

'It was you,' she said. 'It wasn't Mike. It was you who Seth heard at the campsite.'

Zach frowned. 'Seth? What did Seth—'

'He heard you arguing.' Stevie didn't mean to cut over him. The words seemed simply to tumble out of their own accord. 'Ten years ago,' she continued. 'The night you and

335

Olive got engaged. After the others had all gone to bed, he heard you arguing with Abi. And then he heard the two of you getting together in her tent. He thought it was Mike – that they were continuing what he'd interrupted by the waterfall – but it was you. And then it was you who Miley heard visiting Abi's hut last night. It was you who she took out into the garden so that you could talk, and it was you who Miley heard storming off. Miley thought it was Mike, because she recognised an English accent, but it was you. She said you went to the hut and asked to talk. Abi took you out into the garden, but after a few minutes you ran for the door.'

As he listened to all of this, Zach's mouth was agape. Stevie could scarcely believe it herself. She was thinking as she spoke, piecing it all together, word by word.

She tried desperately to order her thoughts. She wanted to be wrong. Wanted some stray detail to trip her up and stop her in her tracks. But she knew in her gut that it was all true. Because she knew, exactly, what she had seen on Zach's phone.

'Abi told you,' she pressed. 'Didn't she? You went to her hut last night to find out why she'd brought you all here. And when she told you the truth, you panicked. You couldn't handle what you were hearing, so you went running out of the hut. And then, today, you killed her to keep her from sharing that truth with—'

'No!' Suddenly, Zach found his voice again. 'No, you've got it all wrong. I didn't kill her. I haven't killed anyone!'

336

'Liar!' Stevie's voice rose to a panicked cry. 'You killed her so that she couldn't tell Olive the truth. And then you killed Mike to frame Humphrey.' She shook her head. 'Why? Why did any of it happen? Why did you sleep with Olive's best friend? Why would Abi sleep with her best friend's fiancé? And why . . .' She swallowed back a lump. 'Why did she put that engagement ring in your rucksack? It can't have been a simple prank. Not with what happened after, in Abi's tent. So what did she hope to achieve with it?'

Zach stared at her, the panicked expression on his face becoming twice as severe at the mention of the ring.

'I don't know what you're talking about.'

He managed to force a little fight into his voice, but Stevie could hear how fragile it was – how close to faltering.

'I spoke to Seth,' she explained. 'He says that on the day you and Olive got engaged, you all rode here on a coach. And at some point during that journey, the coach stopped at a gas station. You all got off and went into the store to buy water and snacks, leaving your rucksacks on your seats. Jazz and Seth were the first to finish up, so they went back to the coach together. And it was there that they found Abi. It seems that at some point while you were all in the store she broke off on her own. Neither Jazz nor Seth thought much of it at the time. But Jazz remembered later that your rucksacks were all on that coach. Unattended.' Stevie swallowed. 'It was one of Abi's oldest tricks. Taking your stuff and planting it in someone else's bag or room.

337

She did it all the time when we were kids, hoping that I'd get in trouble for stealing.'

Zach's breathing was rapid. Stevie could see the thought process that was going on behind his eyes, his mind working at a hundred miles an hour. She could easily see why he was so frightened. No one had ever confronted him on this before.

'This is insane,' he said. 'All of it. Do you really think that I'd go through with the engagement if that was how it happened? Do you not think I'd tell Olive the truth?'

'How could you?' said Stevie. 'I don't know why Abi put that ring in your rucksack, but I'm sure the last thing she expected was that Olive would find it when she went looking for your mosquito spray, and that when you found it yourself later that evening, she would say yes before you'd even have a chance to realise what was happening. Within minutes Olive had you on the phone to her sick mother to share the good news. She told me herself, the nurses cheered for you. And when you flew home the next day, her relatives were waiting at the airport to drive you to an engagement party. At what point were you meant to tell her it had all been a joke?'

This time Zach didn't even try to deny it.

'But why did any of it happen?' Stevie pressed. 'What was Abi hoping to achieve? Why do this to her best friend? And why would you then want to sleep with her after she'd done it? Just what the hell was going on between you and Abi?'

At this, Stevie paused, a missing piece clicking neatly into place.

Suddenly, her mind went back to the text messages she had seen during Abi's second year at York. Thanksgiving. The kitchen in the Blythe family home. Messages on Abi's phone from an unknown number.

Miss you, babe. Can't wait until you're back here.

And then:

I'll do it soon. Promise. I just need the time to be right.
You know it would break her if I did it now.

At the time, Stevie had had no idea what the second message might have meant. If she was honest, she hadn't wanted to know. But while she'd never seen the name of the sender, she'd always assumed it must have been a guy from York. It was by far the most logical explanation for the *Can't wait until you're back here* comment while Abi was visiting home.

Now, though . . .

She stared at Zach, looking at him as if for the first time.

'Olive says she never understood why Abi wanted to be her friend,' Stevie said quietly. 'Why she chose her. But it wasn't Olive who Abi chose, was it? It wasn't Olive she wanted to be close to. She wanted you. Three years she spent clinging to you all in York. Because she was in love with you. And you . . . You strung her along, didn't you?

339

You told her that you would break up with Olive to be with her. But you never did.'

Stevie glared at Zach, her fear momentarily eclipsed by her repulsion.

'How did you manage to keep it going for so long? Why did Abi believe for all that time that you were going to do it? How did you manage to put it off?'

She tailed off as yet another grim realisation dawned on her.

I'll do it soon. Promise. I just need the time to be right. You know it would break her if I did it now.

'Olive's mum,' said Stevie. 'That's how you managed to keep Abi on the hook. You promised to break up with Olive, and you used the fact that her mum was sick as a reason to keep putting it off.' She looked Zach in the eye. 'Did you ever plan to actually do it? Or did you just like having the attention of two women at once?'

'We were students!' Zach's voice rose. 'We were just stupid fucking kids. It's not as if any of it meant anything. What did it matter if I liked having two girls on the go at the same time?'

'I'll bet Abi didn't see it like that,' said Stevie. 'Did she finally realise on that trip that you had never intended to leave Olive for her? Was she simply making a point? *You want Olive? You can have Olive.* Is that what she was saying when she put the ring in your bag?'

Zach stared at her. For a moment it looked as if he might

argue, his eyes wild and his body rigid. At last, though, the fight seemed to leave him, his shoulders sinking.

'How?' he said, his voice suddenly hollow. 'How do you know all of this?'

Immediately Stevie's fear returned. She glanced briefly at Zach's phone on the dresser as if it might provide a way out. Had the screen not lit up when it had, none of this would have fallen into place. She would still have believed it was Olive, not her husband, who had killed Abi.

'I saw your lockscreen,' she said. 'Your picture of Ryan . . . I look at this sort of thing every day for work. I saw it straight away.'

Zach looked suddenly terrified. 'Saw what?' he said. 'What have you seen in my son?' His tone was meant to be hostile, but it seemed he couldn't quite manage it.

Stevie swallowed, suddenly questioning whether she was really brave enough to say the next part.

'Ryan's eyes,' she said. 'Those beautiful brown eyes. They're his father's eyes. Your eyes.' Stevie felt her heart pound in her chest. He was going to make her say it. She took a deep breath. 'And so are Miley's.'

341

52

Zach said nothing. He didn't argue. He didn't try to deny anything. Instead, he simply glared at Stevie, hanging viciously on her every word.

'I think Abi was dying,' Stevie said. 'Diagnosed with the same illness that took our poor mom and grandmother. It explains the pills in her hut – I'd bet anything it's the same medication I remember our mom taking. And it explains the will she made a couple months ago. She was getting her affairs in order. And of course, the most important question she would have to consider was what would happen to Miley after she'd gone.

'I don't know why she kept your identity a secret all these years. Why she made up that story about meeting someone in a bar after parting ways with you all. Perhaps she wanted nothing to do with you after the way you'd strung her along in York. Perhaps she didn't want to manage the logistics of having a parent in the UK and another in the States. Or perhaps she just wanted Miley to herself. But I'd be willing to bet that, once she'd been diagnosed, she decided it was time for you to know that you had a daughter out there. A daughter who would need you once her mother was gone. The question, I imagine, would have been how to tell you.

'Because you aren't like Mike. Mike *loved* Abi. If he'd been Miley's father, and she'd wanted to involve him, all she'd have had to do was call. But you . . . I'm guessing that you wouldn't ever want to see her again. Not after the way she'd engineered your engagement to Olive. Abi will have known that. And I'll bet she also knew that if she could get Olive here, you'd come too. You'd have to. You couldn't have her here, alone with Abi. There'd be way too much potential for her to learn what had actually happened – to discover that the past ten years had been a lie.

'So Abi set up a reunion. She invited Olive, who accepted without so much as asking what you thought, and what do you know? You came too. Abi had you exactly where she wanted you.

'Now, I don't know when she was planning to tell you about Miley. My best guess is that she would probably have waited until the launch party was dealt with. But you didn't give her the chance, did you? You went to *her*. Last night, while Olive and I were following Mike down to the waterfall, you went to Abi's hut. And you demanded to know why she'd brought you here.'

She watched him thinking, seeing the calculations that were taking place behind his eyes. He looked as if he might try to deflect. As if he might lie or come up with an excuse.

But after several moments, he seemed to recognise that it was no good, his shoulders sinking.

'All right,' he said at last. 'All right. Yes. I went to see her. I wanted to know why she'd set this up. Why she'd gone ten years without so much as a peep only to drag us halfway round the world for a fucking *reunion*. But I had no idea that she would . . . I couldn't have known that she . . .'

He didn't finish, seemingly unable to find the words.

'She told you about Miley,' said Stevie. 'While you were out in the garden. You panicked, or maybe you just didn't want to hear it . . . Either way, Miley heard you run out.'

She shook her head.

'You must have been so scared. How were you meant to tell Olive that on the night you got engaged – an engagement that was, itself, a mistake – you fathered a child with her best friend? How would she forgive you? Surely, if Abi's secret came out, you would lose her. You would lose Ryan. The life that you'd managed to build after Abi hid that ring in your bag.'

Stevie paused, taking a breath as she prepared for the next part.

'So you took a flower from the waterfall,' she said. 'You came to see Abi before the party, and you gave her a glass of water that you'd poisoned.'

'No,' said Zach. 'No, I—'

'And you took her phone,' Stevie continued. 'I'm guessing to cover your tracks. Did you message her before the

344

party? Tell her you wanted to talk? Is that how you knew where she'd be?'

'No!'

'And then . . .' Stevie pushed on, terrified that if she stopped she might never start again. 'Then you saw an opportunity in Mike. He'd been telling everyone who'd listen that he believed Humphrey had killed Abi. He'd even told the *police*. So you followed him to the waterfall. You attacked him and you left him for dead, knowing that Humphrey would be blamed for it.'

'No!' Zach said sharply. 'You've got this all wrong. Abi messaged *me*.' He looked at Stevie with desperate eyes. 'She messaged me before the party. Said that she was going to tell Olive the truth about Miley. I ran to the hut, to try to talk her out of it, but when I arrived she was already dead.'

Stevie shook her head. 'Liar.'

'It's true! I swear to God that it's true. I swear on my *son*.'

'Prove it, then.'

'I can't.'

'Why not?'

'Because I deleted the message on my phone. And I . . .' He sighed. 'You're right. I did take Abi's phone. When I arrived at the hut, and I saw that she was dead, I knew how it would look. I knew the police would look at her messages and I knew that I would be the first person they turned to. So I took her phone, I put it in a glass of water, and then I threw it into the jungle. But I can find it again. Please. I can take you to the place where I chucked it away.'

'You think I'm going to follow you into the jungle?'

'Please!' he cried. 'I'm not the villain in all of this. I'm the victim. Don't you see that? Don't you see what Abi has done to my *life*?'

Stevie shook her head. 'Liar,' she said again. 'You killed her. And you're going to pay for it.'

She made another move for the door. Again, he stood in her path.

'Let me go,' she said.

'No.'

'Let me go!'

'I can't! Not until we've spoken about this.' He looked her in the eye, his expression bleak. 'I'm not letting you destroy my life, Stevie. I can't. Please. Just sit down and let's talk about—'

But he didn't get the chance to finish. Moving as quickly as she could manage, Stevie sprang forward, shoving him hard in the chest. She saw the surprise on his face as he toppled backwards, but she didn't wait to see him fall. Instead, she turned towards the sliding glass doors. She would make her escape through the back of the hut, running through the jungle into the neighbouring hut's garden. She didn't pause to wonder if it would be too thick for her to battle her way through. Nor to think about what she might do if the neighbouring hut was empty – if there was no one she could call on for help.

In the end, neither of these concerns mattered.

She had banked on the doors being unlocked. Had put all of her chips on that one escape route. But as she seized the handle and wrenched it sideways, the door stayed defiantly closed.

'Come on,' she murmured, fiddling frantically with the lock. 'Come on!'

With trembling hands she turned the catch, not daring to wonder how close Zach was to regaining his footing behind her. The lock clicked. Heart pounding, she threw the door open, one foot already out on the patio.

But it was too late. Zach had recovered, wrapping both arms around her stomach.

She stamped on his feet, clawed at his arms as she fought to get free. Nothing worked. He held her tightly, dragging her back into the hut.

'Let me go!' she cried out. 'Let me go!'

She heard her voice rise to a shriek, panic now coursing through her veins as she was hauled away from the open door. He's going to kill me, she thought. First it was Abi. Then it was Mike. Now it's me.

'Listen to me,' he growled. 'Just listen to me!'

She felt his breath in her ear, his stubble on her cheek. A scream rose to her lips.

And then he stopped.

Before Stevie could understand what was happening, Zach's arms fell away and she heard him tumble to the ground.

Dashing forward, desperate to put some space between the two of them, Stevie ran through the door and into the garden. Then, her breath coming in short gasps, she turned to see what had happened.

Zach was on the floor, groaning. Around him lay the shattered pieces of a vase, flowers scattered like confetti and water staining the carpet. And standing over him, an expression on her face that suggested she couldn't quite believe what she'd done, was Olive. Jazz hovered a few feet behind, looking on at the scene in pure disbelief.

Stevie and Olive locked eyes, neither seemingly sure of what to do now. Olive looked down at her husband, and then at the hand with which she had wielded the vase. Stevie could see that it was trembling.

After what felt like a painfully long pause, Olive found her voice.

'Are you OK?' she asked.

Stevie stood in shock, searching for a reply. She opened her mouth, and began, at last, to cry.

Part Seven: The Return

53

By the time dawn finally broke, Stevie was so tired that she ached.

After their intervention inside the hut, Jazz had run to fetch help, hurrying back with a small party of police officers who'd hauled Zach to his feet and led him back up to the lodge. He looked unsteady, blood trickling down the side of his face. Stevie wondered if the blow from the vase might have caused a slight concussion. In any case, he'd protested the entire way, trying desperately to convince Olive that he was innocent. She'd walked silently behind him, watching with emotionless eyes. Then, as her husband was put into the back of a police car, she'd climbed into a second, Jazz accompanying her. As both vehicles pulled away from the lodge, disappearing quickly into the jungle, Stevie had tried to imagine how Olive must be feeling, knowing now the truth of how her marriage had come to be.

It was better that she knew, Stevie told herself. It must be.

But that didn't make the prospect of the days and weeks ahead feel any less daunting. She thought of how different things might have been had Abi not put that ring in Zach's rucksack. Olive's marriage had been a lie. Her *life*, even . . . And of course there was Ryan to consider. How could you explain all of this to a child? Where would you begin?

Stevie's heart sank. Olive had a long road ahead of her.

With both Humphrey and Zach having now been taken away, only a small number of police officers remained. Rojas had spent an hour taking down Stevie's account of her confrontation with Zach. She'd glared as Stevie described going into Zach and Olive's hut unaccompanied instead of seeking out an officer, but she hadn't passed comment. When they were done, the inspector had advised that she get some sleep. In time she would undoubtedly need to travel to the police station for further questioning.

By the time the sun began to rise the guests were starting to leave The Midnight Orchid, a steady trickle of taxis and minibuses coming to take them to other hotels. They wheeled their suitcases behind them, still decked out in their blazers and glittering dresses. Some looked glad to be getting away. Others chattered eagerly, as if having enjoyed being present for such drama.

Stevie, meanwhile, stood out on the terrace. Gripping the handrail, she watched as the sun rose steadily behind her, the light spreading over the jungle canopy as if shining directly from The Midnight Orchid itself. She saw a pair of scarlet macaws fly side by side in the direction of the ocean. Somewhere in the distance she could hear the now-familiar call of howler monkeys. For a brief moment, she could see why Abi had chosen this place. And it made her feel all the more despondent at how things had turned out.

As she thought about her sister, Stevie wondered whether she and Abi would ever have stood a chance. Whether, in time, Abi might have finally accepted her as a Blythe.

As appealing as the idea was, Stevie doubted it. Or perhaps it was just easier to tell herself it would always have been impossible, given that Zach had now taken away any opportunity they might have had. He had killed Stevie's sister. Tried to frame her brother. All to keep his own secret buried. Now Abi was gone. Like Joel before her, and Frank and Jane, Abi had become another member of the Blythe family that for evermore would be just a name on a gravestone.

Beside her, Miley yawned. After Zach had been taken away, Stevie had gone back to her cabin, where Alana had still been watching over her little niece. It had emerged that since Humphrey's arrest she had refused steadfastly to sleep, demanding instead to know when she could be taken back to Stevie. Now she lay upon a couple of chairs that had been put together, knees to her chest and a blanket draped over her.

Her eyelids seemed finally to be growing heavy, sleep apparently threatening to take her. Out of nowhere, though, she sat bolt upright, catching sight of something across the restaurant. Then, she let out a shriek so loud it made Stevie jump.

'Uncle Hump!'

Leaping to her feet, Stevie watched as Miley ran across the restaurant and hurled herself into Humphrey's arms. He lifted her off the ground, hugging her tightly. Over her shoulder, he met Stevie's eye.

For a few seconds it felt as if the world stood still. Stevie nodded at Humphrey, forcing a small smile. She noticed that Miley had begun to cry, burying her head in his neck. She had to urge herself not to do the same, well aware that if she started again she might never stop.

Finally, with the sobbing Miley still in his arms, Humphrey breathed a sigh, walking across the restaurant towards her.

'Coffee?' he asked.

Stevie nodded. 'Coffee.'

54

In the end they decided to have coffee in Stevie's hut.

By now seemingly every guest had heard about Humphrey's arrest, prompting dozens of probing looks as he'd reappeared in the restaurant at daybreak. With Stevie's hut being the furthest from the lodge, they would have all the privacy they could want, and somewhere quiet for Miley to finally sleep.

Miley protested, of course. She said that she didn't want to sleep. But that didn't stop her, just a few minutes later, from passing out in Humphrey's arms. She didn't wake as he laid her down on Stevie's bed. She didn't even stir as he went about making the coffee.

Sitting in one of the deckchairs in the garden, Stevie watched her brother work. She didn't particularly want a hot drink, but she didn't want to stop him either. He was there. They were together again. With all the challenges that undoubtedly lay ahead of them, the relative calm of this moment was all she needed.

Emerging from the hut, he slid the glass door shut

behind him, taking care not to make unnecessary noise. He then crossed the little garden, put the mugs down on the table and sank, with a sigh, onto the other deckchair.

'So run it by me again,' he said. 'Abi really called the reunion just to get Zach here?'

Stevie nodded. 'I think she'd been diagnosed with the same illness Mom had. And as Miley's biological father she wanted him to know, so that he could take her in after she'd . . .' Stevie winced. 'After she'd *gone*. But she knew Zach wouldn't come willingly. Not after what she'd done with the ring in his rucksack. He probably wouldn't have ever wanted to see her again. So she set up the reunion. I think she figured that if she could get Olive over here, Zach would have to come too.'

'And after she'd told him about Miley, Zach killed her?'

'I guess he was worried that if the truth came out about Miley, Olive would kick him to the kerb. He'd lose Ryan. Lose the life he'd managed to make for himself after Abi put that ring in his bag. Protecting what he already had must have seemed more important than taking in a kid he didn't know.'

Humphrey shook his head, eyes glazed. 'I still can't believe it, you know. I didn't know Zach well, but I wouldn't have thought he had it in him to kill someone.'

Stevie grimaced, trying hard to dispel the memory of Zach's arms wrapped around her middle. His breath in her ear. She might not have believed it before either. She had no difficulty now.

'And he 'fessed up?' Humphrey continued. 'He told you he'd done it?'

Stevie shook her head. Then, thinking a moment longer, she said, 'It's weird, actually. He admitted to some of it. Like, he admitted to having the motive – to not wanting Olive to know the truth about Miley. He even came clean about taking Abi's phone and throwing it into the jungle, because she'd messaged him before the party to say that she was going to Olive with the truth. But he wouldn't admit to actually killing her. He denied that right up until the moment Olive intervened.'

'I guess he knows there's some of it he just can't deny,' said Humphrey. 'Like the connection to Miley. It would be instantly clear from a DNA test. Likewise, with the phone: if they manage to find it, I guess they'll be able to check it for fingerprints. Maybe even recover that message. But he probably thinks there's a little more room to deny killing Abi. Maybe he's banking on the police believing him if he owns up to some of it willingly.'

Stevie nodded. 'Maybe,' she agreed. She swept a look around the garden. 'What'll happen to this place?'

'I've no idea. I suppose the company will take it over. Rebrand it. I guess it's not for me to know.' He gave a small, sad smile. 'Listen,' he said. 'I know it's early days, but I've been thinking about Miley. I thought I could explore the possibility of adopting her.'

Stevie raised an eyebrow. 'Are you sure you're up for that?'

'To be honest, no. But someone has to, and you've got

357

a life in London to get back to. I love that kid to death. I'd be happy to try.'

Steve nodded slowly. 'I don't have to stay in London. I could come back home. Help out.'

'You'd do that?'

'Yeah,' she said. 'Of course.' She frowned. 'You have to wonder, though . . . Why did Abi turn to Zach in the first place? I know she wouldn't want *me* to step in. She hated how well Miley and I get along. But why not talk to *you* about adopting her?'

'I told you at the party,' said Humphrey. 'Abi didn't like me spending time with Miley. She thought I was too irresponsible.'

'I get that,' said Stevie. 'And I guess I can understand her worrying about you giving her too much candy or taking her to too many theme parks. But surely she would know that if you really had to you'd step up. Like . . . Zach's her father. Sure. But he doesn't know her. He didn't even know that she existed. And he lives in the UK. Is being Miley's biological father really enough?'

'She'll have had her reasons,' said Humphrey. 'But I guess we'll never know.' He shook his head, still in shock. 'I can't believe she just told him out in the garden. With Miley inside the hut. Imagine if she'd heard them.'

Stevie hummed in agreement, taking a sip of her coffee. Then she stopped, looking at Humphrey carefully as she lowered her cup.

She played his last words over in her mind.

Imagine if she'd heard them.

Something about this simple statement felt wrong. She couldn't say what. She couldn't even say why she thought it. But something about those innocent words didn't stack up.

She watched as Humphrey tapped at his phone, glancing quickly away when he looked up.

'What?' he asked.

'Nothing.'

'You sure?'

'Yeah. Sorry. I'm just a little spaced out. I need some sleep.'

She forced herself to meet his eye again, willing a smile into place. He frowned at her, unconvinced.

'Stevie, what's wrong?'

'I said it's nothing.'

'And I'm saying there's clearly something. Stevie, come on. You're freaking me out.'

She swallowed, mouth suddenly dry.

'How did you know that they spoke out in the garden?'

His frown intensified. 'What do you mean?'

'Abi's conversation with Zach. How did you know she had it out in her garden?'

'You told me.'

'No, I didn't.'

'I'm sure you did.'

'No. I didn't. I never said where they were. And I certainly didn't say that Miley was inside. So how did you know?'

'I'm not sure. Lucky guess. Or maybe someone else said something.'

'Who?'

'I don't know.'

He watched her for a few seconds, his expression suddenly becoming serious as he studied her face. 'Stevie . . . Why does it matter?'

She chewed her lip. 'I think we should go back up to the lodge.'

'What for?'

'I just think we should. You stay here. I'll wake Miley up.'

'Wait.' Humphrey shot out a hand, catching her wrist. 'Don't wake her up, Stevie. She's exhausted. Just . . . sit back down, will you?'

She did as instructed, slowly sitting back down on the deckchair.

'Do you want another coffee?' he asked.

She shook her head.

'A water?'

'No.'

He gave her a searching look. 'Why's this bothering you so much?'

'Because I didn't tell you that Abi spoke to Zach in her garden. And I didn't tell you that Miley was inside the hut. So how do you know?'

'I don't.'

'But you just said—'

'Stevie.' He gave a hollow laugh. 'I don't know what

I'm saying. I haven't slept. I've spent the last few hours in a police station, accused of murder. None of what I'm saying makes any sense.'

Stevie didn't reply. She knew that she hadn't told him where Zach and Abi had spoken. And she couldn't bring herself to believe it had been a lucky guess.

She gripped her hands together tightly, trying to stop them trembling as she scrambled for an innocent explanation.

And then it came to her. Their conversation at the bar, just moments before they'd gone searching for Abi. When Humphrey had asked which hut Abi had given her.

Damn, he'd said. *She literally put you in the furthest one from the lodge. I'd offer to swap, but I don't think you'd want mine. I'm right next door to Abi.*

Stevie felt her eyes widen.

'You were next door . . .'

Humphrey's eyes narrowed. 'I was what?'

'Your hut. It's next to Abi's. If you'd happened to be out in your garden when she spoke to Zach you would have heard them. You'd have heard every word and they would have had no idea you were even there.'

'I don't know what you're talking about—'

'You *heard* them, Humphrey. It's the only way you could have known.' She stared at him. 'Why didn't you say anything? Why keep it to yourself?'

'Stevie,' Humphrey said sharply. 'You need to slow down. We're all stressed. We're all grieving. None of us have slept. But you worked it out. You did it, Stevie.

You realised that it was Zach. There's nothing to be gained by—'

'Zach . . .' said Stevie. 'Zach said that he got rid of Abi's phone because she messaged him. She wrote that she was going to tell Olive the truth about Miley. That's why he took it. Because he knew that the message would link him to her death. I thought that's why he killed her. He went straight to the hut and killed her before she could go to Olive. But what if it wasn't Abi who sent that message? What if someone else sent it? Someone who knew what Abi and Zach had discussed and who wanted to give the police something that would point to Zach.'

Humphrey glared at her. 'Stevie. You really need to—'

'What would have happened if Zach hadn't thought to take the phone? The police would have picked it up. They'd have found a message from Abi, saying that she was about to tell Olive the truth about Miley. They'd ask Zach what the truth was. Even if he denied it, they could probably guess. I'll bet they could even make him do a DNA test. Suddenly there's a compelling motive for Zach to kill Abi.

'Zach thought he was being set up. But someone could only have written that message if they knew he would have a motive in the first place. If they knew what he and Abi had spoken about the night before.'

Stevie stared at her brother, eyes wide.

'Humphrey . . .' she whispered. 'Jesus, Humphrey. What have you done?'

55

For a long while, neither of them spoke. Then, at last, Humphrey heaved an almighty sigh.

'Stevie . . .' he said. 'Stevie, *come on*. You'd done it. You'd wrapped it all up. Everyone was happy. Why'd you have to go and complicate everything again?'

Stevie stared at him, mouth hanging open.

'You killed her,' she said. 'You killed them both. God-dammit, Humphrey, why have you done this?'

'Does it matter?'

'Of course it matters! You've killed people, Humphrey. You've—'

Before she could go any further, he shushed her, nudging his head in the direction of the hut. Immediately, Stevie understood – Miley was still there, sleeping on the bed.

'What are you going to do?' he asked.

'I don't know.'

'Are you going to tell anyone?'

She looked at him, heart pounding in her ears.

'Just tell me why you did it,' she said.

'Did what?'

'Humphrey!'

'What are you expecting to happen here, Stevie? I'm not *helping you* accuse me of murder.' He looked her in the eye. 'Look. The cops have someone in custody. A bad person, I should add. Are we forgetting that Zach is the guy who got our sister pregnant the night he got engaged?'

'He didn't mean to get engaged.'

'So that makes it OK?'

'He's not a killer, Humphrey! He didn't do it!' Stevie stared at him. 'All this because you were removed from the company?'

'No. Not the company.'

'What, then?'

Humphrey sprang to his feet, turning his back to her. It was his demeanour that unnerved Stevie most. He was behaving as if she'd used his PlayStation without permission back when they were kids. Not accused him of double murder.

'Back to square fucking one,' he muttered.

'What does that mean?' said Stevie. 'Square one? What's square one?'

He didn't reply, and in the silence Stevie scrambled desperately for an answer. For something that would explain what her brother had done.

'What did you think Abi was going to tell us after the launch?' she asked. 'Before we knew she was sick. When you thought it was Pete she was talking to on the phone. What did you think she was going to say?'

He faced her again, not anger in his eyes but disappointment.

'Why are you doing this, Stevie? I'm the one who cared for you. The one who *wanted* you. Abi never did. If anything you should be *thanking* me.'

Stevie winced. But she didn't stop.

'Why did Abi choose Zach?' she pressed. 'Why would she rather give Miley to a father she's never met than risk leaving her with you? What did you think she was going to tell us?'

He stared at her, eyes boring into hers. 'You look scared, Stevie.'

'Because you're scaring me.'

'You're scaring yourself.'

'Was Abi scared of you?'

'Yes.'

'Was she right to be?'

'Yes.' He smiled at her. That gleaming, charming smile. 'Come on, Stevie. You're almost there. If you're going to insist on putting this all together, at least make it over the finish line.'

Stevie swallowed, trying for a moment to pretend that this was a nightmare she might soon wake up from. But the cogs of her mind were already turning, dragging her unwillingly towards a secret that Humphrey had been terrified Abi might share. A reason for her to be so afraid of him that she would sooner reconnect with Zach than risk leaving him with Miley after she was gone.

Finally, the answer came. And with it, Stevie knew that this was no nightmare. It was much worse.

'You killed Joel.'

Humphrey spread his hands out wide. 'In my defence,' he said, 'the waterfall killed Joel. But it might be true that I gave him a nudge in the right direction.'

'And Abi saw it.'

Humphrey nodded. 'She wasn't meant to be there. I'd suggested to Joel that just the two of us should go check it out. But she came after us. Felt left out, apparently. If she'd got there a second later, it would have been fine. But she arrived at just the wrong moment.'

'She never told anyone?'

'I made sure of it. Told her that if anyone were to find out she would go exactly the same way.'

'That's why she wouldn't let you spend time with Miley. It's why she didn't object to you coasting on all of her work at Conrad Blythe. Because she was terrified of you.' Stevie shook her head. 'I don't understand. I know you said that Joel wasn't the golden boy Mom and Dad thought. But what could he have done that warranted killing him?'

For the first time, a hint of frustration crept into Humphrey's voice. 'I guess there just came a point when I'd had enough. When I decided I didn't want to watch everyone fawn over him and talk about how wonderful he was, while I was the only one who saw him for what he actually was.'

'You were jealous.'

'You bet I was. Why should he have been Mom and Dad's favourite? They had no idea what he was really like.'

Stevie stared at him, scarcely able to believe what she was hearing.

'How long had you been planning it?' she asked. 'The waterfall. Had you been . . .'

She tailed off, unable to finish her own question.

'There was no plan,' said Humphrey. 'I'd thought for a little while about how much better everything would be if Joel wasn't around. But I wasn't sitting there, ten years old, plotting his demise like some kind of Bond villain.'

'So you just *did it*?'

'Sure. We were on that camping trip. He'd spent the whole weekend, as always, being his little shitty self. Getting me into trouble with Mom and Dad for things *he'd* done. When we went to that waterfall I saw an opportunity.' Humphrey gave a shrug. 'I was just a kid. Kids do impulsive shit all the time.'

Stevie took a deep breath, her head spinning.

'So the phone call you overheard,' she said. 'When you got back from Bangkok. Abi telling someone that she was going to *tell the family* after the launch was over. You thought she was speaking to Pete . . .' She paused, her mouth dry. 'You thought that she was getting ready to tell the truth about Joel. You thought that she'd organised those secret meetings with Pete to discuss her position. That she was working out what she needed to do from a legal perspective. And you thought that, having finalised her legal gameplan with Pete, she was going to finally tell the true story.'

Humphrey gave another shrug. 'Something like that. You have to understand, Stevie, that Abi and I have never spoken about what happened to Joel. Not once. I told her what would happen if she said anything, and that was that. I didn't expect her to have forgotten, as such, but at the very least I thought she'd moved on. Clearly, though, with the way she never let me spend time alone with Miley, she hadn't. I couldn't spend the rest of my life looking over my shoulder, wondering if there might come a day when she finally decided to tell the world. And when I heard that conversation with Zach, last night . . .' Humphrey smiled. 'I guess I figured there would just never be a better opportunity. A poisonous flower. An old friend with an amazing motive to want her dead. How was I meant to pass that up?'

Stevie shook her head. 'You killed Abi because she *might* have told someone?'

'In my defence, I thought she was definitely going to. Those secret meetings she was having with Pete . . .'

'Those meetings were to draw up her will! Because she'd found out she was sick.'

'Be fair, Stevie. How was I meant to know that?'

Stevie grimaced. 'You were the one who *told* me about those meetings. That was after you'd killed her. After you'd sent that message to Zach from Abi's phone. You wanted to plant the idea that the meetings were con-nected to her college friends. What were you hoping I'd

368

do? Assume, eventually, that she'd been speaking to Pete about introducing Miley and Zach?'

'Something like that.'

'And what about Mike? Why kill him? It can't have been just to keep him quiet. He'd already told everyone who would listen that he thought you'd killed Abi. The damage was done. So why go after him?'

Humphrey sighed. 'That was just really fucking unlucky.'

'Unlucky?'

'He happened to take a stroll by the waterfall just as I was down there picking more flowers. Ideally, I'd have heard him approaching and hidden somewhere, but with the water coming down I couldn't hear a thing. I had no idea he was there until it was too late.'

Stevie stared at him, unable to believe just how casually he was describing this.

'And what were you going to do with the flowers Mike caught you picking? Put them in Zach's hut? An extra piece of evidence for the police to find after he took Abi's phone?'

Humphrey scowled. 'I couldn't believe it when I heard he'd done that. Even if he did go running to her hut before someone else had the chance to find her, I thought the sight of the body would panic him enough that he'd forget about the phone.'

'That's why you were so determined to find it,' said Stevie. 'Three times you told me that we needed to get the phone back. It was even the last thing you said before the police took you away. I just assumed you were desperate to catch the killer. But you needed it for your cover story.'

Stevie felt sick. She couldn't breathe. She thought of all the time she had spent with Humphrey. The hours in the Blythe family home spent sharing her fears and baring her soul. The hikes he'd taken her on in the White Mountains.

At that she stopped.

The hikes . . .

The way Abi had always insisted that she join them. Never engaging, just trailing behind them, glaring.

She could feel the gears turning in her mind. Something else was coming. Another revelation rapidly approaching.

'She was watching over me . . .' Stevie felt her eyes go wide. Heard the disbelief in her own voice. 'All those hikes Abi insisted on joining. I thought she just didn't want the two of us bonding. That she was saying you were *her* brother. Not mine. But she was . . . she was watching over me. Making sure you were never tempted to do anything similar again.'

The words came like a punch to the gut. Her head spun, as her entire relationship with her sister appeared in a blinding new light.

'I thought that too,' said Humphrey. 'She never said anything out loud, of course. But she wasn't exactly being subtle about it. Or at least, she wasn't to someone who knew the truth about Joel.'

'She was protecting me,' said Stevie. 'All of it . . . Everything she did to have me sent away. Trying to make me look like a thief. Begging Mom and Dad to send me back. It was all to protect me from you.' She felt tears bead in the corners of her eyes. 'I thought she hated me.'

'She did,' said Humphrey. 'Don't kid yourself, Stevie. She never forgave Mom and Dad for bringing another kid home. For replacing one of us so easily. She was never going to accept you. But she didn't want you taking a tumble down a waterfall either.'

'Was I ever at risk?'

'Maybe once or twice. There were moments when it pissed me off seeing how much they loved you.'

At this, Stevie had to look away, wiping her eyes with the back of her hand. Her entire life – her entire relationship with her siblings . . . None of it had been what she'd thought.

'I loved you,' she said. 'I thought you loved me too. You're my brother.'

Humphrey nodded, adopting a mournful expression. 'I know,' he said. 'And there were definitely times when I enjoyed having you around. But if all of this has taught me anything, it's that I really should have been an only child.'

At this, Stevie heard Max's words from the previous afternoon.

Manipulative . . . prone to jealousy . . . a complete lack of empathy or remorse . . . I'm telling you, Stevie, you grew up with a psychopath.

It seemed Max had been right. Stevie had grown up with a psychopath for a sibling. Just not the sibling she'd thought.

Humphrey sighed. 'So what do we do about this?'

'What do you mean?'

'I'm sorry, Stevie. I like you. A lot more than Abi did, at least. But I did all of this to get rid of a sister who knew too much. And now here we are, with a different sister who also knows too much to be allowed to walk away. As I said: square fucking one.'

'Are you going to kill me?'

'It doesn't have to be unpleasant. Abi barely had a chance to work out what was happening before the poison kicked in.'

'You want to use the flowers.'

'I think so.' He thought for a moment. 'OK. Here's what I suggest we do. We'll walk to the waterfall. We'll crush a couple of the flowers into a bottle of water. You'll drink it, and then I'll send myself a message from your phone saying that it was you who killed Abi. I'll say that you were getting her back for how awful she's been to you all these years, and that you killed Mike too, to incriminate me further. But now you've had a change of heart. You're filled with regret, can't live with the guilt . . .'

Stevie now felt so frightened she could barely breathe. The way he had reeled all of this off so casually . . .

More to the point, it all added up. She could actually see it working.

'And if I refuse?'

He looked towards the hut. Towards Miley.

'You wouldn't,' said Stevie.

'I don't *want to*. But how else am I going to get you to play ball?'

She shuddered.

'I'm all in, Stevie. Now, Miley won't sleep for ever, and we'll have a tougher time of this when she wakes up. So what's it gonna be?'

56

She knew her coffee would be cold by now. They had been speaking too long for it not to be.

Even so, as she snatched her mug from the table and hurled the tepid liquid at Humphrey's face, Stevie saw a flash of panic in his expression. Heard him cry out as he flung up his hands to shield his eyes.

She didn't stop to see how long it would take him to realise the coffee wasn't actually scalding. Instead she leapt from her deckchair and sprinted into the jungle.

She wasn't sure how long she ran for, branches and ferns scratching her as she forced her way through. But eventually she stopped, ducking behind the trunk of a particularly large tree.

She pressed her back to it, the bark rough against her skin, and did her best to slow her breathing. Somewhere above her, she heard a monkey moving in the canopy, lightly accompanied by distant birdsong. Then she heard another sound. Footsteps. Someone working their way frantically through the foliage. She held her breath as he passed, terror gripping her so tightly that she didn't trust herself even to breathe without crying out.

He was moving quickly. Hunting her.

She waited until she could no longer hear him, the sound of crunching earth and rustling leaves eventually swallowed by the jungle. Then she waited a little while longer, just to be sure. Finally, when she had summoned the strength to move her legs again, she emerged from her hiding place, hurrying back towards the hut.

She found Miley standing in the lounge area, looking confused. Humphrey's panicked cry must have woken her. That was good. There wasn't time to waste rousing her.

'What's happening?' she asked, rubbing sleep from her eyes.

Stevie didn't answer. Instead, she hurried to Miley's side and grabbed her hand. 'Come on,' she said. 'We've got to go.'

'But why—'

'Please, Miley! Before he comes back!'

The girl looked suddenly frightened, but she didn't argue. Instead, she gripped Stevie's hand as they hurried through the hut, making for the front door.

Stevie reached for the handle. Opened the door. Then came the sound she had dreaded.

'Stevie.'

She felt her blood run cold. Turning to face him, she saw Humphrey standing in the garden.

'Don't,' he called out to her. 'Don't run.'

At her side, Stevie was aware of Miley looking up at

her. Turning to face her little niece, she saw the terror in her eyes.

'Don't!' Humphrey said again.

Stevie took a deep breath. Made a quick calculation in her head. Then, she gripped Miley's hand and ran.

She couldn't outrun Humphrey on the path. Not with Miley in tow. And with her hut the furthest from the lodge, she knew that if she tried he would catch them before they could reach help. So instead she charged straight ahead, back into the jungle. Humphrey was bigger than her. He would have a harder time forcing his way through the trees and bushes. Stevie's one hope was that this would slow him down long enough for her and Miley to achieve some distance. To hide somewhere in the undergrowth and then make their way stealthily towards the lodge.

Within seconds, though, she was lost. Guided more by panic than by any particular sense of direction, she realised with a start that she had lost all sense of where they were in relation to the lodge. She might as well have been running in the dark. And all the while she was aware of Humphrey crashing through the jungle behind them.

They pushed on, branches whipping at her face as she urged Miley to keep moving.

Then, she heard a sound that gave her a flicker of hope.

Running water. She had no idea how, but she realised that somewhere up ahead was the waterfall.

She began to move with renewed vitality. She knew her way from the waterfall. If she could just make it there, she could get them to the garden. They would be safe.

She pushed through the rainforest, ignoring the cuts and grazes that she was picking up along the way. They were getting closer. She could hear it. They were almost there.

Suddenly, the trees parted. A small clearing appeared before them, barely larger than the private garden behind Stevie's hut. Immediately she realised, heart sinking, that she had been wrong.

They had not, as she'd assumed, been running towards the bottom of the waterfall. To the pool and the flowers.

They had been running towards the top.

'Hide!' she screamed.

Miley did so without question, breaking off and running into the undergrowth. Seconds later, Humphrey emerged, his face an angry mess of scrapes and scratches. He looked over Stevie's shoulder. Seeing the water cascading down over the cliff-edge, he seemed to think for a moment, before nodding as if to say, *Of course. Here we are again.*

'It didn't need to come to this, Stevie,' he said. 'You could have just let it be.'

Stevie backed slowly away, moving as close to the edge as she dared. Anything to put a little more distance between them. Before she could stop herself, she wondered if this was how Joel had felt, all those years ago. In the moments before Humphrey had pushed him to his death.

She looked frantically around for something she could use. A rock. A branch. Anything she could wield to defend herself. She saw nothing. Nothing, at least, within reach.

Then, she clocked something on the ground. A root. Jutting up out of the dirt, it was a few feet in front of her, hidden from view by a large fern. Thick and sturdy, hovering at around ankle-height, it was a miracle that she hadn't tripped on it.

'Abi was awful to you,' Humphrey continued. 'Your whole life, she treated you like crap. And she was dying anyway. What does it really matter that she's gone?'

Stevie took a deep breath, knowing all too well that she would only have one shot.

Do it for Miley, she told herself. Don't do it for you. Do it for Miley.

'Because it shouldn't have been her,' she called back. 'It should have been you!' Her voice quavered, and she had to will herself to carry on. 'You don't deserve to be the last Blythe standing. You never did. And d'you know what? If they could see you now, I think Mom and Dad would say the exact same thing.'

It worked. Humphrey snarled, letting out a cry so primal that Stevie scarcely believed it could have come from a human being. And then he ran, hands reaching out to grab her.

Stevie stood there, waiting as long as she dared. Then, at the very last second, she dropped to her belly, hitting the ground hard. She expected he had been counting on a fight. Or maybe for her to dart to the side. But not straight down.

She saw the confusion on his face. Then the panic as his foot caught on the root. Finally, the terror as he lost his balance, his own momentum carrying him forward.

He sailed clean over her, a scream escaping his lips as he flew through the air, over the waterfall and into nothing.

57

Two hours later, Stevie sat in the lobby with Miley tucked closely into her side.

A blanket they didn't need was wrapped around their shoulders, a police officer standing guard over them. They each had a glass of water that neither of them had touched. Stevie ached all over, the countless cuts and scratches that she had picked up beginning to sting, and she had definitely done some damage when she'd thrown herself to the ground to duck out of Humphrey's way.

None of that mattered, though. Not right now. Because they were safe. They had survived.

It had been a little while since either of them had spoken. Stevie wondered if Miley was in shock. She wondered if *she* might be. Whenever she closed her eyes she could see the look on Humphrey's face as he'd disappeared over the side of the waterfall. Whenever she so much as blinked.

She grimaced, pursing her lips to contain an involuntary noise of discomfort as she fought to push the memory away.

He was a killer, she told herself. He killed Joel. He killed Abi. He killed Mike. He was going to kill you, and he would probably have killed Miley.

She knew these things to be true. She knew it in her bones. And yet she struggled to feel it. Any moment now she expected someone to wake her up. To tell her it had all been some horrific out-of-body experience.

'Miss Blythe.'

A voice came from somewhere beside them. It was Rojas. Turning to face her, Stevie saw a curious expression on her face. It wasn't her usual stern, interrogating gaze. Instead there was kindness. Concern, even.

'They're ready to take you now.'

She spoke gently, nodding towards a cop car in the parking lot.

'Are you coming with us?'

The inspector nodded. 'Soon. I need to finish a few things here before I can leave. But the officers taking you are good people. They'll wait with you at the hospital until I arrive.'

Stevie let out a long breath. Then she patted Miley on the shoulder. 'Come on, you,' she said. 'Let's go.'

Miley rose to her feet, clinging so closely to Stevie that she made it difficult to walk. They went like this all the way to the parking lot, passing through the lobby and onto the steps. Every muscle in Stevie's body groaned, but she didn't stop. She just kept moving step by step to the car, her arm wrapped tightly around her niece.

An officer opened the door for them, closing it again

after they had climbed into the back seat. As the engine started, and the car began to move away, Stevie breathed a sigh of relief. It had already been decided that they wouldn't be coming back to The Midnight Orchid. Rojas had offered to have their things collected and taken to the hospital. If they needed further accommodation before returning to the States, she had said that she would arrange that too.

Stevie turned her head a fraction, taking one last look through the back window. The lodge was already disappearing, and she managed just one last glimpse of the pointed thatched roof before the jungle became too dense.

She faced forward again, her cheek brushing Miley's hair.

'It's an hour to the hospital,' she managed to say. 'Maybe even a little further. You should get some sleep.'

'Will you watch over me?'

'Always.'

'You promise?'

She couldn't say if it was fatigue, shock or a mixture of both. But for a moment, Stevie imagined that Abi was with them in the back of that car, watching her intently as she waited to hear the answer to this question.

Stevie met her eye, looking into the face of the sister who had protected her. The sister who, in death, she now understood so much better than she ever had in life.

'Yeah,' she said. 'I promise.'

Six months later

'Ma'am?'

Stevie turned, looking into the face of a broad man in a dark polo shirt. He stood in the doorway, a large cardboard box in his arms. The words *Concord Removals* were printed on his breast pocket.

'Where would you like this one?' he asked.

'Is it kitchen stuff?' She lifted the corner of the lid. 'Yep. Kitchen stuff. Anywhere in here, please.'

The removal guy nodded, carrying the box to the corner of the room. As he did so, Stevie heard Max's voice ring out from her phone.

'Blimey,' she said. 'That's the third box of kitchen stuff so far. How much do you guys have?'

Stevie's phone was propped up on a kitchen counter, Max's face filling the screen.

'I think that's the last one,' she called back. 'To be honest, most of it's come from Abi's old place. Pretty much everything has.'

'Makes sense,' Max replied. 'And my card definitely arrived?'

Stevie held it up for Max to see, the words *Happy New Home!* printed in bright font.

'Hallelujah,' said Max. 'The amount they charge you to send stuff to the States, someone at the post office would have been getting a hiding if it hadn't arrived on time. When's the social worker coming?'

'In a couple hours, I think. Once these guys are—' She broke off, sticking her head through the kitchen door. 'Excuse me!' she called into the hallway. 'That one's going upstairs. Door on the right.'

The guy thanked her, disappearing up the stairs with a box marked *Miley's Room*.

'Sorry, Max,' she said. 'It's a little hectic over here.'

'It's fine,' said Max. 'Why don't I leave you to it? You've got your hands full.'

'You sure?'

'Yeah. We can catch up later. That's if you're sure you're both good?'

Stevie glanced up, looking through the wide kitchen windows into the backyard. Miley was working on a snowman, the New England winter having lived up to its reputation. But it wouldn't be long before the snow started to thaw. Spring was approaching. In a few short weeks the white would turn to green. They would spend their weekends hiking and boating on the lakes, and then towards the end of the year they would watch as the trees turned the famous shades of red and gold.

'Yeah,' she said. 'We're good. Catch you later. And send me some dates for when you're thinking you'll come visit us!'

Max grinned. 'I will do. Have fun. Miss you.'

Stevie ended the call. Before she could put the phone down, she noticed that while she'd been speaking to Max a WhatsApp message had arrived from Olive.

Hope the move goes well today x

Stevie looked at the message, touched that Olive had remembered.

They hadn't spoken regularly since the events of The Midnight Orchid, but they had checked in with one another a couple of times. During those conversations, they'd covered the counsellor Olive had been seeing, who – along with Jazz – had been helping her determine what her life should look like going forward, now that Zach had been kicked out. They'd also discussed Stevie's relocation to New Hampshire and the process of formally adopting Miley. But for the most part they had spoken at length about whether to tell Ryan and Miley that they each had a half-sibling on the other side of the Atlantic.

They would need to be told one day, of course. But not yet. They had all suffered enough emotional upheaval for the time being. Right now there were lives that needed to be rebuilt. Children who needed to know they had a future. There would be time later.

She typed out a reply, thanking Olive for thinking of

them and saying that they should catch up again soon. Then, she let out a contented sigh, looking around at her new kitchen.

The place was bigger than anything she'd pictured when she'd imagined moving home. Not a condo, but a three-bedroom house with white railings and a veranda. A pole over the door for an American flag and a young beech tree in the yard that would offer shade in the summer.

But then, of course, it had needed to be bigger. After all, it wasn't just Stevie living there.

She looked again at Miley. In the end there had been no question of Zach taking her in. While on some level Stevie had been dismayed by his lack of interest, on another she had been glad. As the police car had ferried them from The Midnight Orchid, she had decided that she would be the one to do it. She would brook no argument. If Zach had decided he'd wanted her then Stevie would have fought him. But it had quickly emerged that there would be no need. With Olive's eyes now opened to the kind of man he was, it seemed Zach had more than enough problems to keep him busy without the added question of what was to be done about Miley.

Stevie left the kitchen, going through to a smaller room at the front of the house. The removal guys had already put her desk in there, as well as a chair and an oak shelving unit that had yet to be filled.

She placed her hands on the back of the chair.

At first, her bosses in London had been disappointed when she'd turned down their offer of a promotion, opting instead to hand in her notice. But they had accepted it graciously, understanding the situation. That was, until a week later, when Stevie had been asked to join a conference call with the firm's managing director.

Even now, she couldn't believe her luck. The offer he'd made was for Stevie to continue working from New Hampshire, remotely supporting the team in London when needed, but primarily focusing on securing clients in the States. It had emerged that he'd been considering opening an American branch for some time, and Stevie's change in circumstances had convinced him to take the plunge. That was, if she was willing to accept.

She'd done so on the spot.

Standing now in her soon-to-be study, she reached into a box that the removal guys had deposited, and carefully retrieved two photo frames. Inside one was a picture of Miley and Abi. And in the other was a smiling Frank and Jane Blythe.

For a moment, Stevie held them, one in each hand. Then, she took them through to the kitchen and put them on the counter. She knew this wasn't the family situation that any of them had imagined. But she made a silent promise — one that she had made a hundred times already — that every day she would do them proud.

Hearing the sound of a door opening, she looked up to see Miley coming in from the garden.

'I need a scarf for my snowman,' she announced.

She kicked off her boots, snow going everywhere as they landed with a thump on the kitchen floor.

'Have the guys . . .'

She paused, clocking the pictures on the counter.

Stevie watched her closely. 'We don't need to have these out. If it's too painful we can—'

'No,' said Miley. 'I want them.'

She came to stand beside Stevie, wrapping her arms around her middle. Stevie hugged her back tightly.

'I miss her,' said Miley.

Stevie nodded. 'So do I.'

The words sounded alien, the notion of missing Abi still strange. But she meant it. She missed her sister in a way she couldn't quite express, longing for an opportunity she would never have to thank her. To tell her how brave she'd been. To tell her that she was sorry she'd never understood, but that now she did.

'Have the moving guys got all my stuff out the truck yet?' said Miley. 'I need that scarf.'

'I think so. I've seen them taking a couple of your boxes up there.'

'Let's go. Come help me look.'

Stevie promised that she would, and Miley went scampering off up the stairs.

It would be a long road, Stevie thought. It would take time for Miley to heal. A lifetime, perhaps. And she would need time too. Humphrey's betrayal. Abi's secret. All of it would need to be processed. Some nights since, when she lay staring at the ceiling, she had wondered if she would ever trust anyone again. If she would ever be able to trust *herself*.

But, she told herself, those were questions for another

day. Any day but this one. She and Miley had a lifetime's worth to choose from.

She looked once more around the kitchen. It wasn't what she'd imagined. But it was home. *She* was home.

She reached out, brushing the frame with her thumb.

'I'll take care of her,' she said quietly, meeting Abi's eye. 'I promise. Just like you took care of me.'

Then, with Miley calling for her to hurry up, she turned away from the photo, and began to make her way upstairs.

Acknowledgements

As ever, this book would not exist without a large team of brilliant people. I'm grateful to you all for your hard work and talent, but to call out a few in particular . . .

Thank you to Harry Illingworth. Confidant, cheerleader and the best agent an author could wish for. I'm endlessly fortunate to have you in my corner.

Thank you to editor extraordinaire Emily Griffin, for your wisdom, your guidance and – more than ever with this book – your patience. Your insight and reassurance are deeply appreciated.

Thank you to Joanna Taylor and Alice Brett for your diligence and your keen eyes. Thank you as well to Claire Simmonds for being my sounding board during the early stages of writing this story.

Thank you to Hana Sparkes and Lucas Lockyer for all you do to promote these books. I'm indebted to you both. And thank you to the wider team at Century working tirelessly behind the scenes in sales and production.

ACKNOWLEDGEMENTS

Thank you to Patrick Knowles for yet another breath-taking cover. I'm in awe of your talent, and I know from speaking to readers that they are too.

Thank you to every bookseller who has stocked, sold or recommended one of my books. It's because of you that these stories have reached so many people.

Thank you to Dr Daniel Emlyn-Jones for speaking to me about manchineel trees, and thank you to John Knox at the wonderful Alnwick Poison Garden for putting us in touch. Needless to say, any errors are entirely my own.

Finally, the biggest thank you of all goes to Hayley. It turns out writing a book with a newborn baby in tow is quite a challenge. Thank you more than ever for your fortitude, your understanding and your encouragement. This book, as with everything I do, is ultimately for you and Erica.